CAYU

A MAX DEAN ADVENTURE

BY LARRY MOLLIN

Published by Manhattan Book Group, an imprint of MindStir Media, LLC
447 Broadway | 2nd Floor #354 | New York, NY 10013 | USA
212-634-7677 | www.manhattanbookgroup.com

Printed in the United States of America
ISBN-13: 978-1-7352710-3-3

CAYUGA

A MAX DEAN ADVENTURE

BY LARRY MOLLIN

MANHATTAN
BOOK GROUP

THANKS

The author is grateful for all his book buyers, readers and fans of *St. Malo*, the first Max Dean novel. Love you!

Special thanks go out to Dee, Gary and C. Falk for their reads and valuable impressions of *Cayuga's* first draft.

Also, to Maggie Kelly, and the Manhattan Book Group/Mindstir Media and its editors and designers for continuing me on this novel way in such fine fashion.

INTRODUCTION

If you agree most myths and legends are fiction, then it stands to reason that those that aren't fiction might be fact. The following account will enlighten that notion. It begins in 2009 but references earlier, even earlier, and much earlier times.

I, alone, have been entrusted with the task of penning this recollection to the best of my ability. I have no reason to doubt that what was told to me over the course of two years is not true. Though there certainly may be some misrepresentations caused by the passage of time and the tricks that memory can play. As the ten-year, non-disclosure agreements are now over, certain new details may come to light confirming or disputing the following re-telling. If you should have anything to add or subtract, please contact the author at his website: larrymollin.com.

This publication has been creatively crafted to give it context. It is intended to be a digestible distillation of my own, fact-checked investigation based on interviews with one of the actual participants of this most dangerous pursuit of an ancient weapon of mass destruction, an apocalyptic treasure foretold in early Hindu writings. If that fact already confuses you, do not read on. Otherwise, dear trusted reader, go right ahead and you will be duly rewarded with the whole, amazing Max Dean tale.

It's said that lightning doesn't strike twice. But does that apply to reincarnated lifetimes?

For all the people I have met along the way, this book is for you.
Especially those people I shared experiences with in the Finger Lakes.
You are in it.

Of course, there would be no story here without my wife and muse, Dee,
brother Fred and sister Sandy, sons, Johnnie and Jackson and all the dogs
and the walks where the real writing occurs.

This book is dedicated to my mother, Peg and father, Ed
both now gone but never forgotten.

KALI THE DESTROYER

CHAPTER ONE

It was freakin' May, and it was snowing. Not just a normal, cutesy, downy spring, upstate New York storm, but a mother-humping, total blowing, winter white-out, white-knuckled, icy, wet blizzard that came out of nowhere to dump high and heavy. Max's rental Kia would be no match. Any skid on the banked, downhill, divided, county highway would be epic. Fingers gripping the steering wheel, wipers swishing the slushy snow away, Max stared steely-eyed ahead. He wished he had the aesthetic distance to appreciate it all—the natural beauty of the hill descent, the Northeast afternoon's delicate lighting, the blinding reflection giving brief glimpses of a lake beyond the tree line. He feathered the brake and slowed the car down praying for an exit ramp soon or, at best, a safe shoulder. He was Southern California born and bred and near blinded on this slippery stretch of unfamiliar road, so far out of his element. The fact he was in the Finger Lakes at all showed how needy he had become. It was nearly ten years ago that he and Mei U had walked away from St. Malo, France, with bags full of pirate treasure that cashed out at three-point five mil over the following three years. Max choked on the thought. It invariably led him down the road to revisit all the financial mistakes and bad luck befalling them in the half-decade that followed. No, he needed this job, and when Ella von Tragg tried again to engage him as an investigator, he agreed to meet her in Ithaca and hear the scope of the engagement. It made some sense to Max plus, whether he took the job or not, he could catch up with the only cousin with whom he still communicated. Janey Dean Flatman, originally from the area, was a professor at Cornell University in the anthropology department, and Max was looking forward to telling her about Ella's offer. To his surprise, Janey already knew. Since Max arrived the day before at the small regional airport on a shitty, connecting flight from L.A. through Cleveland, things were that kind of strange.

His client had arranged for him to be picked up, and after reuniting with the widow von Tragg at the Taughannock Inn on the west side of the lake in Trumansburg, Max was off somewhere on the east side of the lake, chasing the trail of this supposed, hush, hush, hidden antiquity that everyone in Janey's department seemed to know about. The deal Ella von Tragg offered was generous with a completion bonus, and Max knew the elderly German lady was good for it. He also knew with even more certainty that it would be a mistake not to believe her outrageous story of a dear, dear friend murdered over a most valuable and most deadly, ancient treasure. It was all irresistible to Max, a victim of the moment, as if treasure hunter was a tag that defined him now, lured him like catnip like crack and luckily made him employable. Of course, those in the know, know Max previously in St. Malo wanted nothing to do with treasure hunting. But perception is everything and Max believed it rarely went in his favor, so he had to say yes. Even his love, his wife Mei would have agreed with him, he thought to himself, on the thirty-mile drive out to the hometown of Ella's murdered friend, Thomas Gill. Now Max was driving back from said Freeville after a wasted trip, empty-handed and feeling information deprived in the middle of nowhere outside Ithaca on a rapidly unnavigable road.

He was sure the best thing he could do was to try to get roadside and sit it out. His passenger, a young, stranded stranger he met at the Freeville gas station minutes before, abruptly lowered the passenger window, unlocked the door, and unbuckled her seatbelt. Max snuck a look over at the girl whom he was helping get to the Cornell campus.

What? You crazy?!

East Indian, by the looks of her, the young lady had told Max that she was a grad student and her own car had broken down. She had a tutorial for which she couldn't be late, *please*. Now the tawny-skinned, somewhat attractive co-ed wasn't so polite. She was screaming something at Max in Hindi.

Shiva rahata, Kali!

That was a nanosecond before she jammed her feet atop Max's, stomping down and hitting the brake and the accelerator at the same time, hard. Max was right. The skid that followed was epic.

The rental car fishtailed first on a strip of blackening ice, then pinwheeled out of control, a strobing blur under the cold, blue heavens. Crossing lanes, the car spun like a two-ton top on the glassy sheened, snow-encrusted asphalt. The good news—the Kia Optima was the only vehicle in range dumb enough to be caught in the spring storm. This would not be a multi-vehicle accident. The less good news—Max's car T-boned the median's concrete barrier clean and launched.

The rotating sedan shot skyward, passenger door flapping wide. Strapped in like a test crash dummy, at the optimum point, in his Optima, Max was ass over tea kettle; airborne enough to see the whole, breathtaking, finger-shaped lake shining in the distance below. Literally, like the Cornell fight song goes, he was:

High above Cayuga's waters…

CHAPTER TWO

The native people believed Lake Cayuga was made in the beginning when the Great Spirit was creating the world. He laid hands on the soft earth to bless it. His imprints filled with water and became the ten major Finger Lakes of which Lake Cayuga was the middle finger of the right hand, one of the biggest with depths immeasurable. The Creator graced the surrounding area with hanging valleys of magnificent gorges and waterfalls.

The Onondaga Nation, descendants of First Men, occupied the region with its five original tribes spread out across what is now most of New York State. Sometime in the 1500s, the assorted clans formed the Iroquois Confederacy. It was a hard-brokered, mutual understanding that gave the Mohawk, Oneida, Onondaga, Seneca, and Cayuga centuries of inter-tribe peace, cooperation, and well-being. The Cayuga tribe had their village by the lakefront that bears their name within the shadow of a great waterfall. It was considered such special ground that every year representatives of the Confederation would travel to gather on Cayuga land for their powwow. The annual conclave was in the natural, concave bowl at the foot of what they called Taughannock Falls after a founding Onondaga chief, Taughannock. Pronounced Tuh-GA-nick, it drops a dizzying 215 feet, making it three stories taller than the great Niagara. Its waters carve a 400-foot-deep gorge through layers of sandstone, shale, and limestone that were once the bed of an ancient sea.

Their lives were honest, and there was enough for all, and then the Europeans came. The fur-seeking Dutch and French trappers, then the power-seeking English. Some good, some bad, some worse. The glory days were over, their chiefs warned. The Europeans were as tribal as the native people without a peace-binding Confederacy and much more violent than the savages they scorned. The English and French waged a ferocious extension of their Seven Year War on tribal lands, known in American history books as the French and Indian War. From 1756 to 1763, New York State was a bloody battleground that split the Iroquois Confederacy. Half the tribes threw in with the English and half with the French. It fractured further thirteen years later when the colonials decided to fight their English overlords. Some Indians backed the neighboring militias, but most backed the heavily favored English army. It was not pretty. It was bitter and bloody. By April of 1777, all the tribes on either side of the conflict were heavily decimated in the fight, in disheartened disarray and done with the white man's wars.

* * *

Chief Wading Bird was in a quandary and did not like his options. The perfumed, English General whose command they had only been under since the week before had foolishly ordered his heavy artillery to be rushed up to the front. The problem was that meant crossing a wide, low-lying creek well known by Wading Bird and his Cayugas. It was early spring 1777, and a driving rain would make the swollen creek impassable for these big, iron guns. It was obvious to even the least-witted brave among them. So, Wading Bird and his men set up camp near the creek to wait it out. The English officers and soldiers had other ideas, and after attempting the crossing themselves with disastrous results, pressed Wading Bird and his men into service. The cannons were mired in the mud and all hands—English, Canadian, Hessian, and Indian—were required now to un-mire them in this hellacious rainstorm. Wading Bird had told Black Deer of the Senecas who had the ear of the English commander that it was best to set up camp as they had done and wait till the creek was calmer. Black Deer agreed with Wading Bird but was no help. Their English leader needed the guns at once and they had pledged to obey. That general with his New York Royal regulars had laid siege to a colonial fort further ahead and needed to take the fort quickly before the push east to victory. A victory that could allow their Confederacy to prosper once again.

Wading Bird admired his optimism. He did not share it. The once friendly Oneida and Tuscarora had pledged their warriors to the colonists, and they gave no mercy to their enemies, even former confederates. It was Indian versus Indian and atrocities had been escalating. The French trappers had taught them scalping the hard way decades before and the new generation of war-crazed braves turned it into a grisly art. It was not just scalps the Oneida were taking. They would skin the feet and whatever else, before removing the heart and holding it up so it was the last thing their victims would see. Wading Bird silently wished his men had stayed home and planted as this was the season. He wished he was snugly wrapped in cozy bear hides with his loving woman who always smelled of lilac rather than shivering and straining in the stinking creek knowing there were battles to come for causes he cared not.

But the Cayugas had no choice. The war had come to them, and they had to take a side. Like the Senecas, Mohawks, and Onondagas, the Cayugas figured the English had more might and once victorious would, in gratitude for the help, block the local farmers, trappers, and new arrivals from moving further west and settling on more tribal land. It made sense. The Redcoats were well-armed and a disciplined lot. The colonials were not.

The soldiers and Indians tried their best to move the cannons in the creek, but the cast-iron guns had other ideas. It was going to be a long night with his Cayugas mumbling and grumbling non-stop about the English dummies. Wading Bird did not stop their yammering. He totally agreed.

You can't fix stupid.

* * *

Eton-educated, Brevet Brigadier-General Barry St. Leger was the luckiest man in the English army. That's what his wife, Frances, insisted. He had been presented a command like no other without any real military experience. Along with his orders to meet up with General John Burgoyne at the head of the Mohawk River, he was given the responsibility to deliver to Burgoyne a secret weapon, the *gift*. At least that's how it was described to him by the personal secretary of none other than Lord North. This covert, ancient armament was shipped to Quebec and placed in St. Leger's custody. It came with a towering, Gurkha bodyguard who was never to leave its side. Encased in a protective iron-lined chest, it was about the size of a small pig and double the weight. St. Leger which he pronounced *Legger* to sound as un-French as possible, was told to never open it and to protect it with his life should anything happen to the Gurkha. St. Leger could tell it had come from India by the Sanskrit writing etched into its lid. When he asked the taciturn, turbaned Hindu officer whose name was Singh what the writing indicated, he was told, *Death*. It was a weapon of mass destruction that would swiftly end the war and send them all back to their motherlands with glory.

So far, so good. Barry's invasion force had made terrific progress coming down from Canada. They had faced only a few skirmishes with colonists armed with little more than pitchforks and hatchets. He had seen what the Senecas and Cayugas were capable of and was glad they were on his side. His troops hardly had to raise a rifle. The Indians did the rest, hungry for the bounty on scalps that the Crown offered. St. Leger didn't have much appetite for the gruesome business, but his wife insisted he harden his heart and exult in every revolting colonist's demise for his men's benefit. So, he did. St. Leger had been instructed to make haste as time was of the essence, and delivering the *gift* was paramount which made his decision to stop and lay siege at Fort Stanwix all the more peculiar. The fort was no threat and had no strategic value. The fighting was to the east. His army could have passed the fort without incident, but Frances thought since it was only manned by roughly armed irregulars, her husband could easily take the fort and then move right along. It would be a major feather in his cap. A celebrated rung on the ladder of a sure-to-be successful campaign.

Unfortunately, the local Americans inside the fort were damn stubborn and fought back for two solid days, firing from behind the safety of their walls. Stanwix did not immediately fall and St. Leger was stymied. The cannons would help immeasurably if they ever got there. When Black Deer, his Seneca in charge of the Indian auxiliary, sent word the cannons had finally been freed from the creek and could arrive by the next high sun, St. Leger was surging with confidence again. He had his men surround the fort outside the firing line and made camp, continuing the siege. Before heading into his own tent for the night, St. Leger looked in on Singh in the tent next to his. The dark-skinned giant was on his knees praying over the crate and whispering the word—

Kali...

CHAPTER THREE

The county road crew, working overtime, had been piling high the accumulating snow alongside the highway when they heard the Kia's tires screech and saw the airborne car coming their way. Jumping off Sno-Cats and plows, tossing shovels aside, scattering for their lives, they looked back awestruck as the car above them rotated a full circle on its way to plunging down. Then it clipped the biggest branch on the only major tree still alive on the roadside. Slowed in its descent by the sturdy maple, the car tilted and dropped into the man-made, white hillock, straight up, nose in. Its airbag exploded open and the driver inside disappeared, sliding into the snow at a ninety-degree angle. From within a scream of pain was heard.

He's alive!

The five workers scrambled to help Max, who was encased inside the car six feet into the pile. They dug at the snow, flashing shovels in the late afternoon sun, and clawed away working hard to reach him. It was the best of humanity on display Max would later proclaim when he had a chance to buy his rescuers a coffee. They were a mixed bag of locals including two convicts on work release. This was the most motivated they'd been all year.

Inside the car, Max could not hear a thing, which was scary. He could feel the icy cold around him, but his eyes were pushed into the airbag now deflated and wrapped around his face, rough on his skin. He was blinded and jammed into this position and could not free his arms or legs. He tried to turn his head and had the distinct sensation that he was bleeding, somewhere. As for his passenger, Max was pretty sure she wasn't still in the car.

...and what was that she was yelling? Something out of an Indiana Jones movie?!

This Max said aloud, and he rejoiced in the sound of his voice no matter how muffled. It was his. He took in some deep breaths with increasing difficulty as the air closed in. Getting light-headed, Max went full grim and figured a benefit to dying could be not having to answer these confounding questions. The hitchhiker tried to kill him. The hitchhiker had jumped out the door.

Fucker!

Before he could waste another labored breath, he heard the high-pitched voice of DeShaun DeMott, a two-time loser for dealing in stolen goods.

Don't you go dying now, dog. Not after that stunt. You hang in!

Chiming in and digging hard for his age was DeShaun's gravelly-voiced, gray ponytailed, hippie cellmate, an illegal ticket scalper named Artie Hicks.

We gotcha, dude, you know it!

Max could tell he was in determined hands and awaiting rescue, hope bloomed. The biggest plus to dying would have to wait. For the time being, he would continue to be angry at his late wife, Mei U, for going first.

CHAPTER FOUR

Take anything with value. But do not kill the high priest.

Scratch that. Not going to happen. Sheffield steel had gone right through his heart.

It was winter early 1774 in Varanasi, India, and the great Bengali drought had produced the Great Bengali Famine. The heat never wavered even in the Punjab, and Lieutenant Philip Pearce was counting the days till he was mustered out and on a ship back to Britain. Pearce's commander's words of warning were ringing in his ears, In his defense, when he was surprised by the high priest, he and his men were looting artifacts for the Crown in a hellish, skull-lined tunnel near a small river temple in the insurgent city. The highest of the high holy, Sabu Shaan was dressed as a beggar, smeared in ashes, smelling of feces and attacking with a frightening Bundi dagger when Pearce whirled and killed his first man ever. His commander was going to come down hard on him. To compensate, Pearce pushed his men further to comb the catacombs for anything that could be remotely valuable. Only later, in his quite decent officer's quarters in nearby colonial Jodhpur, would he realize how much his men had overachieved.

His girlfriend, Aruna, a local beauty, bathed him lovingly while he teased her with the promise to take her with him when he left. It had been a horrible day, and Pearce couldn't have been filthier. The things he had seen. And the terrible mistake he had made in killing the holy man.

He was clothed like a miserable wretch!

-Baba Sabu Shaan was Aghori. They are the thing we are not. We are life. They are death.

Aruna went on further to kill any romantic moment by explaining to him that the strange cult reveled in whatever humans reviled most. They found purity in dirt and degradation. As Hindus believed in re-birth, the Aghori embraced *re-death*. Pearce rolled his eyes and rolled his sweetheart into the clean sheets of his somewhat sagging four-poster bed. He told her after, she could have her pick of one of the treasures he had appropriated as tax collector for the region.

In the corner of his apartment at the bottom of a cherry-picked pile of loot that included a gunnysack of silver vessels, gold candlesticks, and bejeweled bowls was an old, iron crate with Sanskrit writing on its lead lid.

CHAPTER FIVE

Three years later, April 19, 1777, that looted artifact was a tent away from St. Leger, outside what is today Syracuse, New York. Night was falling, in the quiet siege encampment, and St. Leger thought it might be a night where he could give Frances proper thanks and pleasure her. Since the march from Quebec, he had not been able to get good and firm enough to satisfy his wife. Stress probably, she told him. St. Leger, panicked about his normally reliable manhood, had prevailed on Black Deer to have his medicine man recommend something to remedy his situation and the Seneca had delivered. The brew was awful, and St. Leger did throw up on his boots, but to his surprise later, he felt potent. Frances, however, despite her normally stirring libido, had no interest and went right to bed. Blue-balled Barry seemed to have no choice but to toss and turn uncomfortably all night, painfully pivoting on his best erection in a decade.

After midnight, he was rousted, still aroused. A spy had been captured, and St. Leger was out of bed in a snap, hiding his priapism unsuccessfully under his dressing gown. The man, Reverend Yorn, was a Church of England clergyman who had been captured working with an American search party as their scout. Since Yorn's life depended on this meeting with the British General, he tried not to stare at Barry's prominent stiffy. Not possible. He stared; he chortled.

What in God's name do you find so funny?

Yorn was a survivor and had already changed sides twice in two years.

Funny? Hilarious, sir! Outrageous! That your fine soldiers would think I, a man of our God, was with the revolting rabble. I am and always will be loyal to the king.

Yorn fell on his knees and explained how he was captured and forced into service. To prove his point, he proceeded to gush, telling St. Leger of a great, great threat coming his way. A growing, reinforcement force of local soldiers and irregulars under a General Herkimer bolstered by hundreds of scalp-hungry Oneida warriors, was coming to relieve the besieged American fort. From eye level on his knees, Yorn watched as the once steadfast, pitched tent beneath St. Leger's dressing gown slowly and surely collapsed. Not unlike the British's chances to win the war after Barry St. Leger's fateful decisions the following day.

CHAPTER SIX

The local EMTs, Ithaca police, and fire department all were working to get Max out of the half-buried car in which he was trapped. With winds whipping at the sunny, snowy roadside, the jaws of life, a spanking new, bazooka-sized, hydraulic cutting apparatus borrowed from the neighboring town of Lansing, was put to the test. Max's two new best friends were given the job of keeping Max conscious and positive while the rescue pros worked their magic on the crushed car. It would not go swiftly. Artie Hicks, a die-hard Yankees fan, tried first to engage Max in the latest baseball season, going over the stats of the team's whole starting 2009 line-up highlighted by his personal reflection of the athletic artistry of Derek Jeter.

The unnerving sounds of glass shattering and of metal being shredded filled the frozen air, creaking and frightfully moaning. The jaws widened, and metal and plastic cracked and snapped. Crows scattered. Emergency lights whirled red, dyeing the landscape in crimson. Rubberneckers on the highway gawked at the wreck. State troopers slowed all vehicles. The whole window post between the Kia's front seat and back seat was sliced away by giant scissors. The car shifted and dropped again, settling. Max felt sudden pressure on his ribs. He concentrated on getting small. Artie concentrated on his team.

And I know people say Joba Chamberlain…Oh, that big guy's a dirty player. He throws at guys' heads. I say good! You need an intimidator. Scoreboard, baby!

He offered to help Max get a good deal on Yankee tickets. Max appreciated the offer though he wasn't a fan of the team or of intimidation. He just wanted to wait quietly and occasionally wince in pain. DeShaun DeMott took that as a challenge and tried to pump him up.

Man, don't you get dark. As long as you come out with a working dick, you be okay.

That hit home. Max's right hand was pinned to his thigh. Silently, he worked it toward his crotch and, with a burst of effort, goosed himself. His eyes rattled all the way up in his head from the painful sensation. Max sighed happily, shivering under the space blanket they had stuffed in. He nodded to DeShaun.

All good, yes, thanks!

Max shut his eyes and counted his temporary blessings. Like the work crew, DeShaun continued.

Oh, yeah…I hear you…C'mon. dog. Spill it…You an ass or a titty, man? I know you got a hot mama back home.

–She died.

Max hoped that truth would silence them both, and it did. For a full minute. A minute that Max took to remember why he was here and every funky thing that had happened in Ithaca since the morning limo ride from the airport.

***

Can I ask you a question, Mr. Dean?

The local limo driver looked back, lowering the dividing glass halfway so Max's answer could be clearly heard.

Sure.

The young chauffeur who'd been booked by Ella von Tragg to pick up Max and bring him to her Trumansburg hotel, checked his rearview mirror one more time and then stole an over-the-shoulder glance at Max.

Have you noticed...that blue car's been tailing us all the way from the airport? Is someone on to you?

-On to me? What?

Max had been in a lot of limos in his days in the rock and roll world of touring. He'd been in fancier, bigger stretches, pursued by paparazzi, groupies, irate spouses of deadbeat clients, but none had anything to do with him.

No, you must be mistaken. Why would you think—

The driver, Eddie, a junior college graduate with an Eagles tribute band and the business card to prove it, apologized. He had heard it from his girlfriend that Max was a private eye. Candace worked at the hotel and had been doing the advance on Mrs. von Tragg's arrangements. She was the one who first contacted Max off his own security consultant website that advertises his P.I. services. The kid had him. Max had always kept a hand in the business. Any way to make a living in uncertain times. The limo pulled off Route 89 in Trumansburg and up the driveway of the Taughannock Inn, historic lodgings on the shore of Lake Cayuga, at the foot of the majestic falls. The blue, late-model sedan continued up Route 89, disappearing. Eddie, who on weekends handled the band's Joe Walsh impression, did not have a peaceful, easy feeling.

Well, I think it was following us. The girl behind the wheel looked foreign. I got the plate number if you ever need it.

Of course, Max would.

That was clue #1 that Max should have stayed in L.A. and looked for honest work as a TV writer. *Cough, cough.* He still had an agent who took his calls and submitted him for script work. He just hadn't gotten a union assignment in ages. First fiscal year without work, Max lost his

Guild health insurance. With the sub-prime mortgage breakdown causing the whole country to sink into a recession, he and Mei U's once-solid real estate portfolio went underwater fast. They were burning off thousands a month for Mei's cancer treatments. Max tried to get his union insurance reinstated and was told he just needed one paid story assignment and he would qualify for another two years. He knew the showrunner of a tacky, syndicated action show about a private eye and persisted in getting a meeting. In that high-rise office in the black tower, he pitched his ass off. It was an amazing, true detective story that had everything and was perfect for the series Max was sure. The showrunner wasn't. The guy passed in the room. Max, desperate, asked him to please reconsider and told him the truth of his situation. A simple story assignment would help. Not even a full script. The showrunner looked at Max like you look at a tone-deaf busker on the street pushing his CDs on you and said:

Don't you have a friend who could give you an assignment?

Max didn't. None of his friends were in a position to do so. The showrunner sighed.

You need better friends.

In a show of generosity, he made sure his secretary validated Max's parking stub, so it wasn't a total loss. *Thank you very much.* After that, Max had no choice but to use everything they had left. She could beat cancer. He did, a decade before. She was younger and stronger. They bet on her life and he never regretted it. They chased the globe for the newest cure, the most cutting-edge doctor in the U.S., Mexico, Switzerland, Prague. They tried. She died. It had been over a year and a half since, and the pain of losing Mei was still an open wound.

***

It was getting later in the day, and the sun slipped behind a steel curtain of clouds. In the crushed Kia, with the temperature dropping, Max was going numb from the cold. He could hear voices talking to him, but he could not make out what they were saying. All he could sense was the howling wind and a cold void beckoning. Maybe he would die after all. He knew that had its advantages.

On a hill across the six-lane highway, oblivious to pain, a banged-up, East Indian grad student with an unset, compound-fractured left arm and left thigh contusion sat on a big rock staring in the distance at the accident site. A victory roar erupted from the rescuers, and her head dropped. Max was out! Into the dumb air and gurney-rolled quickly right into a waiting ambulance.

CHAPTER SEVEN

Lt. Philip Pearce, all of twenty-seven, in a foreign land in the year of 1774, had not ridden through a landscape as deathly as the eerie miles that stretched south of Rajasthan. Pearce had underestimated Aruna. Exotically beautiful, he had picked her out for only physical comfort but besides being an effective medical healer, she was a patient teacher, wise and forward-thinking. She continued to be the only bright spot about his rapidly ending tour of duty in India. He had never felt real passion for any previous partner and knew Aruna had gotten under his skin, deep into his heart. So much so that he half-wondered if he was being enchanted. And in the same half-thought realized he was okay with it. She was making him do things which a normal man would not do. Like riding out ten miles into a no-man's-land on his only days of leave. They pushed on, riding toward what appeared to be the ruins of a city in the distance.

Aruna had insisted they make the unsettling trip. Once she saw the sacred chest in his apartment and read the Sanskrit inscription, she opened it up and closed it right away. Pearce had no idea what he had plundered from that stinking underground vault on the banks of the Ganges. It was the last *Eye of Shiva*, long rumored to be protected by the Aghori. A thick, tourmaline-covered disc, no larger than a serving platter. Its history was part of the *Upanishads* and many other ancient Hindu writings. According to the wise ones, Pearce was in possession of an unthinkably devastating, God-like force. Aruna grew up believing the stories told. Originally there were three Eyes of Shiva. The First Eye created the world, and the Second cleansed it. The Third Eye's story had not yet been written. Quoting by memory from the *Mahabharata*, Aruna continued.

"Each Eye was a single projectile charged with all the power in the universe."

Pearce always the pragmatist asked if she considered the writings hyperbole. Aruna told him to judge for himself. Raised in nearby Lucknow, she had devoured all the old tales about the catastrophe that befell the Rama Empire.

"An incandescent column of smoke and flame as bright as 10,000 suns, rose in all its splendor...It was an unknown weapon, an iron eye, a gigantic thunderbolt of death which reduced to ashes an entire race . . ."

The closer they rode toward the city that was once called Harappa, the land became more barren. Nothing seemed to grow, though they were not in a desert. Rather than sand beneath their steeds, it seemed to be ash that covered the land. Centuries later, the valley would be scientifically recorded as having radiation levels a hundred times normal. It was a holy place but also a cursed one. Site of the largest city in the Rama Empire, it was once home to a half-million souls, vaporized some 10,000 years before by an enormous explosion, the detonation of the Second Eye. They called it the Second Cleansing. It was one thing to tell her handsome Englishman old stories, Aruna wanted Pearce to see the evidence. It was all around them. Rocks and more rocks vitrified by unthinkable heat, fused together from melting. No life nearby whatsoever—animal, bird, insect. They dismounted and walked the urban grid of ruins. What was once an expansive city of buildings, streets, squares, and life had been totally destroyed in one singular event. Scattered everywhere were fossilized human skeletons of all sizes seemingly baked and imprinted into the ground. Many were holding hands, linked together, expecting their fate. Pearce trembled, Aruna held him. He kissed her with all his might and sighed, cheery amid the echoes of time-lost carnage.

This would be Aruna's ticket back to London with him. Pearce was taking the weapon back to King George himself.

CHAPTER EIGHT

Wading Bird and his men had been rewarded for their herculean efforts freeing tons of war iron from the mighty mud by being pushed double-time through the night and the breaking day to join up with St. Leger. Without any sleep, the Cayugans arrived at the British encampment in time to get new orders. St. Leger, in distress about the advancing force under this General Herkimer, was ordering his Hessians and all his Indians to make haste and surprise attack the revolutionaries before they could reach the fort. His own scouts had confirmed Yorn's story. The enemy army was near. Despite not wanting to risk any English soldiers in this battle, St. Leger had announced he would lead the secret mission. He felt obligated and Frances encouraged it. Despite the obvious danger, his men needed him. She kissed him goodbye as sweetly as he ever remembered and off he went. It probably would have been best for him and history if he had stayed the course. Instead, he succumbed to a mild case of diarrhea and after a mile's march, returned back. His mercenaries and Indians under experienced Hessian command advanced onward.

It was mid-day when Brevet General Barry St. Leger finally returned into the quiet camp. He tried to be as stealthy as possible to avoid any embarrassing conversations. He could see his big guns had arrived and also the rest of the Canadian support battalion which was carrying all the supplies including three wagons overloaded with the Cayugans and Senecan camp belongings. St. Leger was starting to feel better. More like himself. With no reinforcements, the American fort might surrender at first sight of his artillery and they could be back on their way to Burgoyne for more glory. He'd spent a good hour in the woods relieving himself until it hurt.

He assumed this was more payback for the virility potion he drank the night before. Better he just pleasure his wife manually, and not worry about inserting himself. Unfortunately, Frances, his wife, had taken the matter into other hands and other parts. In this case, Singh, the Gurkha, had a naked Frances upside down, her legs over his shoulders in a fine, tantric position. A devotee of the *Kama Sutra*, Singh was making her sing, banging Frances to beat the band when St. Leger entered the tent.

A hush, a gasp, Singh's feeble attempt at an explanation, and an outraged St. Leger, still outfitted for battle, flashed his sword without hesitation. With adrenalin pumping, he screamed, hacking off Singh's head, his long, dark snake flapped out, swirling white goo. It mixed with the blood splatter all over the tent. To St. Leger's distress beneath his britches, shit dripped down his leg. Frances bravely rose up, ignored the smell, and hugged her blood-soaked husband until he accepted the story that she had been raped. The fiend in their midst had one job—to protect the strange *gift* until they delivered it to Burgoyne—and he had failed. Now they both knew that awesome responsibility would be on the not so-sturdy shoulders of Barry St. Leger, a victim of unintended consequences.

CHAPTER NINE

Ella von Tragg lived like a rich, retired movie queen. Bedeviling her eighty-six years, she had Jane Fonda-quality plastic surgery, and a better fashion sense than her friend and countrywoman, Heidi Klum. By 2009 she had buried two husbands, scores upon scores of lovers, all her children, grandchildren, and her best friend Tom Tom (Thomas) Gill of Ithaca. He was the one she missed most. He had taken her from the depths of degradation to the heights of respectability. He had created the wealth and its advantages that Ella still enjoyed. Though he never approved of her many indulgences, he would never criticize her more than once. He was a rare man, confident in who he was and respectful of all he met. A country gentleman but one who understood women as equals. His wife Jeanie was a lucky woman until she wasn't. Tom Tom was never the same after she died in a lightning strike off the Cote d' Emerald nearly twenty years before. Though they always seem to live a continent away, he was a terrific, long-distance communicator. The last few years of his life, the talks dwindled. Ella, however, did speak to him on the phone a few times in the week before his powerboat hit a dock at full speed in the thick, tulle, lake fog.

That first phone call Tom Tom was very energized and excited. He had been given an old Cayuga Indian map to an unusual and storied, hidden relic. He was considering putting together a small salvage crew and jokingly asked Ella for her help. She had to remind him that the last time almost killed her. Indeed, she still bore the hideous, wrap-around scar on her neck where she had been strangled by a twist of fate. Tom Tom had saved her, sacrificing the retrieval of more pirate treasure in the cave that night. Ironically, the man she was expecting today had benefitted decades later, finding what she and Tom Tom had left behind. Tom Tom's death in 1996 was ruled a suicide or an accident by the local coroner. Neither explanation sat well with Ella. She suspected there was more to it and pushed for a police investigation at the time. Nothing changed, the police found a suicide note and last will on his computer and that was that.

And what of this dangerous artifact he had recovered? It was never found among his possessions. He told her he was put on a mission to protect it. That had nagged at her for years. Tom Tom was a beautiful soul with emotions as true and blue as the sky reflecting on the Lake Cayuga waters below her hotel room. He had grown up on these waters, so an accident seemed inconceivable. And suicide while on a mission? Take the coward's way out? Even in his deepest pain, Tom Tom believed he owed it to everyone who loved him to persevere. Ella surprised herself with a laugh thinking of one of Tom Tom's favorite sayings when faced with adversity.

I may have to eat shit. But I don't have to say yummy.

Live like Tom, she always tried to tell herself when faced with troubling decisions. Usually, though, she did the opposite. Ella straightened up in her wheelchair as her latest helpmate, Franz, a Hungarian national and former professional ballroom dancer, came into the room.

Your detective has arrived. He is waiting in the library as you instructed.

Franz did not understand the bond that Ella and this "Tom guy" had first forged on the Brittany coast over fifty years ago. He assumed the dead man was an earlier paramour, which of course, he wasn't. He was, as she often said, *the brother she always wanted.* Not the ones she had. Ella hit the throttle on her electric wheelchair and off she went to meet Max.

Max rose when she entered. They'd only met once, and it was memorable. He was with Mei U in between their two marriages, escaping the madness of St. Malo. The older German woman on the train seemed to see right through them and knew exactly what they had done. It was eerie and awkward too. Especially since Ella's granddaughter and Max had an earlier fling before she had her throat slit. That was in the past, and the lady knew that Max and his friends were victims themselves of the man responsible. Pleasantries were exchanged between them, but one hung in the air.

How is Mei U? I was hoping she'd be with you. Two for the price of one.

Max was prepared for this. Ella sighed and apologized for assuming the young don't die young, then got right down to business. She had been contacted by one of her late friend Thomas Gill's closest work associates.

His name is Wilbur Red Hawk, and he is a Cayuga Indian.

Wilbur told her he had been living in the original Gill family home in Freeville. It was bequeathed to him by Thomas's estate. He was cleaning the basement after a wasp invasion and dropped an antique pipe rack that had held Tom Tom's favorite Meerschaums. Its bottom drawer banged opened and besides pipe cleaners and toothpicks, a small Polaroid photo with a hand-drawn map tumbled out. It was dated the day Tom Tom died.

What kind of relic are we talking? Indian?

-East Indian. If you can believe it. It's ancient.

Ella had a copy of the photo that Wilbur had faxed to her. The quality was sketchy, but it looked like a strongbox with odd etching on it. Max was as confused as Columbus must have been when the explorer assumed he had landed in India and called the original Americans, Indians. Ella was patient.

Inside the chest is the Eye of Shiva. Tom Tom told me it was looted in Varanasi, India, in the latter part of the eighteenth century and lost for centuries after. Franz did some Googling on it too. Thank you, dear. You can go now and please close the door.

Franz did as he was told. With a too-gracious smile to both, he exited. Unlike Tom Tom, *yummy* was a lifestyle choice. Once Ella and Max were alone, she took Max's hand for emphasis.

Trumansburg is where Tom Tom found it. Ten days later, he was dead.

-And inside the chest is...what?

CAYUGA

Tom Tom called it a prehistoric atomic bomb.

Ella did add he'd begun drinking more heavily after Jeanie was killed. Now this disturbing call from Wilbur Red Hawk, a man whom Tom Tom valued. A man who also believed her friend was murdered. The first step for Max would be for him to meet Wilbur in Freeville. She had instructed the old Indian to give Max what he had discovered. It sounded easy enough to Max, who yawned, still on L.A. time. Ella had reserved Max a hotel room and a rental car in Ithaca and he could drive out that very afternoon. Wilbur was a wampum jewelry maker and worked at the Freeville home just on the other side of the lake. Once Max brought her back the map, they could discuss the next step over a fine Taughannock Inn dinner.

We have a reservation for two for eight o'clock. I understand the anise cured breast of Hudson Valley duck is insanely delicious. Is it a date?

Max was good with that and tried not to think she was flirting with him. He pocketed the retainer which he was pleased to see was all cash, and with a chivalrous kiss to Ella's hand, he split, rocking a new gig, rolling into springtime.

* * *

Not. Needless to say, the first step put Max in the hospital. He was in a private room with a view of his hotel of all things, and he hurt all over. With some time to assess, and the wonder of a painkiller, he wondered if the whole trip to Freeville was doomed from the start. When he had arrived at the Wilbur address, the old farmhouse had been burned to the ground. Neighbors shook their heads. Happened the night before. No one knew anything, least of which where Wilbur might be. With that dead end, Max had figured to head right back to downtown Ithaca and meet his cousin Janey at the State Diner for their Bo burger, a local culinary delight he had seen Guy Fieri enthusiastically devour on late-night Food Network. Then the damn snowstorm hit followed by his simple (foolish) act of kindness helping the young, stranded stranger. The East Indian girl who seemed determined to kill him. He could not believe she was not hurting like him or worse. And why did she have to be East Indian? The coincidences were starting to hurt more than his ribs.

Hey cuz. Doctors say, nothing broken, only bruised. They're releasing you tonight.

-And good to see you too, Janey.

She apologized and air-hugged Max. Janey Dean Flatman was a coffee-colored exotic, part African American. She had the prettiest face and smile with interesting wrinkles and a story behind each one. A tenured professor at Cornell, she was a good fifteen years younger than Max, divorced and outweighed him by a few ounces.

I know, I know. I gained some weight since...uh...

-You can say it. Mei's memorial.

Max knew exactly the number of days since Mei passed. All that love and memory they had together. Wondering where it all went kept him up some nights. Existence and non-existence. Time loops where she'd still be alive. Mei was big on reincarnation, and it was a big comfort to think of her being every friendly insect, interested bird, or glorious rainbow.

I used to go out with the emergency resident on call. He says you're a miracle.

Max was buoyed to see his cousin. She was the adopted daughter of his father's baby brother, Mychal, the family's black sheep, long since gone, who was known as "the communist." Not so much for political reasons but because he once lived on a commune. Max never knew who Janey's real mother or father were and was always too hesitant to ask. Janey, on the other hand, was not one for hesitation.

If your client's looking for the Eye of Shiva, you're in luck. I did my first thesis on pre-history India.

Max let out a long, painful moan. In the fate versus free will tug of life, fate was suddenly the favorite. In the hospital hallway, a tall, turbaned man with the look of an academic passed by their open doorway.

Janey gave him a friendly wave.

CHAPTER TEN

Reverend Yorn, the spy, counterspy, survivalist preacher secretly split off from St. Leger's sneak attack force in time to miss the entire, what is now called, Battle of Oriskany. Flanked by tomahawk-wielding Cayugans and Senecans, under the command of the mercenary Hessian Rifles, they ambushed the Americans, bullets flying. In the fierce, hand-to-hand fight that followed, St. Leger's men prevailed, despite a distressing number of casualties. The Americans lost their General Herkimer early on and disorganized and unprepared, had to run for their lives. Only their Oneida warriors kept up the fight and held their own for nearly an intense, bloody hour. What was left of the Oneida fled as well, dispersing in all directions. One thing was certain when the gunpowder clouds cleared—no help would be arriving for the besieged colonials in Fort Stanwix.

Wading Bird had lost two of his most experienced braves, both his sons. Many of his warriors who had survived had also seen family fall in the chaotic clash. Some Indians and Hessians suffering serious injuries were being carried on improvised pallets and might not make it through the night. The Senecan leader Black Deer was angry about the sacrifice they had all made while the English soldiers had remained in the camp. It was the first time Wading Bird had ever heard him waver in his support for the British. Hearts were swallowed as the blanket of fog enveloped their path making their way that much more challenging. Silently, they trudged back to St. Leger's position in tight, single file, physically exhausted and spiritually unsettled.

St. Leger had his fill of up and down incidents since his early return. He'd killed Singh, the secret weapon's protector; he'd directed his artillery officers to move the big guns into the most strategic positions; he'd heard from a scout that his auxiliary strike against the fort's reinforcements was successful; and then he, unfortunately, discovered his encamped infantrymen, in hurry-up-and-wait mode, had gotten into the brandy supply. Imbibing sentries had not detected a scavenging party of fleeing Oneidas who had doubled back and slipped into the Redcoats' camp. Rather than fight, they stealthily stole the two-wagons full of Cayugan and Senecan belongings, rolling them away without notice. Shortly after the discovery, an outraged St. Leger called out his senior officers, meting punishment for the breach. Lashes were one thing but now it was ultimately St. Leger who would have to explain the loss of all belongings to his Indian allies. He could not afford to lose their help. He hoped Black Deer would smooth this all over.

* * *

With night falling, Reverend Yorn climbed down from a leafy oak treetop and headed for the nearest farm where he could beg some food and a bath. He had betrayed the American cause to save his life. An American and a patriot at heart, he would figure out a way to make it up.

And as fortune would have it, he'd soon have his chance.

CHAPTER ELEVEN

Max missed Ella's dinner reservation at the Taughannock Inn but not by much. Released from the hospital, he and Janey cabbed it out to Trumansburg by nine p.m. Max was taped around the ribs and sporting some bandages on his face from airbag scrapes. Upright and walking albeit slowly, they entered the inn's classy old bar that still smelled of whiskey and cigars from as far back as 1879 when it first opened. Ella had first gotten word of the accident from the rental car company, then the police, then the hospital. She was not one to easily show emotion but her quivering lip was a tell; her anxiety was off the charts. They settled into a corner, high-back booth and Max introduced his cousin. With little tact, Ella extended a hand sizing her up.

If you needed a ride, Mr. Dean, I could have sent a limo for you.

Max explained that was not why Professor Flatman was joining them. Max thought she could add important context to what they were after. In addition, she had already heard rumors about the Eye of Shiva. Janey, on the spot, shrugged.

Anthropology department. We're a tight bunch. One of my associates was asked to translate some ancient Sanskrit characters from a fax image of an artifact. He showed it around the department. No one could, but we had an idea what it might be.

Ella had no one to blame but herself for the leak. She'd sought out the translation after receiving the copy that Wilbur Red Hawk had sent. She now realized what Max had learned the hard way. This asset recovery would not be without complication or risk. Franz approached with a water glass and a medicine vial for his lady. Ella thanked Franz and dismissed him before he could join them. He smiled like a professional and retreated off. She popped two small pills.

Did you tell the police about your hitchhiker?

Max had. He believed the student must have jumped when the car went out of control. The police checked and found no body or evidence of anyone involved. They didn't believe Max's explanation for the wild skid.

I think she was trying to kill me. Seriously. Did I mention she was East Indian?

Max hadn't. He let them feel the weight of the oddities, then let it all out. He was followed on his way to Freeville and set up for elimination. Max wanted to know the name and phone number of the limo driver. Ella stiffened.

You don't think the boy, Eddie . . . ?

–No. He got the license number of a blue sedan with a dark-skinned, female driver that followed me from the airport. Now that I think about it —the damn disappearing hitchhiker's abandoned car was also blue.

Max paused, silently wondering if he could best work this job remotely back in sunny L.A., where he had LAPD friends and a Sleep Number bed. His aching ribs were talking, and he was listening. Ella was reading him as usual.

If you want to quit, go ahead. I don't want to be responsible for any more harm.

Ella didn't care about this artifact, but Tom Tom gave his life for it. She cared about who killed him years ago. Max had to admit that it could be the same people who were after it now. Janey had been listening and felt obligated to point out the obvious.

You know...if the Upanishads *and* Mahabharata *have even a kernel of truth...in the wrong hands, the Eye of Shiva could be...Scary. Devastating. Catastrophic. Pick one. Or all of the above.*

CHAPTER TWELVE

Lord North was not impressed. He ran his finger over the lid of the old, holy object from the Punjabi region of India that he had been asked to inspect. It was not even made of gold. How valuable could it really be? It was early April 1775, London, England, and despite pulling some major strings, Lt. Philip Pearce had not gotten his audience with the King. Lord North was next best. With Aruna, his Jodhpur lady by his side, Pearce tried to make the famed British Prime Minister understand the power in the box's mysterious contents. Aruna eloquently presented the background and North patiently listened or at least pretended to. Pearce chorused in having seen physical evidence of the Second Cleansing that obliterated the Rama Empire. North nodded and let out a belch which he did not excuse and sent them off with a promise to get back to Pearce. He would have his scientists look it over. He had more pressing matters with the damn American colonies reacting badly to his plan to tax their tea. Due to the Bengali famine, North had hoped to bolster the sagging revenues of the Crown and his own East India Tea Company. The ungrateful Americans were threatening to declare independence and North was pushing to send more troops and weapons over to quickly quash any thoughts of rebellion. Could this ancient weapon help in the goal? He doubted it and was certainly not going to get the King involved. However, if it was some type of explosive, it wouldn't hurt to send it across the ocean and put it in one of his general's hands, specifically, General John Burgoyne in Quebec, whom he trusted to make use of or even the threat of it. Gentleman Johnny was a master chess player who was an expert at the bluff and regularly beat North when they would get together. Before hitting the water closet, the Prime Minister called for his secretary to find a native Gurkha soldier in the palace guard who could be counted on.

Pearce was disappointed in the presentation. Not Aruna's part, which was near perfect, but his own explanation for not turning the artifact over immediately to his superiors in India. North looked at him like an insubordinate and he was worried. Pearce had also expected some thanks for taking the initiative to deliver it to the King and perhaps even a promotion for his effort. None was forthcoming. He waited with Aruna in the officer's quarters for further word. His fellow officers gossiped among themselves that Pearce's power-play reeked of obvious and onerous ambition. Aruna was oblivious or else the model of calmness. She was grateful to Pearce for bringing her to a country that seemed to value women more. She wanted to seek out higher education and become a writer like Eliza Haywood. Haywood's eighteenth century, romantic novels that preceded Jane Austen, had made their way to Jodhpur and were a revelation to Aruna. The world was changing for women and Aruna felt she too had something to say. She loved Pearce for believing in her and taking her out of poverty and into a culture where her destiny was not so limited. Her lover and love had forged her dream into their dream—to be married soon and happily ensconced in the lively, cosmopolitan world of London. She kissed him with a fire that knew no deceit. Never had she been so optimistic about their future.

Pearce would never admit to her that he wished he had not risked bringing the Eye with him to England. If it hadn't been the clincher to gain passage for Aruna, whom he declared an essential artifact expert, Philip certainly would have left it behind where friends in high places told him it should remain. Indeed, the crazed Aghori monks charged with its care were not going to rest until they got it back. Pearce never told her what he learned upon arriving on British soil. Aruna's family had been tortured after it was discovered she had left with Pearce. The family gave up the fact that it was sent to England before being burned alive in their own home. Nothing positive might come of his reckless action and of one thing Pearce was sure. He never should have killed the holy man. If he or Aruna ever went back, they most certainly would be hunted themselves.

North's reaction came quickly. Pearce received orders to serve three more years for insubordination and to be returned to India immediately with Aruna.

CHAPTER THIRTEEN

By the dying embers of a campfire, Wading Bird waited in the dark for Black Deer to get back from meeting with the white leader. His braves, despite severe enervation, were not getting much sleep. They tossed and turned on the cold, hard ground, frothing with bitterness after discovering all their personal belongings were not protected by the scarlet soldiers and had been stolen by the very Oneida they had routed. With no provisions, the Cayugans and Senecans had been given some charity rations and blankets but had nothing else and seethed inside at the effrontery. This was not their war. Wading Bird hoped Black Deer would have some news to settle the mutiny coming. Black Deer walked slowly toward Wading Bird and sat with him for a while before opening his mouth. Their general was very sorry and promised to make up for everything and more once they reached the river's end at Saratoga. This did not sit well with Wading Bird. Before he could strongly protest Black Deer announced in a hushed voice that he was instructing his men to leave the camp that night. Vanish. They were going home and screw the English.

Fuck them in their stupid, redcoat asses!

Oh, yes. Best laugh Wading Bird had since they had joined the fight. The Cayuga and Seneca would all be gone by the morning, and the British could do whatever the hell they wanted. Black Deer went back to tell his warriors. Wading Bird did not plan on leaving empty-handed. The British needed to pay. It was no secret that one wagon and one tent were reserved for some kind of treasure box shadowed always by the dark giant. Or at least it had been. The giant was gone, and the dozing soldier stationed at the tent that housed the Eye of Shiva never saw them coming. Wading Bird, not knowing what it contained, grabbed the fur-covered chest, whisking it away into the darkness of the forest.

CHAPTER FOURTEEN

Max did not take the pain pills he was given and was the worse for it. Every twitch of sleep had been torturous to his chest. Some weak coffee from the Marriott's free breakfast buffet did not help his morning mood. Janey, on the other hand, was perk plus. Before meeting him in the lobby, she'd been up on campus doing some research, and in the library ran into one of the university's East Indian professors. Sabu Shera had been at the hotel management school for over a decade. He was heavy on charisma and Hinduism, and though a well-respected, campus fixture, carried the air of a mystery man.

Something about guys in turbans. Sexy Svengali, you know?

–Is there a point to this?

Max didn't mean to be rude. He didn't want to process unnecessary, local gossip. Janey explained it was the professor who finally helped with that Sanskrit translation for Mrs. von Tragg. He was in the stacks with one of his graduate students. Poor girl was bruised up and had a cast on her arm. Janey prodded.

You think—

Max couldn't, not till he had a real cup of coffee. He was due at the rental car agency to sign a bunch of annoying papers concerning the crash, and the late, great, totaled Kia that somehow had saved his life. And yes, glory be, since it was on Ella's tab, he elected to take the extra insurance coverage. On their way, they cut through DeWitt Square Park and passed some orange-vested workers cleaning up.

Hey, Max. Look at you

-Man, you be all that and bag of sweet tater fries!

It was his rescuers, Artie Hicks and DeShaun DeMott. Max was thrilled to see them and invited them to the Starbucks across the street. They awkwardly explained they were on work supervision from the correctional facility, but perhaps he could get them frappuccino to go. Max was happy to oblige. DeShaun expanded on the order.

Maybe stop at Al's on the corner. Get a couple of those little tequila bottles.

-Dude, make that two tequila nips, one bourbon.

Artie and DeShaun shot their most persuasive smiles, and Max introduced his two angels to his cousin. To his surprise and delight, Artie and Janey warmly hugged. Old friends. His cousin explained.

I've known Artie since I was a little hippie dancing barefoot in diapers at the Salty Dog.

-Amen

Artie sighed, wistfully savoring those days.

As a teenager, I got to hang out at The Crossing, the commune where she lived. For a short time, me and Bibi, Janey's uh, mom...I mean it was after Mychal and her, uh...

-Never mind. It's cool.

Janey wasn't quite ready to fill Max in on the blanks. He and Janey jay-walked across the street to grab the boys' orders when Max's "Free Bird" ringtone cried out. It was Ella. Wilbur had emailed her that he was at the Onondaga Reservation south of Syracuse and gave the address. Ella wanted Max to drive out to see him. Could he rent a car? The thought of driving hit Max with an annoying thud. He was a click under senior citizen and felt twice that. Ella offered to hire Max a driver when eavesdropping Janey jumped in.

I've got a car and am officially between semesters. Had my last class yesterday.

Max was not prepared for her enthusiasm. She waited for his response, cute as the curious cat. Max remembered when she was more svelte and quite a head-turner. Fortunately, he didn't voice this lame thought out loud. Instead, he silently chastised himself for the fat-shaming and realized, what the hell, he had nothing going on back in L.A. He could only walk through the empty rooms of his and Mei's Hancock Park fixer-upper so many times a day talking to ghosts.

Let's rock.

CHAPTER FIFTEEN

His name was Singh. He was born in Calcutta in 1744 and had been a loyal sergeant for the British East India Tea Company. Not a practicing Hindu, he was a modern man with ambition. He sucked up to his English masters early on and distinguished himself suppressing the local rabble in riots against British rule. He was merciless to his own kind and was rewarded for it. He scoffed at the old Indian ways and was disdainful of his ancestors, which isn't to say he wasn't superstitious and wouldn't occasionally pray his ass off. He still kept an onion and a knife under his pillow to keep Kali from killing him in dreams and believed if he cut his hair on a Saturday, it would be bad luck. In 1774 when he had the chance to go to London as part of a special Gurkha guard, he jumped at it. In England, at times, he hated being treated like a second-class citizen. Other times though, it allowed him the darker freedoms that his white colleagues did not have. He believed his future was bright. Especially now that he was hand-picked by Lord North himself to escort a secret weapon that, if legend held, could end the American rebellion. Was he predestined to lose his head to the sword of Barry St. Leger two years later? That was the furthest thing from his mind on the evening he was raping Aruna.

The fact that Aruna was not on a ship back to her homeland and certain doom was a testament to the love and sacrifice of Lt. Philip Pearce. He had placed her out of harm's way and swore to her before their last kiss that he would return to England to be with her. There was no reason for Aruna not to believe him. He'd always been a man of his word. It had taken all of Pearce's family's inheritance to allow her to stay and all of two days for Aruna to have been violated.

Singh had met Aruna when Lord North's secretary arranged for them to confab with the royal scientists to discuss the artifact. Singh did not know anything about the Eye of Shiva, but he was the muscle that would protect it. Aruna was there to explain its origins. The scientists had studied it with gentle care, fearful of breaking into the tourmaline-covered disc lest it really was explosive. They could not say for sure if it was what the French called a *bombe* and listened with a mixture of curiosity and skepticism to Aruna's stories about its power quoted in the early Hindu texts.

After they had met with the scientists, Singh invited Aruna to a little party that evening. He gave her the address and time. Some Indian compatriots anxious for news from the homeland would be delighted to welcome her to London. Aruna showed up on time to the location and once inside saw only rough bedding on the floor and six naked men, including Singh, standing in a semi-circle. Naïve, she asked where the party was.

You are the party.

When they were through with her, they left her bleeding near death. In the morning, the scientists had some follow-up questions for Aruna and circumstances being what they were, the scientists had to wait almost a full week for her to recover. She did and gave the proper footnotes to the Hindu texts they wanted in case anyone ever asked. Asses covered, I's dotted, and T's crossed, the royal scientists, though conflicted, approved it to Lord North. North's secretary, Sir Ramsdale, a practical and not entirely heartless man, gave Aruna a pittance for her part and another pittance not to pursue her tale of being attacked by Singh and his friends. He was needed by the Crown, and off to the New World sailed the Eye of Shiva and Singh.

In the lost week waiting for Aruna and the royal scientists' approval, across the Atlantic, General Burgoyne and his army marched Southwest from Quebec and could no longer be in receipt of what was now called in spy code, '*the gift.*' Instead, Lord North arranged for Singh upon arrival in Upper Canada to deliver it to Brevet General Barry St. Leger, the next ranking officer and accompany him until it was delivered into the hands of Burgoyne. St. Leger's armed regiment, complete with artillery, Indians, and Hessians, were to come from the west. They would join up with Burgoyne where he would be positioning his army on the banks of the Hudson River at the mouth of the Mohawk. Burgoyne believed with St. Leger's forces, and the already triumphant General Howe's army coming north from Manhattan, they would control the Hudson, the spine of the northern colonies. It would effectively cut off New England, and isolate New York from the southern colonies. The war could be over by Christmas.

And then there was this '*gift*' he was promised to speed things along. An instrument of terror, he was told. Burgoyne liked the sound of that. What he didn't like was Barry St. Leger in charge of getting it to him. The man traveled with his wife. A lovely lady named Frances who once shared her maidenhood with a footloose, young Johnny back in Cambridge on a rainy day in a wonderfully accommodating horse stall. He could still smell her wetness in the hay.

Her memory, however, might not have been quite so fond. He never did write her back. She was just too damn controlling.

Johnny rub this. Johnny kiss that.

* * *

On a crisp and fateful 1777 morning before the sun was even up, Barry St. Leger had satisfied Frances. At least it sure sounded like she had completion. Frances had said it was the start of what should be a glorious day. In her chemise with a blanket around her, she poured tea as they waited for the first rays of day. At sunrise St. Leger had already commanded his cannoneers to fire the first warning shot on Fort Stanwix, and they were standing by. He expected the besieged, stubborn settlers would raise the white flag and they would be on their way with prisoners to boot. In the glow of a lantern's soft light, Frances let him rest his head on her bosom. He took the moment to loudly and proudly reflect on how far he had come from his birth in Kildare, Ireland, to conquering the wilds of America. It was astounding how much he had accomplished. Frances knew the truth and stroked his brow without a word. St. Leger was a lucky sperm club member of wealthy land-owning parents who were titled peers with a coat of arms. Everything had been given to him including his commission. She took the moment to reflect as well on Johnny Burgoyne, whom they would see soon. She had given herself to him at the age of sixteen and the dirty cad had used her. She never knew the word *schadenfreude*, but she was an ardent practitioner. She rooted for Burgoyne's failure and wished him the worst. The very thought that she and Barry would be helping Johnny on the path to any glory put her spun cotton undergarment in a bile-twisting knot.

These inner thoughts quickly went *poof* when St. Leger's personal aide asked for entry. After that, everything crescendoed for Barry in a 1-2-3 gut punch. First, he learned that Black Deer and all the Indians had left camp and took horses and mules. Next, he heard that the sentry guarding the *gift* was dead and the tent empty. And then the clincher. The young corporal blurted it out as simply as he could.

Preacher Yorn here to warn you. Continental Army coming. 1,000 men. Close!

Severe panic shot through Barry St. Leger's whole body. Outside the tent, Reverend Yorn wondered how his story was playing. It was mostly total horseshit. There was a twelve-soldier scout party led by Benedict Arnold coming up the river, but Yorn decided to add the thousand-man thing and see if it stuck. He had steered St. Leger right one time, why not a second?

Inside the tent. Frances steadied her husband. He needed to focus and focus now. The disappearance of the *gift* could be blamed on Singh's losing it, or maybe he gave it to the mutinous Indians. He was Indian too, Frances desperately reasoned.

That's why you had to kill him. Don't say you were defending my honor.

–Who cares about your honor!? We have no Indian troops. Over three hundred of our best fighting men. There's an army smack dab in our path to Burgoyne! What do I do?

Frances slapped him across the face.

March. North. Quickly.

–To Canada? But Burgoyne. . ..

He'll be fine without you.

Without St Leger's men, Burgoyne would not be fine. General Howe who was also supposed to bolster Burgoyne's troops, decided instead for his own ambitions, to march toward Philadelphia and George Washington's army. Alone, Gentleman Johnny Burgoyne would be forced to wave the white flag. And the lost *gift?* It was forgotten by the English in the embarrassment and failure of the Northern campaign. Historians all agree the British surrender at the Battle of Saratoga was the turning point of the American Revolution. The desertion of the Indian tribes and Burgoyne's defeat compelled France and Spain to join the Americans against the Empire. After that, it was never a question of *if* but *when* Britain would give up all sovereignty over American soil.

Before mess call St. Leger ordered his troops to decamp. They folded their tents and marched off to the north, double-time. The confused and bemused, outgunned Americans in Fort Stanwix cheered them off. And Brevet General St. Leger became the only commander in history to ever lose a siege by retreating.

***

Eight miles to the south, the Eye of Shiva, wrapped and secured, bounced on the back of a British Army mule over the rocky greenway that led to the land at the foot of Taughannock Falls.

CHAPTER SIXTEEN

Two hundred-thirty-two years later, in an unleased, vacant storefront, a stone's throw from Taughannock Falls, Eddie Longacre was in a morning rehearsal with his Eagles tribute band. He was joyfully dueling his Joe Walsh Gibson to his cover bandmate's Don Henley Stratocaster. They were channeling the memorable guitar hooks in the instrumental break in "Hotel California" when Eddie's cellphone literally vibrated out of his jeans pocket with persistence, flopping on the floor, ending the song before it was done. It was his girlfriend, a tad irate that he hadn't gotten back to the inn guest who'd been trying to reach him. Eddie apologized and turned the temperature down. He did not want to have any problems on the one night a week they got to be together. Besides, he had taken the initiative with the license plate number. He'd gladly contact the detective himself. That was followed by him slipping in something suggestive. To his relief, she was amused by it and gave him the number with a more suggestive rejoinder. Crisis averted, call ended, he asked for a band break and reached out to Max.

Max was riding shotgun in Janey's late-model Prius. It was easily holding the highway upgrade now cleared of ice and snow. She roared passed a few slower cars, terrorizing Max. He flinched, a bit gun-shy at being on the same road where he'd wiped out. Janey had gathered for Max a folder of pictures and articles on the Eye of Shiva and he was trying to absorb it all when Eddie's call came in. Max was glad to hear from him.

Terrific. About that plate number you got on the blue sedan.

Eddie told him he'd already asked the mom of one of his bandmates for a favor.

She loves me. I got her son into rehab last year, and he's stayed sober. She works at the police station. She'll have the plate IDed for us by the end of the day. As soon as I—

Max stopped him. Too many hinky things had occurred. Maybe it was best if they could meet up later. With Janey's prompting, Max asked Eddie if he could come to his cousin's office on the Cornell campus.

Say seven p.m.? I'll bring us in some Bo Burgers.

—Perfect. With a side of cheese tots, please.

Done.

Max and Janey were on their way north on 81 to the Onondaga Reservation. The hilly, wildflower blooms on both sides of the road were firing up with crazy color and silly, sweet smell, ignited to critical mass over-night. Snow was a far-off memory. This peaceful, bucolic landscape was all a turbulent and important Revolutionary battleground, Janey pointed out.

Along the banks of the Mohawk, you can still find musket shot and broken tomahawk shards.

Max wasn't listening. He was transfixed on a photocopy of a desolate location in Northeast India. The rocks in that landscape appeared melted. More photos showed the ruins of a city and skeletons baked into the ground. Janey looked over to see it as well, a little too long for Max's nervous liking.

Hey, hey, eyes on the road.

—Sorry. That was the city of Harappa. It was the economic and population center of the Indus Valley before it was wiped out sometime around 6000 B.C. Thus, the legend of the Second Cleansing.

Max didn't put in words what he was thinking, but Janey could read his skepticism. A scientist herself, she always tried to keep an open mind. The area south of Rajasthan, she explained, has vast areas of vitrified rock. Rock that only could have achieved that physical state by enormous heat. Other historians explain it as a meteor strike but there is no evidence of meteorite matter. It is all ash and the radiation levels are off the charts.

And then there's people who really understand these things. Like J. Robert Oppenheimer, who's called the "Father of the A-Bomb." You know?

Of course, Max knew. Janey looked over to be sure, and Max directed her eyes back on the highway. Janey chuckled.

Sorry. Well, Oppenheimer clarified that "Father" title. He always said his was the first atomic bomb in modern *times. He was known to be a devotee of the Sanskrit texts. After he watched his first atomic test, he was asked how it felt and he quoted from the* Bhagavad Gita. *"Now I am become Death. The Destroyer of Worlds."*

Okay. Max maybe could buy that there was a powerful weapon created by an early Hindu civilization, from natural elements and primitive Iron Age technology, but...

But? But what? What's your problem?

Max's problem was the simple rules of real estate. He chewed on the thought and got lost for a moment down a dark, uncomfortable, time tunnel.

In 2005, before she fell ill, he and Mei invested their nest egg into buying L.A. real estate like the dumbest of the dumb. They were house flippers. Buy low and sell high, good two years of profit until the sub-prime mortgage crisis infected everything in the economy and *home foreclosure* became the epidemic of the "aught" decade. Originally, it seemed like a no-brainer especially since Max couldn't get steady work as a Hollywood writer after his movie bombed. Max had sold a studio movie script roughly based on their St. Malo adventure tale, and it was going good right up to the casting. On camera, the lead, good guy playing the Max Dean part had eyes too close together and seemed evil. There was no chemistry with him and the Mei U character either. *No one was rooting for them*, the producer told Max at a postmortem drunkfest after it opened and quickly closed. The postmortem on Mei was organ failure. Max still felt guilty that he hadn't done enough to save her. He felt guiltier for feeling an emotional release when she passed. He doubted his ability to love and be intimate with another. That may have died with her. He had loved Mei U, his Viet Nam war bride, whom he married twice. He had no idea how to move on or what his purpose in life was now.

Max? You were saying...Eye of Shiva...your problem? You okay?

Janey was impatient, and he was thankful for the interruption.

Yes. Problem is...Location, location, location. Why would it be in the Finger Lakes of all places, thousands and thousands of years later?

Janey did not exactly have a theory on that, but she did believe it left India in the late eighteenth century.

The Eye of Shiva was looted by British soldiers from Aghori monks in Varanasi, India, sometime during the last years of the Tea Company rule. It showed up as a reference in a 1785 royal scientific journal. It mentions it was examined in London in 1775.

CHAPTER SEVENTEEN

Aruna was hurrying over slippery cobblestone and had to slow herself down or risk falling. It was that awkward twilight before the lamplighters came out. The shadows were longer, and night was ready to pounce. She did not like walking the London streets after dark, or worse, walk St. James Park, which she was cutting through on her way to Downing Street. Aruna had been gang-raped once and that was enough for a lifetime. She was raised Hindu and could have pondered why that was her karma. How her earlier lives had led up to the attack. She could have, but Aruna had buried away that hurt and shame somewhere in the back of her psyche and more than survived the last year in its aftermath. She planned never to mention the violation to Philip if they were fortunate enough to reunite. Through the park, fighting a wet wind, up a most polished alleyway, Aruna reached Downing St. She was hoping to catch Lord North's secretary Sir Ramsdale to thank him and his wife. Ramsdale's wife, Anne, had warmed to Aruna's plight and had introduced her to a well-bred woman who had a daughter with an independent streak and needed a bright friend. The daughter's name was Mary Wollstonecraft and she was a young woman of strong opinions about women and the rights of women. She found a kindred spirit in Aruna. Together, with some philanthropic money raised, they had begun a weekly feminist pamphlet on which Aruna was a featured writer. Since being left alone in her new country, Aruna had never been so happy.

When Aruna neared 10 Downing Street, she could see something was terribly wrong. Bobbies were surrounding the entrance and a hospital wagon with horses uncomfortably waiting. A curious crowd pushed in closer despite the efforts of the police. From the crowd, she could hear prayers and whispers as someone was carried out on a gurney. The sheet covering the victim was glaring, stained red where the face would be and bloody wet around the midsection. Someone had been butchered. A devasted Ramsdale, sobbing and coughing, exited the building in a trance. He teetered toward the hospital wagon when his eyes glued on Aruna in the crowd. He frantically veered right for her.

Please help me!

He embraced a shocked Aruna who gave what comfort she could. It was Ramsdale's wife, Anne, who had been murdered. Aruna was in disbelief, reeling. A turbaned Indian, with the appearance of the dirtiest of dirty beggars, had done this deed. He had been coming around Ramsdale's office asking about the damned Eye of Shiva. Ramsdale had told him it had been lost in America, but the madman wouldn't believe him.

Who was he?

Aruna could tell from the description that it was an Aghori monk. She promised to tell the police all she could. Ramsdale wished Lord North had never sent that *gift* to America where the Indians there would steal it. Ramsdale pulled at the remaining strands of hair on his head, wailing.

Why didn't I just tell him about the Cayugas? Let this evil fall on them.

Ramsdale quaked in Aruna's arms. The hushed crowd's gaze was on them. The closing curtain of night fell to no applause. The pain of reality settled in for a long run.

Somewhere in those shadows, an Aghori assassin watched too.

CHAPTER EIGHTEEN

Evil. The word had spread among the tribes of the Confederacy who had backed the losing side. It was late summer 1779, and George Washington had ordered a systematic, military purge against the Loyalist settlers and the Indian tribes that had allied with the British. Not unlike Sherman's merciless March to the Sea in the South eighty-eight years later, General John Sullivan was tasked with taking the war into the civilian homes of the enemy in western New York and breaking their morale with scorched earth tactics. By the time they were mere miles from Wading Bird and his tribe's home on Lake Cayuga, the old chief had already heard all the devastating stories of brother tribes being chased out of their land, killed in droves and all the crops in their fields destroyed. Terrified Indians who could, were already fleeing north to Canada and sanctuary in the British held territories. Resistance was mounted by Loyalist leader John Butler and Mohawk chief Joseph Brant. They joined up and led an attacking force of hundreds of warriors to halt Sullivan's march. With Sullivan having over three thousand, heavily armed, seasoned soldiers under his command, it was a foolhardy, futile attempt. The Indians and Loyalists were crushed at the Battle of Newtown and the survivors ran off for their lives, their lands confiscated. With shelters gone and food supplies being destroyed, the Iroquois Confederacy was officially over in New York.

Wading Bird was not going to flee north. Not yet. He had something to offer General Sullivan and he was preparing how to present it. He had stowed the Eye of Shiva in a secret cavern beneath Taughannock Falls. The fact the chest was always warm to the touch motivated Wading Bird to seek a damp and cool hiding place. In retrospect, it was a wise decision. He made a detailed map to the stash, using wampum shards on a deerskin scroll. He rolled up the map and placed it in one of his wife's best pottery jars. That was buried behind their longhouse for safekeeping. He would reach out in peace to the American army leader whose name he heard was Sullivan. In exchange for mercy, he would offer him this treasure so prized by the Redcoats. It seemed possible to Wading Bird.

The morning Sullivan's brigade reached Wading Bird's village, there were more than enough reasons that nothing good would follow. And then there was the unnerving cry coming from the lake. Wading Bird believed Lake Cayuga had a soulful spirit and a mighty protector, On-Rah-Dee, Cayugan for green. Old Greeny was a revered sea serpent that lived at the bottom of the deepest part of the lake. In drawings that still exist, it appears to be large and monstrous. A long-necked, marine creature with eyes on each side of its scaly, green head and steel-trap jaws. It had only been seen by a few but all Cayugans knew him, from their dreams and in their songs. On-Rah-Dee was crying, and Wading Bird understood it was a bad sign. Though he was trying to save his people, Wading Bird could not help but blame himself for being too clever. He should not have kept the English treasure box to trade with the white man. He should have offered it to the lake. Now it was too late. He dressed in his finest as did his wife and all his people who had not fled already. They held no weapons and waited for Sullivan.

General Sullivan had no intention of entering the village to offer surrender terms or pass judgment. Instead, he sent ahead his most vicious cavalry yahoos. They swooped in from all sides and blindly struck down Wading Bird whose arm was raised for peace. His whole village was burned, every longhouse, every bountiful field, and all his people slaughtered or scattered. Wading Bird's secret would die with him. The map to the Eye of Shiva would remain buried in a pottery jar by the shores of Lake Cayuga for another one hundred years.

CHAPTER NINETEEN

The things we do for love are nothing compared to what we risk for lust. This jolly thought was rolling around in Walter Newton's head as he dug what would be a four-foot by four-foot by four-foot deep, hole in the ground. He expected it to take all night, maybe even into the morning, considering they also needed an identical hole and a ten-foot underground connecting trench with a three-and half-foot diameter. Walter was strong and the late spring earth was soft and easy to move. There was no thought given to asking anyone else to help. The fewer people who knew of the hoax the better. Walter had a lot to lose if they weren't careful. It was May 1879 and after three years assisting the esteemed Charles Babcock, first professor of architecture, Walter, a Yale graduate, got his chance. He was finishing his first year of teaching design at the university on the hill and could be a future candidate for a full professorship if he walked the straight and narrow. Only trouble was, like his friend, Levi, a former slave and Cornell campus janitor, would say:

Walter, when a woman puts her lips around your love stick, you are going to lose your marbles.

Walter figured only colored ladies or godless gals gave that kind of forbidden comfort during coupling. That was until he met Dearie French. French being the operative word. Dearie was experienced, once lived on the continent, and knew how to make music on the *skin flute* as she playfully called it. She could spell cunnilingus forward and backward and taught it without using words. Make no mistake, she was a lady. She'd been educated and had a degree in Greek and Roman literature from Cornell, class of 1877. Walter had met her when she was a student. A married student. They'd met by the lake, both being fond of competitive rowing, and romance sparked thereafter, despite her domestic situation. Being wed failed to quench Dearie's libido and she told Walter after she'd tongue-kissed him deeply that her husband John understood her peculiar needs.

He just won't tolerate it rubbed in his face. Be discreet, darling.

So, Walter played it exactly that way. Dearie's husband was the co-owner and manager of the Taughannock Inn on the lake. A new lodging and dining venture that had been steadily losing business since its grand opening the year prior. John, being anxious to keep his baby afloat, concocted a giant of an unethical stunt to bring attention and crowds to the inn. With the guidance of a history master at a nearby private academy and a baker friend, they would create Early Trumansburg Man. A petrified, prehistoric giant who would be unearthed by accident on the inn property during a scheduled construction project for a coach house. It had been Dearie's idea to bring Walter into the plot as someone in fine physical condition who could be trusted with a secret.

Sometime before midnight, Walter's shovel hit something that was not a rock. Digging more carefully, he could see by his lantern light that it was an old Indian jar. An ornate pottery piece with a lid. He lifted the cap and gently shook out the contents. It was a scroll of deerskin. Unrolled and laid flat, he could tell it was a map with landmarks denoted with shards of shell. A lot of intricate workmanship had gone into this map and Walter thought there had to be something to it. Despite his curiosity, he put it back into the jar. Wrapping his coat around it, he softly laid it on the grass and continued digging. There would be time for it in the light of day.

CHAPTER TWENTY

The last leg of the drive to the Onondaga Reservation Max couldn't ignore the elephant.

Last time I saw you, you were married? What happened?

Janey took a deep lungful for dramatic effect.

Blame it on Toronto. The only place with weather worse than Ithaca. Nine months of winter, three months of bad skating.

Max could get behind the bad weather factor but patiently waited for Janey to deliver the straight goods, which wasn't hard to figure. Her husband Gord, a working Canadian actor, whom Max had never met, felt it was his manly duty to sleep with every visiting American starlet. After years in Hollywood, Max understood the sex-power syndrome and felt for Janey who had seemed genuinely happy as a married woman. Certainly, compared to Max at Mei U's funeral.

I moved to Toronto for Gord and had a good job at Humber College there. You know, then reality hit. The Fleur de Mal, cheeky panties I found in his laptop bag, saved me from wasting years in denial. Cornell took me back. And yes, since the divorce, I have gained the weight. My psychiatrist says I am trying to be less attractive to men.

Max got a laugh at that. Janey, even with the extra pounds, was always a very attractive presence, quick-witted, loveable, and as much as she hated the word, *perky*. Her Toyota followed the sign for the reservation entrance and drove through. The roadside was dotted with roadkill and a few abandoned cars. They drove on, looking for the address that Ella von Tragg had given and pulled up in front of a well-worn house with a number in chalk on a board by the curbside.

Feeling semi-confident that they had the right place, they both got out. Before they could take two steps, shots rang out and bullets hit their car, pinging it. Max grabbed Janey and pulled her behind the back of the trunk. She burrowed beneath him, clenched like a clam, clinging for safety. Max didn't mind that, good for his ego. He could tell it was a BB gun, nothing serious. Another shot rang out hitting a tree branch overhead. It broke free and dropped down near them. A voice from the house yelled out.

Are you from the school?

-What? No!

A man in his seventies appeared at the front door and waved off the sniper on the rooftop. A teenage Indian girl stopped and put away the BB rifle with the shrug of a shoulder. Wilbur Red Hawk motioned Max and Janey in.

Sorry. We thought you were the truant officers.

Max introduced themselves, and Wilbur nodded with a wistful sigh.

They burned down the Gill house. I had to move back with a daughter. Come sit.

Max and Janey followed him inside. He was a tall man though now somewhat stooped and sported his long gray hair in a ponytail. His wampum jewelry was on display on his neck, wrists, and arms—beaded purpled shelled pieces hand-carved and impressive. The living room was still dark with the shades down, and they settled on a low couch behind a coffee table filled with last night's snacks. There was a big screen TV on the wall and an old Les Paul electric guitar with a vintage amp in the corner. Max liked that.

You play?

-No. That's Em Homer's, my son-in-law's step-grandfather. He once played with Hank Williams. At least that's how the story goes.

Wilbur's daughter came in and put some tea before them. She had a neck brace on and motioned that she couldn't talk. Car accident, Wilbur explained. Max wanted to get back to something Wilbur had said. *They burned down the Gill house?*

Who is they?

Wilbur chuckled drily though not at anything funny. The neighbors told him they saw a blue Ford or Chevy by the house that morning. He figured it was someone looking for the map. Though a bigger question would be how they knew he'd found it.

I was at the Wednesday flea market that morning selling my wampum.

-I would love a bracelet like that.

Here you go.

He removed a bracelet and gave it to Janey, fitting it on her wrist.

Ancestors believe it is good luck to give if someone asks. I can use luck.

Janey was terribly embarrassed and offered to pay for it, but Wilbur refused. She could give him something down the line. Not one to put off things, Janey reached under her sweater and lifted over her head a simple jade necklace hidden underneath.

Ok. Lucky Maori greenstone from the South Island of New Zealand.

Delighted, Wilbur fitted it right on.

Good swap! Where were we?

-Uh, the map?

Wilbur laid it on the table before them and a Polaroid of the relic's lid that Tom Tom had attached. He had made a photocopy of the image and wished he had warned Mrs. von Tragg to be more careful with whom she shared it. Max figured the weak link was getting the photo's Sanskrit translated. Someone at Cornell could have mentioned the Eye of Shiva to someone who understood its value, Janey added. And what is its value, Max wondered.

Did Mr. Gill ever talk about what it was?

-He believed it was dangerous and had to be protected. It was not Indian but Indian.

Max was aware of its faraway origins and didn't want to dwell on how it ended up in Ithaca.

And where is it now?

Wilbur traced his hand on the map, a nautical chart of the lake.

Underwater.

Wilbur was positive this map drawn by Tom Tom, which he had found hidden in a pipe rack, was the real deal. Max needed to rewind to the start.

How did Mr. Gill discover the Eye of Shiva?

-He was given an old Cayugan shell map from a dying friend of his wife. Her name was Marie Sayles.

Janey was delighted. She knew the deceased Marie from The Crossing back in the late '60s. Marie studied drama at Ithaca College and lived at the commune with one of the leaders of the local antiwar movement, Tim Kramer.

Artie Hicks may remember him better. Tim died a long time back. Some accident.

If they needed more info on Marie or Tim, Artie would not be hard to locate. Max wondered if Gill used a translator for the Sanskrit. Wilbur nodded, yes, then motioned his daughter's grandfather-in-law into the room.

They'd like to hear you play, Em. THEY'D LIKE TO HEAR YOU PLAY!

The toothless and near-deaf Native-American, who if he wasn't ninety had ninety-years' worth of mileage on him, sat down by the guitar and fired up the amp. He pulled out a little black pocket comb, broke a tooth off it to use as a guitar pick and ripped into an up-tempo, bluegrass rag. It was magic watching his fingers dance over that fretboard with the homemade pick. Every note clear as hell. Forget all your troubles. A pause in the universe. Even Wilbur's hooky-playing, teenage granddaughter, Tiffany, still packing her BB gun, stuck her head into the room to bob to the beat. Em Homer finished with a flourish and all grateful, applauded with gusto.

Tom Tom loved hearing Em noodle. He'd bring his harmonica and good times, brother. Good times.

The day before Tom Tom died, he told Wilbur he was going to meet an FBI agent at the Taughannock Inn to talk about surrendering it.

What happened?

–Nothing. He said the agent never came.

Next afternoon, after a lousy day of fishing, Wilbur was pulling away from the marina in this truck. He could tell Blue Lightning, Tom Tom's boat, had docked. Wilbur and he exchanged waves. It was foggy but the

Cayugan could see someone else walking up to meet Tom Tom. It was the same foreign student who had translated the Sanskrit, he was almost certain.

Do you remember his name?

Wilbur didn't. Maybe he never knew it. He apologized for having lost a few brain cells on re-entry after Viet Nam.

I usually warn people not to drive for a half an hour after talking to me.

Max and Wilbur, both being in-country vets of the great, hated war had lots to catch up on. Wilbur served in the Navy on a Mekong Delta gunboat. Max was an MP in Saigon. They quickly became wrapped up in playing G.I. geography. Em started noodling some background riffs and Janey excused herself. She thought she could narrow down a search for this former student.

Records from 1996 are easy to get and easy to cross-reference with foreign nationalities.

She also could ask her East Indian colleague, Sabu Shera, for help. Wilbur rose to his feet, suddenly elated.

Shit, Sabu! That was his name!

CHAPTER TWENTY-ONE

His long black hair, unleashed from its turban, hung below his shoulders, dripping sweat on to their young breasts. He tried to ejaculate on both of the girls. He wanted them to experience it all. In a true, traditional, Aghori sex ritual, he would be fucking corpses, but it was 2009, Collegetown, New York, and the elders back in Varanasi, India, allowed the variance. His two, live, sex partners were graduate students from Lucknow, India, recruited to Cornell as helpers by Sabu himself, unlike the monk he replaced, Rama Patel, who worshipped alone. Naked and spread-eagled, they were smeared with ash which came from a pet crematorium not far from his house. The two-story, clapboard colonial just down the hill from campus and across from an old graveyard, was purchased by Professor Patel decades ago and had a deep basement that hid decades of Aghori secret rituals. The East Indian devotee without the arm cast was called Pradeep. The one who had tried to kill Max was Naba. The girls by Aghori law were not allowed to experience pleasure, but Professor Sabu Shera, while savoring his own mystical orgasms, was generous with his grad assistants and let them get off if they could. He was born into an Aghori family and was a true worshipper hiding in the modern world. It was a centuries-old cult within Hinduism that believed the sacred path to holiness went through whatever repulsed others most. They found purity in filth, embraced the perverse, the "left" way to God. Sabu made a mental note to himself to smear the girls in his feces for the following week's copulation and hopefully, they'd be menstruating by then.

Like Rama Patel and the others before him, the main reason Sabu was in Ithaca was to be near the Eye of Shiva. Aghori wise men believed it was fated to be lost here, halfway around the world, at an antipodal point on the globe to Varanasi, India. That day was coming; it would appear and this time he must succeed in fulfilling the prophecy of the Third Cleansing. It was not a fluke that when a call for a Sanskrit translator went out that it would invariably find its way to Sabu. Gill's friends, Wilbur and the old lady, had reignited the search for it again with a newly discovered map. Maybe even the real map. This was a sore spot with Sabu. Years earlier, he had been fooled by Thomas Gill and sent on a fruitless, infuriating search following the original deerskin one that had the Eye sleeping under Taughannock Falls. Professor Shera got the last laugh, killing Gill and getting away with it. Now he needed to fulfill his fate. A fate set in motion he believed, lifetimes ago when he was a high priest murdered by an infidel English army thief. Sabu had made some mistakes in trying to take out the investigator from L.A., but that failure made things better and clearer. Let this Max Dean find the holy treasure and then they will remove it from him. Whatever the risk, Sabu knew he could weather it. He had a tried and true safety net in place. Flaming up a ceremonial, marijuana blunt, he took a long, refreshing draw. Refocused in mind and body, Sabu nee *Baba Sabu Shaan* turned the girls over, whispering in their ears.

God is death. Death is God.

They wept when he destroyed them with a cock as powerful as Kali's sword.

AGNI THE
FIRE GOD

CHAPTER ONE

After half a keg of beer, the conspirators all agreed it was not a half-baked idea. It was a fully baked idea. John French co-owner and manager of the Taughannock Inn was desperate to draw people to his new hotel. Copying what had been successfully done in Cardiff, New York, ten years earlier, French hoped to capture some of the heat that "America's greatest hoax" had provided Cardiff after a "petrified, prehistoric giant" was unearthed there. Sure, it was bogus, but people still flocked to it, and P.T. Barnum himself put a fake of a fake Cardiff Man on tour with his circus. The year 1879 was a time of limited, regional entertainment and amusement that gave birth to the golden age of hoaxes. French and his crew set out to bake a better fake. The plan was well thought out by the hotel manager and his beautiful, nymphomaniac wife, Dearie. She'd brought in Walter Newton, her lover, and he worked doggishly to design and complete the complicated excavation. The plan was for them to push parts of the giant through a connecting tunnel so that topsoil above it would appear undisturbed and the find more credible. Their five-hundred-pound creation of eggs, beef blood, iron filings and cement were fitted into place one fateful midnight with a root wrapped around the giant's thick neck. All that was needed was for it to be discovered by unaware workers.

On a hot July day, the workmen were widening the carriage drive to the inn when one of them felt his pickaxe strike something hard in the dirt. Believing he had come across a boulder, he began to loosen the soil around it. As he dug away the ground, he stopped, and his jaw dropped in amazement. For there in the ground, partly exposed to his startled gaze, was what appeared to be a petrified man. The others rushed over to see too and to carefully unearth the rest of it. In the cavity lay the body of a stone giant! As the local newspaper reported it:

His hands were crossed over his right thigh, while the left leg lay over the right, which was bent up toward the body. Around his neck grew the roots of a nearby tree. To say the men were gripped with excitement is to put it mildly, for they had apparently uncovered the petrified remains of a man who had existed countless centuries before.

The news spread like wildfire, and it was not long before hundreds of spectators were flocking to the scene. Exploitation of the petrified giant naturally fell to John French on whose land it had been found. French and his official photographers enjoyed a period of prosperity. People bought the photos as fast as they could be developed. French was in his glory and Dearie was turned on by his success. Trumansburg Giant mania erupted in the Ithaca area and never had the man been better in bed.

This was not good news for lovestruck Walter Newton. Suddenly Dearie did not have time for him. In the two months following, before the hoax was exposed by the careless tongue of the drunken baker, Walter did not have intimacy with Dearie once, not once. Days and nights of fellatio and cunnilingus lost forever. All the hours wasted studying the *Kama Sutra*, the book she gave him. Newton was so obsessed with losing Dearie it somewhat dampened his enthusiasm for his own incredible find of the Cayugan Indian jar with the mysterious map inside. He did study the deerskin scroll of purple and white wampum shards and picture writing inked in animal blood dyes. He knew with the level of workmanship that it was no ordinary document. Being an experienced reader of blueprints and survey maps, he was intrigued. He believed it indicated the location of a dangerous treasure hidden under Taughannock Falls. It was a secret he longed to share with Dearie in their afterglow. On the last day of his life, Walter Newton carefully rolled up the map, put it back in its pottery piece, and hid it in his attic beneath old sheet music for banjo, from his Skull and Bones days as a Stephen Foster impersonator.

Camptown ladies sing this song, doo-dah, doo-dah.

Whether he had an intuition that he might never come back to the house he owned near the Cornell campus, or whether he was paranoid about the dark, foreign-born boarder he'd taken in, will never be known. All that is certain is Newton went to the Taughannock Inn and outside in the garden, he told John French that he loved Dearie and she loved him. To prove it, Walter kissed Dearie hard right in front of John and his hotel guests. A challenge to a duel might have been fairer, but the enraged French let his new shotgun roar out in response. Walter died on the spot which was a most fatal option he may not have considered, considering his bold action. Dearie grieved but only for a moment. Walter had made it possible for her to fall in love with John once more. After French was acquitted of all murder charges by a jury of his peers, Dearie never cheated on her husband again.

Wading Bird's jar with the map to the Eye of Shiva would remain in that Collegetown attic undisturbed for another one hundred years until the summer of 1969. Marie Sayles, upset with the young man with whom she shared a bed, was up in the attic trying to find some peace in the crowded Crossing commune. She moved a box of moldy, music sheets, and banjo strings and uncovered a decaying, cardboard carton. It contained an authentic piece of native pottery with a curious old map inside and Newton's notes. Walter's detailed interpretation of the map would make it easy for Marie and her peacenik friends to find the lost weapon of mass destruction.

CHAPTER TWO

Max was getting used to the pain in his ribs and the absence of painkillers. He was determined not to take them for fear of enjoying it too much. He'd always been leery of opiate-based drugs and was happy knowing his cousin had some simple Mexican weed in her office which would ease his mind after dinner and let him concentrate on the things he needed to be thinking about. He was a professional and had learned on the job while an MP detective in Saigon decades before. He had a method of working that he hoped to get back on track. It bothered Max that whenever he was starting to feel better, he remembered that someone out there had tried to kill him. That would likely be the same person or organization responsible for the death of Ella von Tragg's friend, Thomas Gill. All somehow about the McGuffin. In classic Raymond Chandler or Dashiell Hammett crime fiction, it would follow that the bad guy would be a double-chinned, fat man pulling the strings. Damn, if Max wasn't starting to feel like a marionette. The sooner he could expose the fat man, the sooner he could turn it over to the authorities and be back in L.A. to see the jacaranda trees turn purple. Unfortunately, he had to admit, the thought of home was not really enticing Not a carrot or a stick's worth of motivation there. He realized how fortunate he was to be working at what he did reasonably well and not dwelling on the other side of life, his anti-life. He was also enjoying the hell out of being with Janey. That was an unexpected bonus.

Wilbur had given Max Tom Tom's map to where he stashed the Eye of Shiva. Ella wanted to fulfill his wishes in getting the relic back into the right hands, which begged the question who that might be? Its provenance was unclear. What was clear was that Gill had planned to surrender it to the

FBI in 1996 but something changed that. Wilbur believed he hid it again according to the map within an underwater structure, a long-forgotten, man-made, Erie Canal lock that helped link Cayuga and Seneca Lakes in the early nineteenth century. Its retrieval on paper would require a not-too-deep (per Wilbur), diving session, and Max was delighted to learn Janey was also a certified scuba diver.

It will be interesting to see if I can fit in my wet suit. If not, I am crash dieting, I swear.

-Janey, you will not have to. We can rent gear.

Hey, I need the peer pressure. Play along.

-I think you look fabulous. Meat on the bone. Shake your tail feather, you know.

That's not helping.

Janey flashed Max her most adorable smile, and they got out of her car in the faculty parking lot for Warren Hall, the four-story weathered, stone edifice that housed Janey's office. The sun was sinking slowly and by the looks of it, either color would soon be exploding on the western horizon or else it could get snuffed out by some low-lying clouds. Max had an armful's worth of steaming take-out from Jack's Collegetown Grill. Janey was already regretting it.

I shoulda got mine wrapped in lettuce. You gotta remind me.

Max promised Janey he'd be more vigilant. Inside the campus building, up one flight of stairs, down the old, marble hall, and into her rococo office, Max suddenly felt stressed. His own undistinguished academic career started gnawing at the gut. He was literally overcome. Janey sat him down and felt his forehead. He explained.

Honest. I will have a nightmare tonight about not graduating because I missed a final exam. Which did happen. And then in the dream, if I can get to the classroom, I can write a makeup test, but I can't find the building. I'm in slow motion. Happens every time I step on a college campus. It's pathetic.

-You need to eat. And hydrate!

She pulled out some bottled water from a little fridge and cleared her big desk of her books, papers, and various cool and creepy archaeological artifacts. Max laid out the fully loaded burgers and fries atop an old madras shawl that she used for a tablecloth. Max thought it best they wait for Eddie, who would soon be joining them. It was six minutes after the appointed time by the antique cuckoo clock on Janey's mantle.

How long do you have to wait for a professor before class is canceled these days? Asking for a friend. Five minutes? Ten? Fifteen?

That was a sore subject for Janey.

Students should never leave till notified the class is canceled. Good students know that.

-So that was my problem. I hope Eddie gets here soon. If not, we can split his burger.

See. Not helping.

* * *

Eddie would not get there. At 7:06, he'd parked his off-duty limo with his band gear still inside in the visitors' lot and was walking briskly across the suspension bridge to meet up with Max at Janey's office in Warren Hall. He'd spoken to his bandmate's mom at the Ithaca PD and she came through big time. The car, a blue 2007 Chevy Malibu, was registered to the FBI. Yes, roger that, the FBI! And the same car had recently gotten a ticket near the Freeville Chevron for not being moved on a snowplow day. Hello? He couldn't wait to tell Max. The old suspension bridge was a steel span marvel that crossed a hundred feet above the Fall Creek gorge and its rushing white water and rock bed below. It was magnificent despite its troubled history as a magnet for student suicide leaps over the decades. Indeed, as of this writing, starting in 2014, a protective cage was put over the bridge to prevent further misadventures. In 2009 however, there was no such protection.

Eddie had crossed the bridge numerous times. Especially when his girl-friend Candace was a student. He knew the campus and expected to be biting into his Bo burger within minutes. He would have been on time, but coming up University Avenue, he thought he saw the blue car parked down at the bottom of the hill across from the cemetery. He had slowed to take a picture of it and sure enough, he was right. Max was smart in not speaking anymore over the phone, Eddie thought. Should he have been more careful? Who had he spoken with on the phone? The police of course and…He paused a moment to recall and take in the sun bursting through the clouds as it set. He thought he was alone on the bridge. He was wrong. Coming for him were two tawny-skinned co-eds. One with a broken arm.

CHAPTER THREE

Tom Tom would have to be careful. He knew the park ranger schedule and believed he had a nice window of time before dusk to get himself behind the cascading water drop from the nearest and driest point. It would have been a lot easier in 1969 for Marie Sayles and the kids from the commune to access the caves behind Taughannock Falls. No nanny-state-mandated supervision back then. The thundering sound of the water was hammering right through every inch of his body, a vibrating condition that was disorienting to say the least. It was 1996 and multimillionaire Thomas (Tom Tom) Gill was not in the best of shape. He was seventy-two years old and unsteady in the rushing water, knee-deep in foul weather gear and waders, towing an inflatable tire around the edges of the waterfalls' natural pool. If anyone did see him, they would think he was insane and call 911, an eerie figure trudging through the mouth of the mist. His miner's hat lamp reflected off the moisture in a random rainbow. Tom Tom doggedly pushed on with purpose, something he hadn't had as of late.

* * *

He had been drinking hard for seemingly the whole year since Jeanie fried off the coast of Brittany. Bad luck, bad curse, dumb, dumb decision for him to go back. There was no need to return to St. Malo, a bored, treasure hunters' one-last-time because you can never have enough. Jeanie had been the victim of a lightning strike, a one in ten thousand chance that had extinguished the light of his life. Tom Tom believed he was to blame and had been punishing himself for it ever since. He was living in his boathouse on Lake Cayuga, having an early breakfast of day-old Chinese and straight-up Tito's when Wilbur called him to relay a call to the Freeville farmhouse from an old friend of his wife's. Marie Sayles was dying and asked to see him.

Marie lived on a farm on the north side of the Susquehanna River near the Pennsylvania border in Broome County, less than a hundred miles south as the crow flies. There was a decent airfield in nearby Johnson City, and Tom Tom had stopped over more than a few times to gas up his favorite Cessna. He sobered up best he could, mouth-washed up better, and flew off to see her. Jeanie knew her from the late '60s. Marie was a drama student and lived in a downtown commune called The Crossing. A townie in a college town, Jeanie was naturally insecure and greatly valued a friendship with the young actress. Jeanie always said it was Marie who challenged her as a wannabe writer into finding her own voice. Seeing her friend became impossible for Jeanie after 1969. Tom Tom had heard some of the story and knew the bottom line. Marie had vanished, assumed to be living under another identity in some kind of witness protection program. It was best, Jeanie was told, to forget her.

***

Tom Tom hadn't been into the cave under the falls since he was a beer-swigging teenager. It smelled piney sweet in the sickening dampness. He sloshed through the waist-high water. There was the same old graffiti upon graffiti on the walls and other subtler signs that if he looked carefully were the ones plotted on the deerskin Indian map of Marie's that Tom Tom had put to memory. He switched off the light on his hat as instructed and a fanciful, somewhat faded, luminescent, spray-painted, day-glow, pink arrow appeared on the cavern roof, pointing the way. It was the long-ago work of Marie's friend, the artist, Suzie Sunshine. *Damn hippies,* Tom Tom always thought and was glad Jeanie wasn't one of them. Hearing Marie's story, he had nothing but admiration for her now. He was also grateful. She had put Tom Tom on a mission, and nothing gave him more life than that. All his old instincts and knowledge surged inside. He hadn't had a drink since he had seen Marie. He figured to find this relic and float it out atop the inner tube. The correct crevasse was marked by inlaid shell shards set in originally by Wading Bird though Tom Tom wouldn't have known that. This indicated a vertical split in the rock that would lead to an inner crawl chamber with shale shelves and another painted signpost clue of Suzie Sunshine. Its opening was high up and difficult to reach. The rock side was slippery with moss, and there was nothing to hold on to. Tom Tom tried to balance on the inner tube while carefully standing up to get eye level with the crevasse ledge. His fingers grabbed the shale ridge to steady but unanchored the rubber tube shifted away. With an expletive and an awkward splash, Tom Tom disappeared into the black water.

CHAPTER FOUR

Aruna was setting up the new classroom in Newington Green, London, when her partner and roommate, Mary Wollstonecraft, arrived. It was a school for dissenting young ladies, those not of the Church of England faith, and the two had great expectations for their coming educational experiment. Mary apologized for being late, but she had stopped at the General Post Office and there was a letter from Lt. Philip Pearce of Calcutta for Aruna. Aruna's heart jumped the moon. She hadn't heard from Philip since he was sent back to India almost three years earlier. She sat down and at curious Mary's urging, Aruna read the letter aloud with a trembling hand.

November 29th, 1779

My Darling Aruna,

I miss you so much and have suffered knowing I was not able to write you sooner. Please forgive me. I have had to be secretly re-assigned several times for my safety. By next year's end, I will be leaving India and coming back to London for good if that's what you want. I know by now you have heard of the heinous attack that took the life of your family. I am truly sorry for that. My life in hiding had been very difficult because I am a marked man of the Aghori. I long for the days and nights I can hold you in my arms without fear. I long to feel your sweet breath on my lips. I—

Mary couldn't hold it in any longer. She let out a long, wistful sigh. Aruna closed her eyes. Her hand drifting down over her ripe, pregnant belly.

Forever, my love, you are my forever. Love, Philip. P. S. I have heard nothing of my gift to the Crown. Do you know what became of it?

***

Four months later in a cramped, darkened officer's apartment in Calcutta, by candlelight, Philip held up a letter in his hand and read her reply out loud with bated breath.

Dearest, dearest Philip,

I count the days till you arrive. So much has happened since you had to leave. Most of it wonderful. I can't wait for you to meet my friend and colleague Mary. She has saved my life, and maybe I saved hers as well. Together we are doing exciting things that will advance the cause of women in Britain. I have mourned my family's passing and so many tears later, I continue to mourn. I cannot blame you for being loyal to your nation, now my beloved nation. Please be careful. An Aghori monk was here in London. He was captured and hanged for the brutal murder of Anne Ramsdale, the wife of the Prime Minister's secretary and a friend. The news of your gift is not good. It was delivered to America to end the rebellion but according to Sir Ramsdale, it was stolen by a savage tribe of Cayugas. No one knows what has happened to it since. It worries me at night but perhaps being lost is its fate.

Pearce paused and looked up to the shadows. He held the letter in his left hand and a pistol in the right. It was trained on an Aghori monk who was seated on the floor before him, hands clasped behind his head.

I've told you everything I know. The bloodletting must stop. It is with native people in America. Indians! Perhaps that is how it was meant to be.

Pearce lowered his pistol. The Aghori lowered his arms and nodded. He rose, with a finger to his nose, and shot a wad of snot at Philip before exiting. With a gasp of relief, Pearce wiped the mucus off his cheek.

CHAPTER FIVE

Max took a deep drag of the joint he'd rolled from Janey's old pot stash. How old? Last time she had smoked was two years or so before. Gord, her ex-was a boozer, and potheads and boozers do not get along. So, Janey gave up weed to give the marriage a real chance. It didn't matter, of course, and by the second drag of Max's fat rolled doobie of questionable quality, Janey low in personal tolerance for the flower, was flying, talking non-stop about how the glaciers' retreat had formed Taughannock Falls and the incredible gorges and the bubbling creeks. She jumped to Wilbur Red Hawk and how amazing it was to meet an actual Cayugan, a vanishing tribe. She spun the true tale to Max about the first inhabitants of the Finger Lakes and their amazing Iroquois Confederacy.

Eventually, six warring tribes signed conditions of peace, and it held for centuries.

She was on a roll. A teacher you'd want, and Max did.

The same concepts for a cooperative union of colonies Ben Franklin shamelessly borrowed nearly intact for America's first Articles of Confederation in 1781!

Janey loved that there was so much history right under their feet, which wasn't to imply she ever got to professionally explore it. She was kept busy on course, field trips to Egypt or Crete, but never the university's backyard.

Just not sexy enough for those alumni endowments, eh?

Janey immediately apologized for saying *eh*. A product of her marital Canadianization and swore to never say it again. She was ready to move on. She was ready to love again.

Easy for you, you're young

-Oh, Max. Life is illusion. Maya, the Hindus call it.

Janey made him smile, and he couldn't stop. He was stoned too, and charmed. He kept egging her on like an A-student and they split Eddie's burger by the 7:20 mark. She circled back to the Cayuga Indians, obsessed with a train of thought about the Eye's chain of custody from its home continents away. It had ended up in upstate New York of all places. Janey had a clap-your-hands, inspired notion and started measuring distances on an old-fashioned desk globe with a piece of string.

Considering all the landmasses that have shifted since time began, the Finger Lakes are like the antipodal point to Varanasi, India, origin of the Eye of Shiva. See. Halfway around the world give and take a few degrees. Antipodal. That's weird, eh? I mean, not eh, just weird.

Max laughed, fascinated, but peering out her office window, he was more curious at the emergency vehicles he could hear and see arriving below. There had been an emergency off by the suspension bridge as far as Janey could tell. Max hoped it had nothing to do with Eddie, who was now very late. Janey knocked on her wooden desk two times at the thought and wiped it once. Max spooked, knocked wood too before they both hurried out.

The campus police were setting up yellow tape, and Max and Janey learned from a colleague in the growing crowd that there had been another suicide. Max looked over toward the bridge and damned if it wasn't his little hitchhiker huddled with some Ithaca PD who were taking notes. Sabu Shera's graduate assistant was crying, wiping her eyes with her broken wing in a cast.

Fuck me!

Among the gathering looky-loos, Janey spotted her turbaned colleague moving through the throng. So did Max.

Is that him?

Janey nodded. Wilbur had told Janey and Max that after Tom Tom's death, he went to the police and gave Sabu's description and identity as someone who had been with Thomas Gill before his boating accident. Nothing had come of it, and the authorities ruled the death a suicide. While Janey and Max watched, Professor Sabu was let in under the yellow tape to join the police who seemed to know him. He comforted his young assistant who appeared shaken up. Max had no idea what was going on. It felt like when his car was out of control and he was helpless, expecting to die, ready to die. What was that song he'd wished he'd written? "Jesus Take the Wheel." Fate or Free Will? Cause or Effect? Maya! Too many answers beyond all human knowledge.

Max was very high on stale, brown pot, and he was bumming hard to boot. All that was clear in this moment was someone was dead. Took a header off the bridge and splattered on the rocks below. Max would love to treat the limo driver and his whole band to a weeks' worth of burgers if Eddie was not the body they were climbing down the gorge to retrieve. But he knew it had to be. Janey did too. This was not a coincidence. Max was thirty-two sleeps away from another birthday north of sixty-five, and at the moment, felt even older. He wished he could go to bed and dream about blowing his college career. *Please.* Sensing Max's unease, Janey put her arms around him and hugged him close.

We got this, cuz.

CHAPTER SIX

Tom Tom had tumbled into the swirling dark pool of water under Taughannock Falls. His rubber waders were filling up, making it even harder to rise, sinking him lower. For secrecy's sake, he'd attempted this retrieval alone, and it was obviously not the best of ideas. When he fell in sideways, his head glanced off a sharp, underwater rock, and he could feel himself bleeding. It felt oddly calming. He was conscious enough to sense the cold water penetrating every pore of his body and to feel the mounting pressure in his lungs. He seemed to be suspended in a dark womb of water that could be his grave. All that drifted through his mind like a distant siren song was that he must come through for Marie. Not because she was a friend of his dear, departed wife but because as a soldier, he believed bravery should be honored especially if it could not be recognized. Marie was dying and already on a morphine drip when Tom Tom got to see her that one and only time. He had been planning his own death before that day. He'd had convinced himself there was only one thing left that would set things right with Jeanie. Carbon monoxide would be her embrace. He composed a last letter on his computer and allocated his assets. Wilbur would get the old family house and farm in Freeville and a yearly salary, the rest of the estate he divided among cousins and friends, environmental non-profits, local libraries, and veterans organizations. Ella von Tragg was named executor. Tom Tom had planned to take his life in the boathouse the day he got the urgent message to see Marie. Did Jeanie from the great beyond have something to do with stopping him? It made Tom Tom wonder, and that itself was a vital spark.

* * *

Marie was remarkably upbeat, considering her state. She was grateful he'd come and proceeded over the next two hours to relay a tale of tales with an apocalyptic Third Cleansing warning for a chaser. Tom Tom had forgotten to bring a flask and had to listen to Marie without the benefit of alcohol. The more she talked, the more ashamed he felt. She'd sacrificed so much. She needed to live. He wanted to die. She was laughing. He was crying. She made him give his word.

* * *

Tom Tom had failed Marie. That shame tripped the right synapse, jump-starting his lifeforce, propelling him blindly toward the water's surface. Pulling himself up on the ledge, Tom Tom's soul bulged, anxious for oxygen again. He would come back to find it. He had to.

* * *

Thirty years earlier, two hippie chicks, their communal boyfriend from the commune and his dog, blazed the same path. They had the benefit of Walter Newton's expert, interpretive map notes, long since destroyed. However, they were under a distinct handicap, two of them were tripping on LSD. It was an early August late afternoon and Marie, their designated, non-tripping guide, in cut-off denims and a peasant blouse, led the way, a knapsack of supplies on her back. Suzie Sunshine, her best friend, had hoped to get in the water and was topless and bottomless under a see-through white sari. A tie-dyed headband kept her gorgeous, red hair somewhat in place. With her leather bag of paints and goodies slung over her shoulder, Suzie was full of acidy cheer and had been marking their way with paints. Tim Kramer, their old man, so dark and gloomy as of late, was into the simple beauties and rubbed his cheek roughly against the rough bark of a tree that lined the path to the falls. Marie shouted.

Careful! You're bleeding.

-Babe, your heart's not in it less you spill a little blood.

Tim used the blood to draw war paint on himself and kissed them both, wildly whooping in between. Che, his husky, bark-whooped too. They had purposely waited till the random hikers and sightseers had left, and they had the place to themselves. Tim jumped from rock to rock, pretending to soar, and Che followed his every move. Marie was glad she made the others come. At first, neither Suzie with whom she first shared the secret map nor Tim who finally was out of her doghouse, seemed too interested in treasure hunting. Then a quiet weekend landed, and the weather was irresistible. At the mouth of the falls, Suzie took off her sari and naked, swam around the edge of the cascading water, disappearing behind. Marie and Tim with rain ponchos and umbrellas sloshed their way around and under into the cave, goofing on the echoes. Standing on a rock, Suzie stretched up and spray-painted a long, pink stripe on the stone ceiling. Tim stripped down and picked up a laughing Suzie, carrying her back into the water, motioning for Marie to join them.

Make love, not war!

It was more than a slogan. It was a lifestyle for the three that year. It was beautiful when they all came together, perfect even for Marie, who wasn't on acid. Che howled too, as if experiencing the same delight. Marie hadn't seen Tim so relaxed in weeks. It was 1969 and Tim was a busy man mobilizing a September antiwar demonstration that was coming right up. He'd invited some heavy hitters from the movement for speakers and had entertainment planned too. The Bread and Puppet Theatre and anti-establishment, activist rock acts like McKendree Spring had already committed. It was going to be a big deal. Unknown to the others, Tim also was expecting a member of a new group, the Weather Underground. Like Tim, they were impatient with the progress of the peace movement. The level of violence to be utilized in the name of peace was always a sore point in The Crossing commune's discussions late at night. Tim thought their voices were no longer enough and wondered what it would take on the homefront to make the government end the war in Southeast Asia. Whatever that was, he was good with it. He had sacrificed a scholarship at Cornell, leaving school mid-semester, to lead the local draft resistance. He was planning to burn his card the night of the fall gathering. That's why Marie and Suzie allowed the relationship. They believed Tim would soon be going to Canada, or worse, would be arrested. So....

Girls say yes to boys who say no.

It was the least they could do, plus they both loved him and each other. Not that things didn't get complicated. If they hadn't, Marie would never have been up in the attic. Never would have found Walter Newton's notes and the old Indian map.

After the wet and wonderful threesome, Tim was ready to go home but Marie insisted they had to at least give a look. It was supple Suzie who first slithered into the tight, inner crevasse, followed by Marie, whom she helped guide inside. Tim and Che hung below, laying out, listening to the magic music of the falling water. Inside the chamber, with Suzie holding the flashlight from her pack, Marie could follow the map notes and identify the tiny shell symbols on the rock wall that were the markers. They found Wading Bird's hiding place for the *gift* with not much trouble at all.

The trouble came after they brought it home.

CHAPTER SEVEN

Lt. Philip Pearce paced in front of the *HMS Leominster,* which was loading supplies and passengers for its trip to Canada. He was expecting Aruna to meet him at the Plymouth Dock. He had only been in England for a few months and was already leaving. He'd seen the love of his life once since being back in England. Aruna had been off on a women's crusade with her friend and business partner, Mary Wollstonecraft. They had a small, dark child they were bringing up together. Their work, setting up church classes to educate poor women, had taken them traveling to Birmingham in the north. Despite the distance, Aruna promised to meet Philip in Plymouth in plenty of time to accompany him on their trans-Atlantic crossing to Montreal. He had her bags already stowed aboard. Aruna's promise was almost up. Philip sat on a bale of dry goods feeling his own bale of woe. Things had gone sideways, and he was steeling himself for boarding without her. After seeing Aruna and her friend's relationship, Philip knew something had changed in the innocent, colonial girl from the Punjab whom he had whisked to London. He was happy for her and her free-spirited life but was crushed in mind and spirit. The ship's last boarding horn sounded. Stiff upper lip was all he knew. Aruna's message was clear. Their lives were no longer tied.

Pearce hoped to head south from Canada to the Finger Lakes area of New York. His destiny was to discover the whereabouts of the Eye of Shiva. Like the Aghori, he could not rest until it was retrieved. Sir Ramsdale had been helpful in gathering all the information he could about General St. Leger's aborted mission. Philip gathered himself. It was time. Last-minute passengers hurried to get aboard. Pearce joined them. Waiting another second seemed as painful as the nasty slice of knife he'd endured from a crazed monk before he left India. Phillip climbed up the gangplank with a heart dropping like an anchor that would never rise.

* * *

Aruna was going to miss the boat. She had every intention of meeting Philip and boarding with him and baby Caleb. Fate got in the way. More accurately, a woman scorned. Mary Wollstonecraft did what she could to sabotage Aruna leaving. She was not in love with Aruna, but she loved working alongside her, and they had their cause. She selfishly faked illness and neediness until Aruna would have it no more and they set out for Plymouth on what had seemed an impossible journey. On good days, it was two days of travel by wagon or carriage, more by horseback or by foot. Aruna was prepared to do them all if need be. Mary had given her a boost in life's possibilities, and she loved her like a sister. It was with Philip Pearce though, with whom she shared a higher purpose. They both needed to find the Eye of Shiva or be shadowed by its darkness forever. Aruna believed once it was returned to its home in India, she and Philip would be free to begin anew; he as a father to Caleb and she as the wife of a man who respected her. Mary had taught her a woman should be no man's wife. The only exception was if he treated her like an equal. That was Philip Pearce. And he was honest. More honest than she had been about Caleb. She intended to fix that. Someday. When Aruna hit the crowded path to Plymouth Dock, she took off sprinting through the busy way with Caleb in her arms.

Pearce stood at the rail, watching the deckhands untangle the gangplank rope. The heavy timbered accessway had stalled halfway up. They released it and it plunked right back down on dock so they could raise it up again cleanly. Pearce saw her first and screamed.

Stop!

The startled deckhands made way for the hard-charging Aruna. They grabbed her, lifting her aboard without losing a beat, hoisting the gangplank so the voyage could begin. The *Leominster's* sails billowed with feminine pride and she pulled away from shore and into the wind. On the dock,

Mary Wollstonecraft had finally caught up. She was crying and waving at Aruna and Caleb. Aruna waved back heartily before kissing Philip with pent-up passion.

They would reach the Finger Lakes five hundred thirty-five days hence. And get a surprise visit from an Aghori monk on day five hundred thirty-six.

CHAPTER EIGHT

After the suspicious death of Eddie, Max was worried about Janey's safety. He did not want her going home alone, and he suggested they both stay at his hotel that night. It wasn't a come on. He offered to get her a room. She didn't want him to shoulder any unnecessary expense. It was already late. They stopped first at her house a few blocks from the Ithaca lakefront. Max stood outside on sentry duty while she went in to grab some items for the night. Max saw a car go by twice with a young woman behind the wheel. He didn't recognize her or the silver Toyota, but he took note. The sleeping arrangement was going to be awkward, but they were adults and family (not technically) and it was a king-sized bed. Both made the best of it. Under the covers, Janey wore her flannel pajamas. Max had on an old Rolling Stones Voodoo Lounge T-shirt and his boxers. They said good night, each exhausted from the upsetting day. Neither wanted to think another second about the next step. Janey almost wished she had classes, but they were done. What she had was way too much free time to invest. She was fascinated by the Eye and its journey and terrified of the thought it could be as powerful as described. Though Max was quite serious when he asked her to bow out, she would not consider it.

First to fall asleep was Janey, and he was tickled by her light snoring. He had to admit it was comforting to be in bed with a warm body. And what a body. He tried to ignore it, but Janey was a full-figured gal. She kept rolling over to him, changing positions, in a seemingly, restless dream. He did not move away after the first time. Thigh on thigh, butt on butt, damn if he didn't get an erection he was ashamed of. Or was he? He had not been intimate with any woman since Mei U's death. It brought up a hunger in him that he was thrilled he still had. It all seemed wrong at first light and he arose feeling guilty. Janey spoke first.

Don't take this the wrong way. I had a dream about you last night.

-Oh, no. Did I look like Woody Allen?

Janey surprised him with a hug.

What was that for?

-I don't know. It's a new day, and we're alive. Your limo driver isn't.

That sad reality hit home. They cut through the park to grab breakfast and formulate a plan. Janey wanted to go to the police and tell them what they knew. Max was reluctant to go to any authorities without more. He was, however, curious about the information that Eddie may have died over. Eddie had said a member of his band's mother worked at the police station and that would be a good place to begin. Max also wondered if Janey could set up a way for Max to meet Professor Shera.

Sure. Do you need a cover story?

-No point.

Gotcha.

Halfway through sharing some halfway decent, corned beef hash and scrambled eggs, Max and Janey were startled by a tap on the restaurant window of their booth. It was Artie Hicks in casual clothes sipping from a Starbucks cup. He playfully modeled his non-correctional facility attire doing a pirouette. Max motioned him inside.

I got out last night. Good behavior. If they only knew…Oops, shouldn't have said that.

-Order some breakfast. You're on my tab.

Thanks. Hey, I scored some Orleans reunion tickets, next weekend at the State Theater. "Still the One"...Just sayin'.

Max appreciated but hoped to be back in L.A. by then. He wondered if Artie knew anyone from Desperado, a local Eagles tribute band. He did, knew the whole band.

Eddie's the best. Hard-working kid. He used to sell for me.

-He died last night. Police think it was suicide

Artie's shoulders went up high, and he scratched his head. Trying to hide a troubled breath, he squeaked a sorrowful moan. It made no sense to him. Max asked if he knew who in Eddie's band had a mother who worked at the police department. Of course, Artie knew.

It's a small town when you're an eligible bachelor.

Artie had married twice. Janey remembered the first. She was at the wedding of Artie and Rhoda Seven, in the woods with all the flower children trimmings—drums, drugs, doves, and a swimmable pond. Janey swooned thinking it about it.

I had my first real kiss, skinny-dipping. I was...He was...

Janey immediately blushed in front of Max. She tried to explain the '60s mores that she had been born into. Max let her off the hook. Artie felt obliged to add.

Last big bash with The Crossing. After that, it was over. I've got some great photos.

-Once Tim died, and Marie and Suzie disappeared, everything got strange, including my Dad. I mean, you know, Mychal.

Goodbye, high times.

Max didn't hear what they were saying. He was focused on something he should have asked Ella. Could Franz, her plus one, be trusted?

CHAPTER NINE

This time Tom Tom was more prepared. On a warm, moonless, 1996 night, he came to Taughannock with Wilbur Red Hawk, and together they got behind the falls and into the cave. Wilbur was younger and stronger. He pulled himself up and into the chamber, helping Tom Tom within. Once inside Wilbur lit up some white sage he had brought along to sanctify the space and chase away evil. Tom Tom closed his eyes in prayer and listened to his friend's chanting. It steadied him and steeled him. When Wilbur was done, Tom Tom took the flashlight and they looked for Wading Bird's shell markers and Suzie's drawings. It was a piece of cake like it had been for Marie and Suzie thirty years before him. They moved the big, round stone blocking the high, dry hole and reached in and slowly pulled it out. Dusting it off, Tom Tom saw the embossed, Sanskrit figures just as Marie had described them to him on her deathbed. They wrapped the relic in a Hudson Bay blanket they had brought along and lowered it out with a rope sling. Believing he had fulfilled the hardest part of his promise to Marie, Tom Tom felt some satisfaction and the soul-rush of human validation. They sloshed out from behind the falls. He couldn't wait to call his old friend Ella. Under cover of darkness, he and Wilbur walked right out of the park, and down the hill to Tom Tom's big house on the lake gingerly carrying what Tom Tom had been told was a primitive, nuclear explosive.

* * *

CAYUGA

When Marie, Suzie, Tim, and Che got back to The Crossing with the same relic in 1969, they had no idea what they had. Nor could they imagine, like a hot potato, it would be put back where they found it four months later.

CHAPTER TEN

Newly married Aruna and Philip Pearce with young Caleb settled in the township of Ulysses on the shores of Lake Cayuga in the Fall of 1785. The war had been over for years, but Philip was still viewed with suspicion among the locals. His family had survived, traveling on money from Philip's army pay, and in Ulysses with his engineering background, fortune had smiled on him. The timing for his skill set couldn't have been better. He quickly got a dream job with an ambitious land developer named DeWitt who was laying out the infrastructure for a new city to be built between two steep hills that rolled down to the shimmering lake. He planned to call it Ithaca for the hilly city in Greece and a population influx was expected. Since Sullivan's Raid in 1779 had eradicated the Cayuga villages in the area, that land was confiscated by the military and became the Central New York Military Tract. In two-acre lots, it was being doled out to veterans who fought on the American side. Location was decided by rank and degree of service. The officers got the sunny side of the lake. The enlisted men got the shade. Squatters or Tories who backed the losing side were evicted with no compensation for lands they had developed. Every day since Aruna and Philip had arrived more and more veterans came for their land and DeWitt needed surveyors. Philip became one of his best. It was amazing to Aruna that they had stayed in America and not gone back to England. They had come driven by a singular reason and that reason was shockingly derailed the day after they arrived.

Aruna remembered it well. Philip was out hunting for their dinner. Caleb, who was almost nine, had been out picking fruit. Being newcomers, they had erected a tent and Aruna was inside mending her growing boy's tunic. She could hear he was back, outside talking to someone in English and it sounded to her like that someone had a Punjabi accent. Frightened, she pulled back the tent flap and there he was. Caleb was talking to an Aghori man, a tall, brute of a fellow, though he was not dirty and was dressed like any other settler. Aruna rushed out and grabbed Caleb. The man flashed a toothy smile and put a hand up in a peaceful gesture. He spoke to Aruna in Hindi.

I mean you and Lt. Pearce no harm.

Aruna would have liked to have taken him at his word, but how did he know who they were. The man whose name was Jovan would not say. He had been in the area for a while and hoped she enjoyed living by the lake. He and his wife lived nearby. He pointed behind him and Aruna could see a woman in a wide-brimmed sun hat, loaded with bundles, waiting for him. She was a white woman. Jovan was trying his best to make Aruna comfortable. He motioned his wife over. The woman was young like Aruna and looked frontier tough, which made the warmth of her smile all the more surprising. Jovan introduced her as Emily. Aruna replied with her name. Caleb, fully East Indian himself, introduced himself, standing ready to protect his mom, whom he could sense was scared. Jovan clasped his hands and bowed his head.

Can I talk to Lt. Pearce?

Before Aruna could answer, Philip did. He'd returned with some fowl in one hand and a musket in the other. He approached cautiously. Jovan bowed his head again and welcomed Pearce. So did his wife, relieved to see another mixed-race couple.

Best of the day to both of you. I hope we can be friends.

Night descended. Aruna cooked on an open campfire. The others sat around it and made small talk. Jovan and Emily were starting a family. He worked at the local grist mill. She tended a garden that produced squash bigger than Jovan's head. She would drop some off for Aruna. Aruna was proud of her husband. Despite all the travails with the Aghori, Philip had the decency to invite them to share dinner. After they had eaten Aruna's fine meal of guinea hen and apple mash, the small talk ended. Jovan spoke his mind.

I was sent here by my master to find the Eye of Shiva.

Immediately Philip assured him they would help him find it. He felt responsible for any harm caused, and he apologized. He told Jovan if they could find it, they intended to ensure its return to the proper custodians.

That would be a mistake.

Philip wasn't sure he heard him right and asked Jovan to repeat that. Jovan explained that if they began searching for it, they would discover like he did, that it was a Cayuga chief named Wading Bird who stole it from the British General St. Leger. He brought it back to his village, and when the war went wrong for his tribe, he hoped to use what they called the *gift* to bargain for their land and crops, and hopefully their lives. Unfortunately, Sullivan's march, like Sherman's march later, scorched the earth and spared no one. Stories passed down among the native people say there was a deer-skin scroll in a pottery jar buried somewhere near the deserted ruins of the main Cayuga village. The scroll is a map to where the *gift* was hidden by Wading Bird. Pearce and Aruna were amazed at how much was already known but puzzled why Jovan hadn't looked for it.

You could say I went native. Lake Cayuga is my home. It is a paradise of plenty.

-He got used to the winters.

His wife, Emily, tried to keep it light. Jovan took a breath before explaining more. His gestures became larger. More emphatic. The fire's glow on his face showed the intensity of his inner struggle.

It must remain lost. My hope and yours, too, is that it never lands in the hands of another Aghori. If it did everything and everyone, as far as we can see, even further, will be destroyed, melted into the ground by the power of the Third Eye.

Pearce poked a stick to stir up the embers and tried to process this. Jovan explained that after it had been stolen by Pearce, the new, high priest, protector of the Eye, and Jovan's master, declared it a sign, all foretold. The fact that it had ended up halfway around the globe validated the new prophecy to the faithful.

They believe it is a call for the Third Cleansing. Like it cleansed the Rama Empire. Like Agni, the Fire God demands. A massive die-off! In death, life grows the path to Shiva.

Jovan hung his head. Emily comforted him. He looked up with tears in his eyes.

I stopped believing.

-We fell in love

I am a bad Aghori but a good Christian. As long as I am alive, the Eye will sleep.

Aruna stroked the hair of her drowsy child and felt great peace. Philip squeezed her other hand, electricity running through them, jolting them into a hopeful future.

And the Eye of Shiva would continue to lie undisturbed for centuries and a day, in that dry hole, in that cavern behind Taughannock Falls until found by two flower children of the Dove generation. The thrill of their discovery would soon be eclipsed by the fear of it falling into Hawk-ish clutches.

CHAPTER ELEVEN

Why would the blue car that had been following Max, the same car driven by the student who tried to kill him, be registered to the FBI? Max did not see that complication coming. He could not have gotten that information without Janey. She consoled the mother of Eddie's good friend who worked reception at the Ithaca Police Department. Tillie Greenhutt was a mess.

He was my friend too. He loved playing detective. Coulda been a policeman.

The police were not considering investigating further because there were two witnesses who saw him jump off the bridge. She answered before Max could ask the next question.

They were graduate students. I can get the names. Foreign, I think. Suicide and Eddie? No! He would have to be drugged or pushed over.

Tillie couldn't keep it together and excused herself. Max wanted the names, and Janey would follow up. They both knew one of those witnesses had to be Max's *Kali*-screaming hitchhiker. His phone's guitar-solo ringtone jolted to life and seemed entirely inappropriate. It was the call from Ella von Tragg that Max had been expecting. She had heard the terrible news about Eddie from his bereaved girlfriend. Max stepped out of the police station to take the call.

***

Candace, the bright and efficient Taughannock Inn's assistant manager with a Cornell degree in economics, was wracked with a deep, roiling hurt. Her legs were so wobbly, she literally couldn't stand up. Her boyfriend had killed himself and she did not know why. Ella felt the young girl's pain but did not have the right words. Franz could do that. He was Hungarian. She drove her wheelchair off into a quiet corner of the inn's lobby to talk to Max, her own consternation swirling. Being a German of a certain age, she did not have the gift of empathy. Untimely deaths of loved ones were all she'd known. Ella had lost her dashing, young husband in World War Two when she was all of twenty-two with a child to boot and another on the way. They'd been married under a year when he left for a frontline command. She'd survived the war years in style being a friend of Eva Braun and shared many responsibilities with Eva including carnal ones with the Führer. Ella had paid for her unconscionable behavior during the war and any person who could legitimately judge her anymore had secrets of their own. After Germany surrendered, Ella was trapped in an abusive relationship with a Russian officer who beat her like a hooker with no price. It all changed the year after the Allies' victory. While retrieving her husband's body in Brittany, she met Corporal Thomas Gill. Together they fulfilled her late husband's destiny and recovered a fortune from the sea caves of St. Malo. That money Tom Tom invested for Ella in his passions which including pioneering TV cable and waterfront real estate. The wealth that was accrued enabled Ella to never need a man again. Franz joined her and smoothed her hair with a soft touch.

You have a spa appointment.

Ella brushed his hand away. The loss of her friend, her American brother from another mother, was all that consumed her. Knowing Max would be asking, she thought Candace would have the name of the translator that was hired. She instructed Franz to ask for it. He didn't have to. He remembered.

Professor Sabu something. How many could there be?

Max was not comfortable talking on the mobile. Before Ella could get into what he did not want to get into, Max quickly proposed they meet somewhere. Janey suggested the State Diner, a low-key eatery on the outskirts of the city. Ella agreed and kept the conversation short. With no limo available, she could have Franz drive her. The time was set, and the call was over. Franz kissed her neck. With practiced effort, she stood up from the wheelchair and gave him a hug. He really was a dear. Franz, on her cue, hugged her and held it, just the way she favored. Tom Tom never approved of her lovers. Ella never understood why he didn't take on ones of his own. Why be alone? That thought made octogenarian Ella blush. She remembered fantasizing that Tom Tom might look to her for solace as a new widower. They were almost the same age. All the time he had known her, he had never come on to her. And she always did her best not to flirt which had come so naturally to her. He understood how important it was that they be friends. Though she wouldn't tell Franz, since they'd been in Tom Tom's hometown whenever Franz kissed her, Ella closed her eyes and pretended it was him, her perfect man. Tom Tom always said he'd saved Ella from hell. If he really cared, she thought, he shouldn't have died thirteen years ago for a stupid, stupid, old box.

CHAPTER TWELVE

The Weather Underground, a militant, antiwar group responsible for a series of terror bombings in the 1970s, were in their infancy when Billy Duncan arrived in Ithaca in early September 1969. The infamous group started as a radical wing of the SDS, the Students for a Democratic Society but split off over tactics. The Weathermen were not just hell-bent on stopping the Asian war. They wanted to start a new American Revolution. Their slogan was *Bring the war home*. Let America suffer like war-torn Viet Nam. That would lead to riots in the streets, young whites and blacks fighting together, toppling of the establishment and social change. That year all the antiwar groups, from the most nonviolent to most extreme, had planned a three-day, October protest in Chicago, The Days of Rage. For their contribution, the Weathermen secretly plotted their first national wake-up call. Needing a rehearsal before Chicago, Billy, one of their leaders, had chosen Ithaca and their local September protest to practice some mayhem. He had heard through the Movement of a campus activist, Tim Kramer, who could be trusted and planned to meet up with him. Billy had six sticks of dynamite in his motel room by the lake and had been tutored by a brilliant University of Wisconsin engineering student named Karl Armstrong how to set up the fuse and timer. Billy planned to use the upcoming demonstration in DeWitt Park for a diversion. The cops would be all over it and he would be free to plant the bomb elsewhere during the night. The leaders all agreed. Whatever target Billy hit, needed to be empty. For the dress rehearsal, they wanted it to rain bricks not blood.

***

The Crossing commune was its usual, late afternoon, divine madhouse. Nine-year-old Janey, the sole commune kid, was on the porch helping the house's official den mother, Elaine, sort through buckets of berries they had gathered by the falls. Janeykins, as she was often called, was planning to sell them to the crowd at the demo and make some extra money for the house. Elaine was the oldest in the commune and wisest. She had once been a professor at the college. Her husband, Richard, was a great poet, and he ran the commune's press. They were counter-culturalists and the people in the commune had gravitated to them. Bright, challenging, and believers in social justice, they brought out the best in most. Inside the house, the elaborate stereo was playing a trippy Dr. John album and all the shades were drawn. Morris, a theatre student, was rolling joints by candlelight, taking a pause from learning lines for a new play. Richard was in the back running the press. He was donating to the cause, printing out the instructions to beat the draft. Janey's mom of the moment, Bibi from Belchertown, and Janet Planet were making bread in the kitchen. Serenading them on guitar was Janey's adoptive father, Mychal. He was a musician and a dreamer. Janey's real mother was long gone. A black, studio singer from New York, Teresa left to make it in Hollywood, Mychal had heard. Mychal was Max's father's baby brother. He'd dropped the last name of Dean and only went by Mychal. The kitchen was hot and crowded, rich with yummy smells. Che, the dog, lay by the stove, eyes open, waiting patiently. The ladies were baking, and Mychal was showing off flashy guitar picking while improvising protest song lyrics.

War raging, boys dying
Makes me sick at heart
Heroes and herpes, baby, you know
Are just a letter apart

They couldn't hear the fight going on upstairs in the attic.

* * *

Marie and Suzie had a battle on their hands. Tim only got interested in the relic when he found out it was some kind of ancient explosive.

That's so bogus, so untrue!

Ever since they had brought the old chest back to The Crossing, they had sworn each other to secrecy. Not knowing what they had, Suzie drew sketches of the characters on the box's lid so Marie could research it at the Cornell Library. Tim did nothing, absolutely nothing, he couldn't have cared less.

I've been busy getting the demo organized. Gimme a break.

Working with books on Sanskrit translation, Marie had a hunch, despite how outrageous and inconceivable it seemed, that what they had discovered from an old map stowed in their attic, was a fabled, powerful weapon dedicated to Shiva. It was hard to keep it quiet. Word got back to an East Indian professor in the hotel management school, Rama Patel, who knew Sanskrit and ancient Indian history. He examined the sketches and was more than curious. He demanded to see the Eye in person and the girls put him off, concerned about his aggressiveness. Tim was no better. He was on his way to meet a very important movement visitor and intended to let him know about their incredible find. The girls, sensing the same bad vibe, were protective. Voices got angrier.

Who? Who is so important?

-He's a leader of a new splinter group of SDS. They are done with peaceful protest. They can use this. Even the threat of it. If used right, it could help bring this country to its knees!

Tim was adamant, but Suzie and Marie held their ground. They made him swear on his mezuzah *not* to mention it. Worn down, Tim swore to them he would keep the secret.

***

The Weathermen needed to recruit some solid soldiers, and Tim had come highly recommended. Billy hoped Tim would help him coordinate the best target and time. He was already late, and Billy was annoyed. He took a snort of methamphetamine and turned up the volume on the bedside radio tuned to the Cornell station. Janis Joplin was singing right to him, taking a piece of his heart. He believed down to his soul in what he was doing. He knew while he may never be understood, his beliefs would be loud and clear. One more bump of speed and Billy wished Tim would set him up with some of the commune girls he had mentioned. He didn't figure Tim would also tempt him with a mini atomic bomb.

CHAPTER THIRTEEN

Tom Tom's home had been burglarized shortly after he brought the Eye home and started researching up at the main library on the Cornell campus. If there was one thing Marie regretted not telling her dear friend Jeanie's husband before she died, it would have been:

Don't go to the library and talk to a Professor Patel.

Tom Tom didn't meet Patel, who was retiring that summer of 1996. He met his graduate assistant who showed up after the second day at the campus library. Tom Tom was reading an early translated version of the *Mahabharata* and was taking notes. It verified the stories of the three Eyes describing it as a weapon of devastating force just like Marie had warned. His heart was pounding. It mentioned a Third Cleansing. Enthralled and sober almost a week, a miracle in itself for, Tom Tom didn't notice that someone had sat down next to him. It was a bright, energetic East Indian named Sabu Shera. He was in a tan turban and was smartly dressed in a red, sleeveless pullover with a collared, white shirt beneath. He loved to talk Hindu antiquities and gave Tom Tom his phone number. Tom Tom reminded the student it was a quiet place and got back to his reading, hand cupping the small Polaroid of the artifact's lid that he'd taken. Sabu whispered:

I know the history of the Eye of Shiva. I believe it is located near.

He leaned closer to Tom Tom. He could translate Sanskrit; the librarians would attest to that. Feigning naivety, Tom Tom tested Sabu.

Why would the ancient Eye be here...in Ithaca of all places?

-Do you really want to know?

Unfortunately, Tom Tom did and was hooked. They moved out of the quiet zone into a nearby campus coffee shop. Tom Tom bought the grad student a tea and he had black coffee for himself and settled in. Sabu spun the tale, a chain of custody, pieced together from 1774 to the very day in 1996. He started at the beginning of its theft with Lt. Philip Pearce. Following its path to London through Lord North to America and Barry St. Leger, Wading Bird who brought it to the Finger Lakes, Walter Newton, Marie Sayles...

And now you...

If Tom Tom had found it, Sabu could help him get it back to where it belonged in Varanasi, India. Tom Tom said he would certainly think about it. *If* he found it. He thanked the young man and left with an eerie feeling. He was not shocked when the same night his place was broken into. In a positive sign that he was taking better care of himself, Tom Tom had been out grocery shopping at Wegman's. When he returned, he could tell someone had been inside searching with care. Nothing was taken, least of which, the relic. Paranoid, Tom Tom had stowed it away in an Ithaca storage locker that afternoon. After the break-in, Tom Tom stayed away from Cornell and considered his options for it. He wondered if Marie had gone underground to avoid people like Sabu. Or was it the FBI that was after her? His wife had believed Marie was in a witness protection program, but that could not be true.

Her last words still tortured him.

***

Marie was on a morphine drip when he got to see her that one and only time. That time he was half-sloshed, and she was pale gray, skin on bone, in a bedroom that smelled of life's opposite. He had seen Jeanie's old photos of her from The Crossing. She was stunning in the most natural way, a bohemian vision of the time. Illness had transformed her, stolen every shred of pulchritude, and left a shell eager to move on. With urgency, she gave him the maps and as much information as she could about the Eye's potential danger. One intense instruction session and she was spent. Breathing heavily, in and out of clarity, she repeated over and over how grateful she was Tom Tom had come. She knew he was a good man and the right one to take it on. She could not handle the burden any longer. He asked if she considered surrendering it to the FBI.

No! No!

Agitated, Marie was animated, advising against it. When Tom Tom questioned that, her lips tightened, and her face contorted. She wanted to answer but could not speak, erupting into a frightening coughing fit. Her quaking body was shaking the IV stand. Tom Tom grabbed the metal pole to stop it from toppling over. Marie was spewing out blood and pointing at him. Her long, bony index finger grabbed hold of his vodka-stained shirt, pulling him close. As a spasm wracked inside, she tried to force out words that sounded like:

Know what...not to do!

A hospice worker in the kitchen, who knew Marie by another name as a beloved high school drama teacher, rushed into the bedroom and asked if Tom Tom would step out. It took a good five minutes for it to quiet inside. When he was finally allowed back in, Marie was snoring weakly in a sleep from which she would never awake. Tom Tom would be left to ponder the meaning of her last words.

Know what not to do.

Which made it even more perplexing when he got a visit from FBI agents the day after the attempted robbery at his house.

CHAPTER FOURTEEN

Naba Gupta resisted the irresistible urge to scratch under her plaster cast. She had come a long way from the University of Lucknow in India to the premiere MBA Hotel Management school in America. When Professor Shera recruited her a few years earlier, she had no idea how radically her meaningless life would change for the better. She let the itch work through her body, she would not give in to it. She was so much stronger since she had become an Aghori initiate. She was so much more an entity with purpose. And then there was the way Sabu used her body. That was her path to God and a meaningful death. She had sworn to obey the Baba Sabu's every command, which would explain why she was holding back an urge to pee as well as itch. She was staking out the State Diner, sitting in the rain with a poncho hiding her face at a bus stop across the street. Pradeep Vijay, her sister Aghori and initiate like herself, had dropped her off on her way to class. Sabu said despite everything, it was important to keep up their studies. Naba read her ethics textbook, glancing to see the old woman being helped into the State Diner by Franz, her tall, distinguished man friend, holding an umbrella. He had been feeding Sabu information for the last week. Pradeep had been ordered to gain Franz's cooperation when the money wasn't sufficient. She complained afterward to Naba that the man knew nothing about fucking and smelled too sweet. Naba buried her head into the book upon seeing the L.A. detective and Professor Flatman enter the diner shortly after the old woman. A meeting was on just like Franz had said.

Franz hated what he had become but saw a clean start starring the new Franz soon. How long could the old lady live? Especially now, with her stress level mounting. Her stupid devotion to her dead friend had certainly put her in a risky condition. She had him rush order more heart medication and a defibrillator, then made him practice using the device and timed him, *the bitch*. Franz didn't care what the dark, turbaned professor was up to and planned to stay on his sunny side. The whole Eye of Shiva thing was likely a story. Sabu had said his people have the right to have their religious artifact returned and that was good enough for Franz. Then there was the two hundred in cash for each and every tip that Franz provided. Nothing better than a side hustle. The bills folded nicely in Franz's Alexander McQueen silver mirrored bifold wallet that Ella had given him. Sabu also delivered on his *bonus* and Franz especially enjoyed the chance to experience young flesh again. He was certain the girl Pradeep had never had a lover like him. He'd been with Ella for seven years and was not yet fifty. If she would just die, Franz could look forward to a tidy, yearly allowance after her death, he believed. That would work well in Budapest, where the women were always generous, and opportunities abounded to indulge his passion for ballroom dancing. Inside the State Diner, Ella asked Franz to wait outside. He smiled with supreme unction and was out the door. Stepping toward his car under an umbrella, he felt like he was being watched. And damn if he didn't like that. Like his dance club, crazy, DJ cousin liked to say:

Sheet's startin' to get real.

It was chilling for Ella to realize that this Indian professor whom Candace had found to translate Tom Tom's photo might have been Tom Tom's killer. Max slowed her roll. He had read the file Ella had sent before taking the assignment. It was from another private detective she hired in 1997 right after Gill's death on the lake. That detective had hired a forensic computer guy who confirmed a suicide note from Tom Tom on his PC. It was written ten days before he died.

That was before he got the map from the dying girl, Marie, something.

—Sayles. She changed identity after 1969. It would help to know why she was in hiding.

Max cautioned Ella on sharing any more information with Franz or Eddie's girlfriend, Candace.

Was that a suicide too? Is that what you believe? Tom Tom and Eddie both killed themselves?

Max calmed Ella down. He was trying to present to her how the police were looking at it. He believed like her. Enough coincidence and incident, and he felt certain Professor Shera wanted the Eye of Shiva and is, and has been, prepared to kill for it. Janey hated the thought of that.

He always seemed so charming. This is very disturbing for me. He's a colleague.

-What's disturbing to me is that this student, the one who tried to wreck me, was driving a car registered to the FBI. So, what does that make Sabu? Big snitch on campus?

Their lunch came. Greek salads for Janey and Ella, and for Max, a fully dressed burger with a fried egg on top. It got an eyebrow raise out of Ella.

Bo Burger.

Max tore into it. Janey raised her fork brimming with cucumber and faked gusto.

More eating. Thanks, Max.

CHAPTER FIFTEEN

DeWitt Park was filling up early. The empty bandstand set up between the two enormous red, white, and blue painted Revolutionary War cannons was a chaotic tangle of microphones, cords, and musical equipment waiting for someone to make sense of it all. A big, tie-dyed banner behind it proclaimed STOP THE WAR. The P.A. was playing "Everyday People" by Sly and the Family Stone. The upbeat rhythms gave the sunny, hot September 1969, Ithaca morning an air of heightened anticipation and empowerment. Something big was coming. Anxious hope for a better world hung heavy. There was also a healthy dose of fear permeating the hearts of the boys who could soon be required to serve in a war that was not going well. The latest news out of Washington burned through the crowd. Student deferments would no longer be given carte blanche this semester. Instead, male students would need to sustain a B grade point average to continue to receive the coveted 2-S deferment. Without it, the prospects of being drafted as a 1-A and shipped to Nam were nearly unavoidable. That personal panic dripped from the long-haired, underclassmen along with sweat from the increasing humidity. By ten a.m., it was already seventy-eight degrees. Students back at Ithaca College and Cornell for the new semester kept arriving at the park and jockeying for good positions to experience the event.

Around the perimeter of the park were information tables manned by committed volunteers, including Marie Sayles and Suzie Sunshine in their love-in finest. Marie, a dove painted on each cheek, was a vision in a long, diaphanous peasant dress. Suzie had stayed up late and fashioned a fuchsia bra with peacock feathers shaped into a peace sign to work with her pink capri pants. They hawked pamphlets for everything draft related, from ways to fail the physical to transportation vouchers to emigrate to Canada. Other counter-culture groups added to the vibe with hippie wares for sale, homemade eats, and more handouts; Whole Earthers with teepee and geodesic dome plans, tarot card readers, Hari Krishnas. Threading through the crowd were costumed members of the Bread and Puppet Theatre's giant puppets who would be performing later. An Uncle Sam on stilts garnered the most attention and most friendly *boos*. There were giant, wooden soldiers, giant pig puppets, large gray puppet ladies, jugglers, acrobats, and clowns. The crowd was resplendent in T-shirts that all held messages either declaring their favorite bands—Hendrix, The Doors, Beatles, or antiwar declarations—*Love is Not Healthy for Children and other Living Things, Hell No We Won't Go, Viet Nam Vets for Peace*. The Black Students Coalition all came in together in black T's and berets. Uniformed, local cops were there in droves, state troopers on motorcycle and horseback kept their distance with a cautious eye on the proceedings. The police were armed with service revolvers and batons. Parked further off on the street at their staging area, riot police in full gear lounged, waiting to see if they would be needed. Plainclothes fuzz were easy to spot with their short hair, in white shirts and brown shoes, milling through the park. Bibi from Belchertown with Tim's dog, Che, Janet Planet, Mama Elaine, and Janey operated a Crossing commune table selling breads and berries. They were doing a brisk business to little Janey's delight. Cruising the tables was a trio of young, townie freaks, among them Artie Hicks, long, blond hair held in place with a leather headband. He was with his buddies, Happy Jack, a conga drummer, and Danny V, a pot pusher in a coat of many colors, who had a knapsack filled with nickel bags of Oaxacan high test that he was looking to transform into one color—gold. Danny had a pet squirrel, Mr. Natural, that everyone knew. It rested on the right shoulder of his long, thin frame and delighted the kids. While Janey fed Mr. Natural, Danny closed a deal with Janet Planet, one baggie for one loaf. Everyone was happy. Tim, head of Students Against War, took the stage as MC. Introducing himself, he worked up the crowd, mic in hand.

How's everyone doing? You ready to stop this fucking war!?

Everyone except the cops roared, and away it went. Tim laid out the program of musical acts and speakers going on until the negotiated curfew of ten p.m. There would be Nam vets back from the frontlines speaking up, educators, draft counselors, one comedian, and an intermission. After that, a performance of the noted, street theatre group from New York City, the Bread and Puppet players, would take over with their antiwar parable, *The Grey Lady Cantata*. Tim teased an infamous, mystery guest who would appear and blow everyone's mind. The crowd was ripe. There would be dancing after the speeches and the headlining bands would take it all home. Then Tim got serious. There were young men among them who at sundown were going to come up on stage and show their personal commitment by burning their draft cards. He asked if others wanted to get on the list.

We need to declare who we are and who we will not be! We. Are. The. Future!

The crowd was his. Another roar. Police pressed that much closer. Tim segued to the campus rabbi who looked a lot like Allen Ginsberg. He wanted to bless the day with a prayer and a song of solidarity that everyone knew. Opening up a harmonium, he began to pump it and sing to the accordion-like sound.

"We shall overcome..."

The crowd was singing along with the rabbi. All knew the words. It was morning magic.

"We shall overcome. . ."

Everyone was swaying, reaching arms to connect singing over and over with the rabbi in a holy trance.

We shall overcome one day
Deep in my heart
I do believe
We shall overcome one day

Tim joined Marie and Suzie and Che, who jumped up on to Tim at first sight, dancing on his hind legs, licking his boy. Tim gave Che a rough petting down and then softly kissed both the girls, surging with adrenalin. The event was kicking off right. Marie was proud of him but bummed to the core, knowing he'd be heading for Canada soon. Suzie was fighting tears.

You're gonna have to split. Feds are here!

–I'm not getting arrested. I'm not burning my card.

The girls were a mixture of surprise and relief until Tim whispered why. He was joining up with the Weather Underground.

It's the only way for me. After tonight there's a good chance I will have to go into hiding.

Tim took a breath to compose himself while his two lovers looked at him with big, keen eyes. This was not going to be easy. He huddled the girls close and told them he had mentioned the Eye of Shiva to the Weatherman he had met with.

I'm cutting away during the intermission to show it to him.

Lied to and betrayed were flash feelings Marie and Suzie barely navigated. Before they could voice a powerful protest, Tim had to run back on the stage to get the next act introduced. Mama Elaine sensing something amiss came over to find out. Marie was beside herself.

Tim is so fucked in his head!

Elaine knew. Tim had told her about the Weathermen and had her support. She tried to get the girls to see his point. It's about doing his thing. Everyone has to fight in their own way, and Tim is listening to his heart's voice. Marie was not about to accept that psychobabble from Elaine without a challenge.

Have you read the Weatherman manifesto? They are copying the Panthers! Burn and bomb their way to a revolution.

Elaine was their spiritual leader. She thought for a moment and delivered her final pronouncement.

So be it. We need a revolution.

The rabbi finished to great applause and Tim took the mic.

Far out! Far out! Let's keep that vibe alive. Please welcome one of my favorite people, a communal brother. Awed to call this artist, friend. Let's give it up for...Mychal!

Barefoot, Janey's dad took center stage with a leather-strapped, acoustic guitar, slung over his overalls with a *Keep on Truckin'* T-shirt underneath. He stood grinning before the crowd adjusting the mic. At the tables in the back, The Crossing members paused to give him focus especially little Janey, who kept shrilly whistling with two fingers through two missing teeth. And damned if her daddy didn't hear her and wave.

Janeykins, I see you! Ha! Hey, how you all doing? What a mess we are in!

Max's disowned Uncle Myk, the Dean family *no-good-nik*, was a sensitive folk singer with some technical ability and no ambition. Even when he played in the Village, people always said, *dude could fingerpick*. And he did, launching into an upbeat story song of Pete Seeger's about the stupidity of the president. The crowd settled in, spreading out blankets, relaxing for a quieter listen. Deep in the throng, Danny V was closing a two-bag deal and Artie Hicks was sealing a deal to ball later with a very groovy co-ed. Mychal hit the chorus and some of the hard-core folkies sang it with him.

We're waist deep in the Big Muddy

And the big fool says to push on.

Rhoda Seven, a spirited cosmetologist, future Mrs. Artie Hicks, and friend of the People, was giving away free, rainbow-colored lollipops, moving through the mellowing crowd. The sun was almost at its zenith, and the temperature had bumped five degrees. Rhoda's pet kitty Eloise, a sweet yellow tabby, was perched comfortably on her shoulder. If an aerial view were possible, it would show Rhoda Seven under a big, flower-rimmed, sun hat and Danny V's long, curly, black locks, inexorably drawn towards each other, weaving through the crowd at off angles from different directions. At the nexus where they finally intersected, reaction was instantaneous. Her cat faced his squirrel, eye to eye. Eloise lunged right at Mr. Natural with a toothy hiss and a claws-out swipe. The startled squirrel jumped off his human and scampered off. Cat jumped off her human and tore after squirrel, followed by Danny and Rhoda cursing at each other in pursuit of their pets.

On stage, Mychal finished to polite applause except for his enthusiastic Crossing family and Tim took over. He was going to be introducing a true warrior of the Movement and wanted everyone's attention.

Why are we here? Three words!

The audience fired back with a random litany. Tim gave focus to the three-word message on the banner upstage of him. He crooned into the mic, paraphrasing the famous Dylan song.

The answer my friends is not blowing in the wind. It is hanging right here. Stop. The. War!

–Stop the war! Stop the war! Stop the war!

The crowd chanted back. The black student group gave Black Power salutes in rhythm. Professor Rama Patel was not the only teacher interloping on their students' off-campus affairs, but he was the only one in the crowd not watching the stage.

His dark eyes were on Marie Sayles.

CHAPTER SIXTEEN

Max stepped out of the State Diner to let Franz know Ella was ready to roll. Franz was smoking a cig, snuffed it out without a word and headed back in. Before he followed him inside, Max noticed the same poncho-hooded young woman sitting at the bus stop in the rain. He couldn't make out her features, but she'd been sitting there waiting way too long. While Franz helped Ella out the front door, Max slipped inside and grabbed Janey moving her back into the diner towards the kitchen door.

Hey, I didn't get to say goodbye to Ella.

–It's fine. Consider it a French exit.

That was what Mei U used to call leaving a party without saying goodbye to the host. Also known as an *Irish goodbye*. Also known as whichever nationality you wanted to burn as too rude or too drunk to respect social niceties. Max led Janey briskly through the hot box of a kitchen. The two short-order cooks, engrossed in flipping meat and shaking deep-fry racks, didn't even raise an eyebrow. Max and Janey disappeared out the rear door and down the back-alley. Janey followed Max somewhat in the dark.

Are you going to tell me what's going on?

–Being careful. In case we're being watched, which dollars to donuts we are.

No more food. Even in metaphors!

Across from the State Diner, Naba stood and removed her poncho hood. The rain had stopped, and the sun was trying its best to brighten the day. The detective and his friend were not going to be coming out. He was clever, and she had lost him. She knew she was due punishment from her master. He knew what would pain her most.

***

Tacking through side streets Max and Janey made it back to the hotel. Inside the lobby, they were immediately ambushed by Artie Hicks.

I got some photos of The Crossing. You gotta see 'em.

Up in Max's *do not disturb* room, Artie spied their luggage; Janey's pink overnight bag and Max's suitcase opened with his clothes half out. It looked obvious to Artie that two people had been occupying the unmade bed. He grinned when Max denied they were a couple. Janey blushed.

We're kind of cousins.

-I never judge.

The fading color photos of The Crossing were a '60s time capsule. No art director or wardrobe designer in Hollywood could have dressed the commune main characters with more authenticity. Janey shrieked on seeing herself in a group shot wearing a tie-dye wife-beater with basketball shorts and high-top, glitter running shoes.

I loved those sneakers!

Janey savored each pic, then passed them on to Max. They were mostly of Artie with different, commune ladies and some from the wedding after the commune went kaput. It was a Be-In, Day-Glo world Max had missed. He was a soldier in-country when they were under incense clouds reading Hesse by candlelight. He knew from experience and the passing years that more than him, these young people in the photos actually did help stop the war. The homefront had spoken. Thankfully. Every Viet Nam vet Max ever knew felt little satisfaction or appreciation for the sacrifice made. It was all proven by history to be a colossal mistake. The brotherhood among them, however, was real as blood and oxygen. Max was looking forward to catching up with Wilbur that afternoon like he'd planned. He had purposely not shared that nugget with Ella. Max held up a group shot from the living room of The Crossing.

Who do we have? Left to right.

Little Janey, her dad Mychal, Morris, Robert, Dee, Planet, Claudia 2, uh, Ganni. Elaine and me. Check it out. I think I had the longest hair.

No...Marie Sayles?

Janey looked at Artie. They both shrugged.

It was after Marie was gone, I guess.

–And before the FBI raided the commune. See, Suzie's shredded American flag that they took is still up on the wall.

That stopped Max. The FBI raided the commune. Did they remember why? Each had a different explanation. Janey was told it was about the riot that happened during the rally in the park. Artie said she was totally wrong.

Really? Your friend Danny with the squirrel was crashing at our house! He caused the riot!

–That's what Mychal probably told you. Everyone else knew the FBI was looking for a bomb.

***

They didn't find any bombs at The Crossing in 1969. The two Syracuse-based, federal agents, however, did enjoy giving the commune a long, slow toss while ogling the braless denizens. In 1996 a different generation of no-nonsense FBI were determined to search every inch of Tom Tom Gill's lakefront property; the big house, the boathouse, hell they searched the original outhouse and didn't find it. Tom Tom played dumb to federal agents, none of whom he knew. There were some local police in support with a bomb squad on the ready. They knew Mr. Gill as a great and generous Ithacan, an esteemed citizen, a philanthropist that never forgot about the police and fire departments. Tom Tom could have lost it and poured a drink while they pored over every nook and cranny. He thought about it, how it would taste, and how it would let him forget whatever needed forgetting. He had been planning his suicide and then Marie distracted him. As if Jeanie was directing her to direct him. He had flown off again to see Marie a few days earlier, but she had already passed. So, the promise stood and promising her was like promising Jeanie. Amazing the tricks the mind can play in making fateful decisions. Tom Tom would need to move the relic from his storage locker before they realized he had one and got a warrant. He had a temporary, hiding place in mind, and it made him laugh to think about how Ella would react when he told her.

Before the agents sent everyone home without any bombs, Tom Tom saw a civilian sitting in the rear seat of the Feds' dark gray Lincoln. He was almost certain it was the grad student Sabu. When the car pulled out, Sabu, sensing Tom Tom's stare, lowered his tinted window and waved. Tom Tom wished it was a wave of goodbye; only he knew better.

CHAPTER SEVENTEEN

By 2009 Sabu had tenure as a professor in the hotel management school of the university. He had learned a lot interning for Rama Patel. Enough to know the old man was useless. If it hadn't been for the theft of the Eye of Shiva centuries ago, Sabu never would have left Varanasi as a devout Aghori. It was getting harder to stay faithful in such exotic comfort, but he knew where his allegiance lay. Once he retrieved the Eye, he would fulfill the prophecy handed down to him. The Finger Lakes would be cleansed like the prophecy of the high priest demanded. Despite Sabu's ability to live a split life, misgivings still crept in like they had with other Aghori posted in Ithaca in the generations before Sabu, before Patel. He had heard the story of the first, Jovan, who after only two years had taken a white wife and stopped searching for their prize. Rama Patel failed too. Sabu would not. He felt the pull of destiny. He was not going to succumb to any distraction. It crossed his mind and gave him comfort that he was still young at forty and as good at duplicity as he was at fucking his acolytes. He had other students who flirted with him, but he knew his limits. Where Patel had gotten timid, Sabu had learned from his limitations. Patel was always worried the FBI would be on to him. When Sabu had his chance, he volunteered himself to the federal agency. They needed a campus informant and he was their man. Over the years, he'd served up more than a few juicy tidbits for the bureau, leading to the arrest of a faculty oxy chemist and dossiers on campus student activists. By 2009 his equity with the Feds couldn't have been higher and it gave Sabu a bulletproof confidence. He could feel this life's meaning was nearing fruition. He would miss this part of his journey and believed his past lives had all led him here. His re-death would be as sweet as this life.

With that Western elation of a job well done, Professor Shera finished a graduate-level talk in Barton Hall on Food Service Management: Theory and Practice. He was popular with students and had a mess of them around him after his lecture. He answered their questions quickly and headed for his office. He was expecting an update on the detective's whereabouts and checked his phone for messages. A text from Naba was disconcerting and the missed call too with no message from Pradeep. It could sense opportunity eroding. His first call was to his contact at the FBI in Syracuse. They spoke once a week. Sabu was going to tip them about Professor Flatman, whom he heard might be coming into possession of a stolen antiquity. It couldn't hurt to go on the offensive. It wouldn't be a high priority for his agents at first but if he added in a ritualistic murder later, they would snap to.

* * *

Aruna was fast asleep in the arms of her husband when she first heard the midnight pounding on the door of the fine cabin that Philip and Caleb had built on high ground. She thought it was part of a reverie of awakening. They'd been in Ithaca over eight years, and things had fallen into a nice routine, certainly for the men of the family. Aruna had been struggling ever since her son became a man and her responsibilities as a mother waned. She longed to be working with her friend Mary Wollstonecraft again. More knocking! *Wake up!* She'd been keeping a journal about her experiences on the American frontier but felt guilty not to be helping advance the cause of her gender. When she tried to speak up locally on issues pertaining to the exclusion of women in important matters, she was promptly put in her place. Philip pleaded with her not to make waves. It was detrimental to his career. So, she tried to pack away that spirit, but it wouldn't be still. She lived vicariously through her friend Mary, and all that she had accomplished in England since Aruna had left. Her book *Vindication of the Rights of Women* was heralded in London and got more than a conversation going in polite society. Aruna planned to discuss a visit to England and hoped Philip would support it. The pounding on the door persisted. It was no dream. Philip arose and answered it. It was their friend Emily covered in blood, Jovan's blood.

CHAPTER EIGHTEEN

A raven-haired, Joan Baez look-alike, folk singer trilled on from the stage. The heat continued to climb. Danny V. was up a tree literally. A big oak in the park was the sanctuary for Mr. Natural escaping Eloise, Rhoda Seven's cat. Rhoda got hold of her cat who couldn't outclimb Mr. Natural and now the squirrel would not come down despite Danny's pleading. So, Danny handed his backpack to Artie and went up to get him. That caught the attention of a local cop who promptly ordered him to come down. Danny V. told him it was his pet squirrel and he had to get him back. Poor baby was scared out of his wits. Danny V. climbed higher. No one was paying much attention yet, except the lone cop whose orders had been disregarded. This was not going to end well. The folk singer on stage finished to some applause and Tim took the stage.

Alright. I think it's time for a special guest before our intermission. Please welcome a teacher who cares, Professor Al Eyas.

A professor in a doctoral, black gown and black, velvet tam took center stage. He was bearded and from under his cap flowed long black hair. Those in the inner circle knew it was the much loved and respected, former Cornell campus priest, Father Daniel Berrigan in disguise.

Two years before with eight others, he had destroyed all the military draft files at a facility in Catonsville, Maryland. They had been tried and each sentenced to eighteen years in federal prison for destroying government property. When it came time for Daniel Berrigan and his brother Phil to surrender, they were no-shows and on the run as fugitives, rumored to be in Sweden. They were the only priests ever to be on the FBI's Most Wanted list. It was dangerous for Berrigan to be here, near his own campus but such was the level of his commitment to stopping the war. The two FBI agents in the crowd were too busy cooling in the shade of a park maple tree to take much notice.

Bless you all for coming today. These are challenging times. I am hearing people here saying change is not coming fast enough. Our voices are not being heard. We need to seek more militant methods to be taken seriously.

Rama Patel had been raised among the Aghori family in Rajasthan. He had been groomed and educated to live in the Finger Lakes, where the Eye of Shiva had been lost. He'd been on watch for five years and had begun to believe it was only an apocryphal tale from olden times. That was until he suspected some hippies may have actually found it or at least a map to it. Now it seemed very real to him and he felt the pressure. All that stood between him and eternal glory were two, silly, white girls. As the "professor" on stage continued, Rama glanced at the two disinterested Feds and made an impulsive decision. He went straight for Marie and Suzie. At the sight of him approaching, Marie tensed and gave Suzie's hand a warning squeeze. Ignoring Patel, they concentrated on every word of the speaker on stage.

I can tell you for a fact, it may or may not be possible to turn the U.S. around through nonviolent revolution. But one thing favors such an attempt: the total inability of violence to change anything for the better! So, stay the course! We are winning!

The crowd cheered at that, lifting the spirits of Marie and Suzie, who hoped Tim was listening. Patel waited for the crowd to quiet down. He was close to the girls and made sure they heard him.

If you give it over to the FBI, they will use it for the war.

Marie froze at that thought. She knew in her heart that it was not an option for that very reason. Patel would not be denied or ignored. Emphatic, he grabbed Marie by the shoulders and was in her face.

It needs to be returned to the Aghori people!

Three uniformed policemen moving through the crowd, pushed by giving Marie the diversion she needed to break free of Patel's grasp. The cops were hurrying toward the big oak tree where a situation was developing. Artie's voice cut through the clamor.

Help! They're trying to arrest Danny!

Danny was up on a lower limb. He was balanced, standing on tiptoes trying to get Mr. Natural to come down a few branches and get a nice juicy cashew he was flashing. The cop at the base of the tree was ordering Danny this, and warning Danny that. He had a daughter who had run off to San Francisco with a long-haired bum, and he was no friend of the tribe. He was banging on the tree with his baton, getting more steamed at being ignored. Danny had no intention of complying until he safely had hold of Mr. Natural. The crowd near the tree was no longer focused on the stage but on the very real, *hippie versus pig* drama playing out right before their eyes. Mr. Natural wanted that cashew and was coming down when the Ithaca cop emboldened by the arrival of the other cops started climbing up after Danny. Elaine was trying to reason with a sergeant. Marie, Suzie, Bibi, and Janey looked on, breathless. The climbing cop grabbed hold of one of Danny V's well-worn, black Herman engineer boots and started yanking. Danny kicked his boot free and caught the side of the cop's head. *Ow!* The cop reached for his sidearm but could not get the holster open. Little Janey was crying.

Leave him alone. It's his squirrel!

The others were echoing it. The crowd good and baked by the sunshine was getting outraged too. Mr. Natural freaked, went higher up the tree, and so did Danny. So did the cop! The other policemen pushed close, forming a circle around the tree, batons raised high. How sad and ridiculous it must have looked to the prince of peace, Berrigan, on stage. And then from within the crowd, someone threw the first bottle. It smashed against the oak tree, glass shards flying. Followed by a rock that hit the back of the sergeant. Followed by police chasing into the crowd for the perpetrators, swinging batons, bringing the heat, as a good old-fashioned, late summer riot hit next level. On stage, Berrigan begged the assembled to back off and keep cool. A trash can went airborne taking out a duo of cops. Horseback police moved in, upping the ante followed by the riot squad. With their federal-paid-for new visored helmets and plexiglass shields, they'd been savoring the possibility that something like this might happen.

Some park-goers, including Rama Patel, scattered for their lives, others, including Artie, Happy Jack, and the black students, dug in harder, fighting back with whatever they could. Another trash can was set ablaze. An ice cooler hit the shield of a SWAT teamer. An agitated Berrigan was gesturing wildly, pleading hard over the P.A. He took off his dumb cap and the wig came off too by accident. For the first time, one of the FBI guys noticed what he'd been missing. *Father Berrigan!*

Tim made his way through the confusion. He was using the commotion to split. He whistled for Che, and his husky came running. Marie and Suzie spotted that and were on it. He tried to wave them away.

I am coming back!

-You are not going anywhere without us.

While more police arrived, the Commune Three made their way out to a side street where Tim's beat-up, red and white International Harvester jeep was parked. Under a blanket on the rear jump seat was the Eye of Shiva. Marie looked at Tim like he had two heads.

Are you insane?! This shitbox doesn't even lock!

-Shut up! Get in!

Marie, Suzie, and the dog squeezed into the car with him. Suzie climbed into the back and put the relic on her lap.

Damn, it sure does get warm. That's freaky.

-Billy will know what to do with it.

The police presence had tripled, and the crowd was being pushed out of the park under orders shouted by numerous bull horns. Some students, black and white, were being arrested and cuffed. The FBI agents were searching all over near the stage area, but the fugitive Father wasn't around. One of the brown-shoed agents got on stage for a better vantage point. Below him passed two giant puppets at his eye level. A bald eagle puppet was leading a giant Uncle Sam out of the fray and toward safety. The Uncle Sam saluted to the agent. The distracted agent saluted back. Inside the puppet was Daniel Berrigan, spirited clean away to fight another day.

High up in the big oak, Danny V. watched below. The riot soon de-escalated to a whimper. He had Mr. Natural on his shoulder again and with no one pursuing him any longer, Danny lowered himself down the tree and strolled out of the park like the happy wanderer he was.

CHAPTER NINETEEN

Wilbur had wanted to meet Max at Taughannock Falls. He had come early to have some moments alone in the sacred place of his ancestors. He sat cross-legged at the edge of the creek at the foot of the great water drop in the deep bowl. Mist hung heavy and saturated the air in a natural, cool sauna. Sweat beads burst on his forehead. He thought of Wading Bird. The last wartime chief of the Cayugas had hidden this dark treasure from a faraway land where people were also called Indians. That always made Wilbur wonder. Before they recovered it from the secret cavern behind the falls, Tom Tom had asked him if he could de-code Wading Bird's map. Wilbur liked to feel the deerskin. It was extraordinary in its workmanship. He translated it with the help of his Uncle Em. It described in shaped, shell shards the location of something dangerous called the *gift*. It was easy to imagine Wading Bird's village of longhouses and the expanse of fields, middens by the lake with piles of freshwater clam and mussel shells. So much happiness and then so much pain having to lead the tribe into a dead-end war. The Cayugas paid dearly for their allegiance to the English. Though it wouldn't have mattered if they had backed the Americans. The Oneida did, and their lands were also confiscated by General Sullivan who did not care to distinguish which tribe was friend or foe. There were few triumphs in war. Few sides that were the right side. Whatever was learned was forgotten over and over. Call it cognitive dissonance or institutional ignorance, as a species we swim upstream getting nowhere, Wilbur surmised. God, he was depressing himself and wondering why Max was so late. Like Max, Wilbur had seen that futility firsthand. He sat head bowed in a place of peace where the tribes met every year to re-forge that humanhood. Where did it all go?

It was said among his people you cannot step in the same creek twice. It was pointless to dwell on that sadness. He knew Tom Tom had been killing himself with drink and he couldn't stop him. Somehow the deerskin map gifted him back his life. More than ever, Wilbur was determined to help Max Dean finish his old friend's mission.

Max had made sure they weren't followed. Artie did them a solid and slipped out of the hotel in Max's jacket with an umbrella shielding his face. He drove Janey's car back to her house while Max and Janey slipped out the hotel service entrance and went to a cab stand by another hotel and got a ride out to Trumansburg. Dropped off at the top of the falls, Max and Janey waited till some tourists moved on and stood by themselves at a scenic viewpoint with a restraining, split-rail fence. It overlooked the entirety and was spectacular to behold, the water gushing down two hundred fifteen feet. Now Max understood why Wilbur wanted him to meet where it had originally been hidden. Overwhelmed by the majesty of the moment, Max reflexively pulled Janey in tight, shoulder to shoulder, in a comforting embrace. Perhaps it was the magic of the falls or her own wish-fulfillment, but Janey mistook Max's gesture and turned on her toes and kissed him on the mouth. He didn't resist. She seemed so needy. Or was he the needy one? It was strange, almost foreign, and he felt like a confused teenager when it broke. Janey blushed.

I'm sorry. Was that wrong?

-I don't know. I...let's try again, and I will tell you.

This time Max did the kissing, and it felt fine. Right or wrong would have to come later.

CHAPTER TWENTY

Billy had aced his crash course in bomb-making with the Weatherman's best engineer. He felt confident as he wrapped six sticks of dynamite with care attaching the timer and fuse, double-checking his work while he went along. He had the discipline to have succeeded in almost any career. Perhaps if his studies had felt more relevant during his brief time in Madison as a University of Wisconsin freshman, he might have pursued that early dream of being a country doctor. He was not yet twenty-five and late at night when he allowed himself to think of a life after the revolution, he believed he would study medicine again. With Tim Kramer's advice, he had decided the ROTC Center on the Cornell campus would be the best target. It would be empty after nine o'clock and with the demo at the park planned to go all day into the night, Billy liked the low-risk factor with the pigs elsewhere. It would make a loud splash and give the new collective confidence to try something more explosive during the upcoming Chicago Days of Rage.

Tim would be by later, and Billy wanted to have everything ready. Billy liked Tim on first meet and believed he could become a valuable member of the group. Tonight would be a good test. When Tim had insisted Billy take a look at something special, something ancient, something unthinkable with immense power, Billy agreed. The Eye of Shiva? It all sounded a little hippy-dippy to Billy who considered himself a soldier. The sound of a vehicle pulling into the motel parking lot in front of his room sent Billy pushing the curtain back to peek out. It was Tim arriving and he was not alone.

Not cool!

Suddenly uptight, Billy stopped his task and headed outside to divert them from entering his room.

You're early.

-There was a little problem at the park. This is Marie and Suzie, from The Crossing.

Billy nodded, barely looking at them, Tim held a blanket-covered object in his hands. Billy apologized but was busy. It got awkward fast. Tim stayed the course and reminded Billy about this special item he wanted him to see.

Can we come in and discuss it with you? Like to get your thoughts.

-Another time, man. Come inside. You and I need to talk.

Suzie reached over and took charge of the Eye. Tim flipped the keys to Marie and made plans to see them later. Marie and Suzie were not upset at all at the rudeness or the turn of events. This Billy was super creepy, and they couldn't wait to split. Tim sent Che off with the girls and trailed Billy into his room at the Driftwood Inn. The dog didn't listen. He trotted after the men. Billy held the door open, letting Che in.

It's cool. I love dogs.

By the time Marie got Tim's jalopy jeep down the road and into third gear, an explosion rocked the area and their world. It seems a distracted Billy wasn't as good a student as he thought. One unwrapped wire crossing another and *ka-boom!*

Billy, Tim, and Che were blown to kingdom come.

BRAHMA, GOD OF CREATION

CHAPTER ONE

Wilbur couldn't stop a grin. The universe was always surprising him. He had made his way up to the top of the falls' viewing area and stopped upon seeing Max and Janey mid-smooch. They seem to be tasting each other like a new flavor. He could wait. They backed their heads away and caught some air; Max saw Wilbur and flushed like an old horn dog. He stumbled for some words to cover. Janey beat him to it, sweeping it under nature's own rug.

Such beauty should be celebrated, don't you think?

Max joined in, ushering them off in the blazing spirit of denial.

Let's roll.

* * *

Wilbur's old Ford Bronco was from a time before there were SUVs. It was a truck and had the suspension system to prove it. They bounced hard over unmarked, dirt roads for the next half hour, their heads barely missing the top of the truck cab with every bump. What made the ride enjoyable to Max and Janey was listening to Wilbur sharing with them the lake's secrets.

They say Cayuga's a thousand feet deep. They're wrong. It's bottomless near the middle. That's where the On-Rah-Dee sleeps. Some call her a sea serpent with a bad attitude. We consider her holy.

Janey was all over that, and Wilbur was happy to fill her in on the local legend which was as real to the native people as Loch Ness was to the Scots. On-Rah-Dee would appear whenever the lake was threatened. Ole Greeny was a dangerous, enormous sea creature with a long, green neck, big head, and a temper. Mysteriously splintered ships were reported in newspaper accounts as early as 1829, and foggy Greeny sightings through the decades continued to fuel the legend. You don't want to get on the lake's bad side, Wilbur added. His ancestors made annual offerings to ensure a good relationship with the sea beast. Janey was fascinated and that fascinated Max who was starting to see his cousin in a new light. She had a childlike curiosity that made her adorable and, damn, if he didn't start wondering about things he shouldn't be wondering about. Janey peppered Wilbur with questions.

Is there photographic evidence? Is Greeny still alive?

-No, but nothing dies forever.

Wilbur wasn't giving anything away. He stopped the old Bronco on the edge of a bluff that overlooked two lakes and shut off the engine. Silence descended. He urged them to listen. Slowly they became aware of what he hoped they would hear.

Is someone beating a drum down there?

-Hey, I was going to ask that.

Both were all ears, reacting to the distant sound of "drums" coming from the lake below.

Scientists want you to believe the sound is caused by the release of natural gas between the lakes. We know it's my people. They're here.

Stepping out of the car, with reverence, they stared below at the lakes. Lake Seneca seemed to be higher than Cayuga. Wilbur pointed out the closest shore.

That's where the old canal was dug to link the lakes. We will need to get into the water at that edge, according to Tom Tom's map.

It looked straightforward to Max. Assuming the weather would cooperate, they could scuba the following day, he thought. Janey, too, was on it.

I'm free. Is it a date?

Max set it for the three to return and see what they could find. Janey offered to get an archaeological excavation permit if that would help secure the area.

I can get one cleared in the morning, and we could legally rope it off and keep away any interested parties.

Max thought stealth would be better. He was amazed Tom Tom, ex-military, didn't give in and hand the relic over to U.S. authorities. Wilbur thought long and hard.

He got spooked. Was proceeding with caution.

–I wonder if it's worthwhile to find Marie's caregivers. They may know more.

Janey loved a research project and was stoked to try to track down the hospice helpers from that time.

Professor and Private eye. Two P's in a pod, don't you think?

Max did and tried to stop himself from being so enthused with every little thing Janey said. It was *defocusing* him. He wasn't even sure if that was a real word, but he felt it. It had been a long time since he'd had that buoyant, untethered feeling.

The ride back was on smooth asphalt to Max and Janey's relief.

CHAPTER TWO

The late September sunrise was cresting over East Hill when Mychal wriggled into some patched jeans without underwear, slipped on a pressed, T-shirt and an oversized, hand-knitted sweater. He dressed without a sound while Bibi slept naked on the bearskin blanket of their waterbed. Before exiting the room, he grabbed the guitar case but not the guitar and walked out of the room without a glance back. Down the still dark, second-floor hallway of The Crossing house, he ducked into the room Janey shared with someone's niece who was crashing at the moment. Mychal kissed the child sweetly and tucked in her blanket. She was not his by blood but the love child of an ex-wife's previous lover. Mychal had parented as well as he could for almost Janey's whole life and was her legal guardian. The commune's women, led by Elaine, did the rest. Janey had six mothers, they all joked. Janey's birth mother Teresa, Mychal's ex-wife, was always somewhere in the back of Mychal's mind and heart. He kept in touch with her and accepted her deficiencies. He no longer saw any point in making Teresa feel guilty for her abandonment of Janey when the child was not yet three. People don't change, especially selfish artists. Teresa was a rolling stone with a beautiful and powerful voice. Janey's real father she surmised, could either be Bob Dylan, or a jazz drummer, but most likely, her manager from Chicago who OD'ed a month before Janey was born. Mychal had met Teresa while she was still pregnant, fell in love, and made an honest woman of her. That was a relationship killer for Teresa. Recently, she had washed out in Hollywood and soul spent, last wrote Mychal that she was trying to get centered and was off to India. She left a forwarding address, an ashram in Varanasi. Nothing surprised Mychal about Teresa. Or about the future which Mychal was convinced, with the Viet Nam war raging, had been canceled. He stepped out of the house, not surprised to see Robert on the porch watching the sun rise drinking his morning breakfast tea. He was a poet and nature, he said, fed him well. Something was always being born or dying and writeable to Robert. He also had an eye on everyone since Tim blew himself up and Marie and Suzie had disappeared. With the FBI watching The Crossing, Robert was watching too. Especially after spying an Indian man, Professor Patel watching their house from the cemetery. He'd heard from his wife, Elaine, that Patel had been asking about the girls.

You're up early.

-Gig on the other side of the lake. Back tomorrow.

Maybe the girls will show up for it.

Mychal sighed and shrugged. *Crazy chicks.* He was not a good liar but was working on it, and he thought Robert bought in. He walked to his old Chevy Nova parked up University Avenue in front of the cemetery. The leaves were already turning golden in the early autumn light. To his relief, the car started on the first try. To his dismay, it started pouring.

Traveling north along the Lake Highway, Mychal wished he had the pot for Suzie. He had stuffed into the guitar case a care package of clothes and personal items she and Marie had requested but couldn't score the ounce of weed. He had been sworn to secrecy and was as solid a friend as the girls could ever want. It was Mychal who had set them up in a safe place, at least for the short term. It was another tribe, deep in the bush, off the grid. He once jammed with one of the main denizens of this back-to-the-land community called Noman's. Orloff was a drop-out med student and mad as mud which could have been another name for the commune.

Noman's was a good hour's drive into the bush along a creek. Avoiding a deer, Mychal almost bottomed out on a half-hidden log, almost got stuck in a huge, brown puddle, almost questioned his sanity but finally arrived. Inside its chain link gates, the compound contained four large geodesic domes lining a rocky river with a few out-buildings. The octagonal structures covered in tarps and plastic for roofing were the main housing. A cleared area of hilly land was terraced farmed and other sections were demarcated by their functions—outhouses, workshops, mill, laundry. It was once a little utopia that had been unraveling for a good, or not so good, year or so. Last time Mychal visited, he was buying Orange Sunshine acid tabs from a Noman's member who got popped a few weeks later at Harper College in Binghamton. The commune had become somewhat of a refuge for the wanted. A hole-in-the-wall kind of place where suspicion was rapidly replacing love. Orloff was doing Mychal a big favor taking in the girls. Mychal knew the arrangement would not last unless there was a quid pro quo. He hoped to be able to trade something and in return, get sanctuary for the girls through the winter. By spring, he thought he could get them to Canada. Or maybe their fear of being found was just paranoia and they could come back to civilization.

In a lean-to shelter, Suzie and Marie huddled on the ground by a small fire, looking like a portrait of misery. They hardly looked up when Mychal approached. When they did, their moods went from bummed to groovy in a bright flash. It had been three weeks since they'd been in hiding. The hippie commune had ostracized them and tension abounded. Mychal couldn't believe they were sleeping in the open air. They would have to earn some housing, Marie told him. They offered to help in the kitchen and garden and have been doing whatever they were asked. It's the nights that have been hard and getting colder. Suzie lifted up the towels she'd been using as a pillow and as a headboard, the iron box that held the relic.

Keeps my head warm.

-I told her, it can't be good for her.

--What is that? What's inside that box?

Neither girl answered. Suzie opened the guitar case and started pulling out the goodies.

Did you bring any pot?

Mychal tried to explain. Suzie and Marie's spirits tightened. Orloff joined them. He wore coveralls over a ratty T-shirt and, on a bad day, looked eerily like Charles Manson without the charm. He had been a good musician and student until methamphetamines morphed him into a hateful hippie.

What the fuck, man? We gotta get a few things straight about these beautiful babies. Ass, grass, or gas. This is Noman's. No one stays for free.

The few twenty-dollar bills in Mychal's wallet soothed the beast. Orloff moved off but not before giving Suzie a hard kiss on the mouth.

I think she's coming around.

When he was out of their sight, Suzie wiped it off with her sleeve. Mychal distributed the items from the guitar case and tried to get them to reconsider hiding out.

You did nothing wrong! Just tell the FBI, Tim was on his own.

-Did they find his car?

Yes.

--Then they have our fingerprints, don't they?

It was a communal car. It's true.

-There's more to it, Mychal.

Marie and Suzie had no choice but to finally tell him. Mychal had no choice but to believe them. The thought of handing over the Eye of Shiva to the FBI made Suzie physically ill. And there was no way Marie was surrendering it to the freaky Indian professor.

Or fucking Orloff. I wish we never found it!

-But you did.

CAYUGA

Mychal stayed at Noman's the day and night, and the next day too, fearful of enemies within and without.

CHAPTER THREE

February 10ᵗʰ, 1796

Dear Aruna,

I hope you are sitting down as you read this shocking news.

Aruna sat, bracing for the worst.

I got married. Yes, for the sake of the child, I thought it best. That's right, I am also pregnant.

Aruna let out a sudden shriek that had Philip running inside with a musket in hand. She apologized for the outburst and continued reading Mary Wollstonecraft's first missive in months.

Virtue can only flourish among equals, and my William has pledged his compliance. As you know, Aruna, I do not wish for women to have power over men but only themselves and I still strive for that ideal. I hope, my dear friend, you do too. I long for the day that you return to England and we can carry on our mission together. I want you to know, never have I been so happy as I am with a full belly of life inside me. I hope you are experiencing unbound happiness with Philip and Caleb too. I miss you all terribly and wish you good fortune. My baby is due in four months and the only thing that could make the blessed event better would be to have you by my side, sister. And between you and me, I think it will be a girl.

Yours in loving friendship,
Mary

Aruna couldn't have been more delighted for her old friend. That pleasant thought was a convenient place holder for the horrid images that had been occupying her psyche since Jovan was murdered by an Aghori monk. The monster had recently arrived in Ithaca, and the local sheriff was on the lookout for him. There had been a search for the dark-skinned, turbaned, wanted man but it had come up empty and the other constables assumed he may have fled the Finger Lakes. Philip could not allow himself to believe so. He and Aruna had sheltered Emily since the heinous deed and were on guard. All were glad that their children, now grown, were living away on apprenticeships for their chosen skills. The danger of another Aghori attack clung to them like the spring mud piles and snow building up outside their door. Philip had been preparing for something like this and thought as a surveyor, he had an edge in finding Wading Bird's map to the Eye of Shiva.

If it is still there, we will find it before him and destroy it.

Aruna and Emily both believed searching for the map was risky. If the monk was still around, it would make them more of a target. It was Aruna who first voiced an option that became a workable plan. It had started out as a seed in her mind when she wrote her friend a return letter.

March 28th, 1797

Dear Mary,

Oh, what wonderful news! All health and good luck from all of us in America. A girl! I know it will be true. I am counting the days. As happy as I am for you, I cannot hide my feelings about my current situation. There is a monster that is bent on destroying us. You know of what utter terror I speak. Another of those murdering fanatics wants our blood, and

the only way to stop him may be to take his life first. Should he suc-
ceed in retrieving that object that haunts us still, there are catastrophic
consequences. I swear any action to thwart him is justifiable. It is so
outrageous that no authorities here believe the enormity of the danger
that hovers. I have never revealed to you what I have learned since,
but understand that relic has an ungodly power of destruction and he is
bent on unleashing it. Sweet sister, I had thought to return to England
this summer, but circumstances prevent it. Keep talking to that little lass
inside, she will be the lucky one to have you as her mother.

Fondest, deepest love,
Aruna

Back in her Cambridge flat that Mary shared with her new husband,
William Godwin, she trembled with bolts of fear at her friend's predica-
ment. A monster was afoot, and she worried for poor Aruna's fate.

And what is this ungodly power?

Heart racing, Mary mused, talking to her unborn daughter. The horror
of it all curdled the feminist crusader's blood. She hoped her little girl did
not have nightmares from it. The baby who would be born on her due date,
also would be named *Mary*. Known by her married name, Mary Shelley, she
would give the world nightmares for centuries as the creator of *Frankenstein*.

That illustrious, literary future would never be known to Aruna's illustrious friend, Mary Wollstonecraft. She died in childbirth that April.

CHAPTER FOUR

Janey never knew her real father, who died while she was in Teresa's belly. Her father for the formative years was Mychal. She rarely thought of him anymore and when she did, she didn't think much. After The Crossing experiment in communal living broke up, Mychal asked Elaine and Robert to take in Janey and they were happy to. They bought an old farmhouse outside the city and Janey helped Robert with the poetry mag. She had her own room and two former college professors as foster folk. No mother, no father around, she told her classmates she'd been kidnapped as a baby by fairies. When Mychal died in early 1971 outside Buffalo, New York, she was in junior high school, excelling in math and science. She was driven, well-read, and well-versed in academics, and also hip to the very real, happy/sad world of adults. Tough and sharp except where it came to matters of the heart, Janey had her share of lovers and serious relationships. At fifty-two, she no longer trusted her own instincts when it came to men. That was what was so unnerving to her. Max Dean was all she could think about and she thought when she dared to, that it couldn't end well. He was seventeen years her senior, but Janey found him sexy as hell and as virile and fit as the young intern from the hospital that she recently bedded. She needed to catch her breath and in the stylish, Victorian-era ladies' restroom of the Taughannock Inn while getting her bearings, she lost track of time.

* * *

Max was sitting with Ella in the cozy library of the posh inn. Its paneled walls were decorated with a timeline of framed photos depicting the property's history including an original, gelatin emulsion print of Dearie and John French with the excavated Trumansburg Giant. There was no photo of Dearie's spurned lover, Walter Newton. While Max filled in the grand dame on their findings, he kept glancing at the door, wondering what had happened to Janey. He and Ella began discussing scenarios should they retrieve it successfully. To whom should they turn it over? The official options, local police and FBI, seemed compromised. Both had degrees of uncertainty. Of one thing, Max was certain, he did not want to give the Eye of Shiva to Sabu Shera, whom he suspected of being behind Tom Tom's murder. The best they could do without hard evidence was to prevent him from getting his hands on it. Ella had contacts with the Museum of Natural History in New York City and wondered if that would be a safe landing for such an historical artifact.

Tom Tom donated generously there. Let them figure out if it is dangerous.

Max needed to think about that. He excused himself to find Janey.

Have Franz come in. I need to take a pill. He's waiting in the lobby.

–Will do.

For safety's s sake, let me get you lodging at the inn tonight. One room or two?

Max thought about it and put up two digits. Ella looked bemused, swiveling in her electric wheelchair for a peek through the bay window at the lake's sunset colors.

Life is for loving, I always say. Live while you're able.

* * *

Franz was not in the lobby. He was in a back hallway pretending to tie his shoe while listening to someone on the phone in the inn's main office. It was Candace, the inn manager, the late limo driving, Eagles tribute bandmember's girlfriend. She was not working but had returned to the inn to grab her iPad and hopefully sleep. If she could ever get her mother off the phone.

Mom, I will explain when I see you in the morning. Because...Because it's complicated! The only witnesses may be his murderers...No! The police say suicide. They believe the girls...Yes! Eddie said one of them was driving a car registered to the FBI...

Max didn't find Janey in the lobby, but he did spot Franz eavesdropping by the open, hotel office door. Max busted him, bellowing out with hand signals.

Hey Franz! Ms. von Tragg. Library. You.

Franz put on an innocent look and pranced off, jaunty jolly. Candace, head in the doorway, watched him fast-stepping away and pulled the door shut behind her. Max had a feeling about Franz, and it was hinky at best. Since Janey had gone off to use the ladies' room, Max knocked on its hand-carved oak door and whispered her name. Janey's voice struggled back.

Max?

–Are you, okay?

I don't know.

Max didn't hesitate. He went inside, and Janey was sitting in a low slung, purple velvet chair by a makeup mirror. She was trying to replace some makeup, but tears were making it difficult.

It's nothing. I'm over-tired and under-hydrated.

–That's it?

And...I think I'm falling in love with you. Which is dumb. Yes?

More tears. Behind her, with his hands gently on her shoulders, Max kissed her neck. Janey sighed, eyes clenching.

Are you upset?

-No, happy.

That's good.

She brushed the back of his hand with hers. Their eyes were meeting and melting in the mirror when her cell phone's old school ringtone jarred the perfectly, perfect moment. Janey showed no interest in getting to her mobile that was vibrating somewhere deep in her genuine Coach purse. Max succumbed.

You're not answering? What if it's Sabu?

-Fat chance. Sorry, not fat! That's the F word. Max, he doesn't have my cell number.

To prove her point, with an exaggerated effort, Janey went into her bag and checked the ringing phone's display screen.

Shit. It is him!...Hello, Professor Shera?

CHAPTER FIVE

The night before Walter Newton was shot by John French, he had an upsetting dream. His dear Dearie French, the woman who had opened the pulsing gates of erotica to Walter, starred in a reverie that was surreal even by reverie standards. Walter was sitting while bound at the wrists and ankles to a straight chair. He was being forced to watch his beloved blow the Trumansburg Giant. Much to Walter's consternation, Dearie seemed up for the challenge. To say the big, stone man's erect member was enormous would be like saying the ocean was wet. And it seemed to take an ocean and an ocean's worth of effort to wet his dick by the way Dearie worked it up and down. It was no skin flute she played but a skin telegraph pole of virile superpower. Dearie's mouth seemed to be elastic and spreading wide, she deep-throated the behemoth's glory. Walter was feeling the strain, pushing against his binds until his orifices bled. It felt like he was the one blowing the damn Giant! Thankfully, the dream broke before the Giant climaxed and the dam burst. Walter was jolted awake, sweating, breathless. He could not get back to sleep that night. Not with those vivid images clinging to his mind's eye. The nightmare would not fade by morning and very well propelled him along his fateful path later that day.

His brother, Thad Newton, had no idea what had happened to Walter other than what he read in the original 1880 police and coroner's reports. He did not go to John French's trial. He knew little of Dearie, or fellatio, or Walter's dreams. He lived and practiced dentistry in Chicago and was in Ithaca to dispose of Walter's house on University Avenue and get a proper headstone for his burial plot. Impatient but practical, Thad felt if he couldn't get a good price for the property right off, he would hold on to the house and raise the rent of Walter's foreign boarder. Kick it down the road and maybe its value would increase. While he was rummaging through some storage boxes up in the attic, Thad found a pile of sheet music for banjo and felt a twinge of sadness bordering on pity for his wayward, underachieving, younger brother Walter. Their sibling rivalry was finally over. Thad was going through the musty pile when he noticed a glimpse of native pottery stowed beneath. Before he could pull it out, there was a clamor outside the house. From the attic window, he could see a horse-drawn, police wagon clanging a warning bell pulling up to the cemetery across the street. Pedestrians were pointing and two uniformed coppers went running up a path disappearing among the tombstones. Curious, Thad put back the sheet music and descended.

The crowd had grown by the time Thad joined the rubbernecking. As they all craned to see, the police appeared with a dark-skinned, long-haired, naked man in custody. He was covered in ashes. Word spread he had been spied by a mourner inside a gated mausoleum desecrating a corpse. Thad's skin crawled, and his blood ran cold. The fiend was Walter's East Indian boarder.

The house across from the cemetery was sold that week to the first buyer who offered, and Thad Newton left Ithaca without looking back. Brother Walter would rest for eternity in a grave marked only by a number, fittingly, *No. 69*.

CHAPTER SIX

Walter Newton's home had been designed and built originally by Philip and Caleb Pearce in 1792. Generations of the Pearce family happily resided in the white, clapboard two-story, colonial-style house with the big porch. Over the centuries, it was usually painted white with dark trim and had looked across to the city cemetery forever. The storage in the attic seemed to grow denser with each successive owner pushing Walter's trove deeper into forgotten territory. When twentieth-century members of the Pearce bloodline tasted professional success and wanted to express it with a bigger home on the lake, the white house was sold. That led to a succession of owners, some of whom lived there and improved it, and others who rented it out to college students and ignored it. Elaine and Robert with their Crossing commune improved it or a least they thought so. Besides the wonderful flower and vegetable garden they added in the 1960s, they were the only residents to paint every one of the house window frames with a different color trim. The result had neighbors sarcastically calling it the Rainbow House. When the commune ended, the property was bought by Professor Patel. He loved the location, the smell of the dead so close, so tempting. A covert, Aghori guardian of Shiva, Patel was the one who added a secret basement where the faithful could practice in private below the world of unbelievers. Patel had done the dirty work and had achieved every goal asked of him but finding the Eye of Shiva. He had set up Sabu well in Ithaca, and it was the one thing for which Sabu was grateful to his predecessor. He thought about how he had worked behind the old Aghori's back to finally get him recalled in dishonor.

His disloyalty to an elder was not a pleasant thought, but it occupied a good minute while Sabu was pissing into Naba's open mouth. His graduate assistant with the broken arm was on all fours, naked, her chin up and dripping with the yellow overflow. Sabu had made sure to drink profusely before so that his stream would be memorable. She had failed him, and he was using her as a urinal. When he finished, he made her suck every last drop and then he held her mouth closed until she gagged and vomited. That, he made her eat too. Sabu had not seen Pradeep come down. She witnessed her friend convulsing on the floor and reflexively went to help.

No, leave her. It will stop.

Naba's spasms did stop, and she lay on the concrete floor in a pool of her own waste, hair matted with sweat, body covered in regurgitated chunks, and clots of blood. Pradeep's head was down, and she cowered in front of him. Sabu was unhappy with her as well and lifted her head up, so she was on eye level. She squeaked.

The detective and Professor Flatman are upstairs waiting in the living room as you ordered.

–Good. In the cage. You will be punished as well.

Sabu moved Pradeep along to a large dog cage in the corner that was used for discipline. He lowered her head, and in she went. He did not lock the door. He did not have to. She sat cross-legged, watching her master move up the stairs to the main floor. Inside her, hate for him and belief in him rendered her impotent, a vessel. From behind the bars of her unlocked cage, she called off to her groaning friend.

You're going to be all right. Brahma loves you. Shiva sees.

* * *

Upstairs, Max and Janey waited. Sabu was willing to meet with them, and they came right over after his call. Sitting in the living room which smelled of pipe tobacco, Max could tell Professor Shera loved his books. Shelves of tomes were neatly stacked everywhere. Janey shrugged.

He is very well-read.

-Apparently.

In a hushed tone, she whispered the word *arrogant* and told Max her one, extensive interaction with him was working on a faculty committee a year back. Moving closer, she continued, sotto voce.

He was a fucking nightmare to the other teachers. Such a bully. His way or the highway, control freak, kind of thing. You know what I mean?

Max did. He also believed bullies were towers of jelly when threatened themselves. They could hear his footsteps coming down the hall and readied themselves. Sabu had showered and changed into his casual, professorial look—old cardigan, Burberry shirt, and chino trousers. He brightened upon seeing them and graciously fibbed.

So sorry to make you wait. I was in prayers.

* * *

Outside the house, Franz waited in a rental Lexus for Janey and Max. Catering to rich old women like Ella was a lonely and self-deprecating career. He'd despised himself for far too long about it. Relaxing in the comfort of the night, he felt at peace with his decision to extort money from the creepy Hindus. He knew that somehow, they were all involved in the death of the limo driver. He knew because he had leaked the information about the boy being on to them. He stretched his legs down to the toes. It felt so good. He would find the right time to turn the screws on Sabu and dance free of Ella von Tragg.

* * *

Inside the white house on University Avenue, the polite conversation led by Janey ended quickly when Max laid his cards on the table.

Professor. I am here to investigate the death of Thomas Gill. You were the last one seen with him.

Sabu took a moment before speaking. He didn't deny seeing Tom Tom late on the afternoon of his accident.

That was a long time ago.

-Thirteen years.

He was fine when I left him. Like I told the police when I was interviewed.
Max shrugged and pushed ahead. He could tell this face-to-face would go nowhere, but he wanted to score some points.

Why are you following me?

-I could ask you—why haven't you gone back to L.A.?

You mean, after one of your students tried to kill me. How's her broken arm healing?

Sabu appealed to Janey.

You understand antiquities. There is a lost treasure of Shiva that we believe Mr. Gill had stolen.

-And when he wouldn't turn it over to you, you killed him?

That was not what Sabu wanted to hear from his colleague. He doubled down, eyes on Max.

The police said it was a suicide.

-Yeah, they do that, don't they? We understand this antiquity could be a bomb capable of major destruction.

So the legend goes. We know it as a holy object. If you find our treasure, would you be kind enough to return it to the Aghori people? There would be a large reward.

Max assured him he would consider that. If he was looking for it, which he was not.

Of course.

—So why wouldn't Mr. Gill give it to you? Or surrender it to the FBI?

The FBI is always an option. They have an office in Syracuse.

—And they lend you their cars. What do you do for them?

Sabu surmised he had nothing to gain with this meeting and excused himself. He had to get back to his interns. He rose with a scorching glare to Janey.

I'm very sorry you're involved in this dangerous business, Professor Flatman. I would think you of all people would have respect for the preciousness of the past.

—I have respect for human life. The Aghori worship death. Prophecy speaks of a Third Cleansing, doesn't it?

That was a conversation stopper for Sabu. He smilefucked them and pivoted out. Lies and goodbyes were swiftly tossed to and fro, and that was it. No big whoop.

Moving off to their waiting car, Max told Janey not to say anything more about it until they were alone. Franz held the door open and Max got in the backseat with Janey. He directed Franz to their hotel where they could pick up their things to take up Ella on her offer for them to stay at the inn. Max had planned an early start to their day. The night though, was another matter. Sinking into the soft leather of the Lexus, Max's flesh surged with electricity as an exhausted Janey's head dropped on to his shoulder and he could feel her close. So close, her lips were on his ear.

One room or two?

CHAPTER SEVEN

Mychal did not expect Teresa, his ex-wife living in India, to write him back so quickly. He had asked her if anyone she knew there had heard of the Eye of Shiva. To his shock, she had and was living in the region of its original home. Not only that, but she also had learned of the prophecy of the Third Cleansing and the devastation foretold if it was ever found again. The Aghori monks who thrive off the Ganges' dead were its guardians and continue to search for it, she added. She wondered why Mychal would ask such an esoteric question. Discussing it, she had discovered, will bring attention from the Aghori, who are fucking scary. Those words were ringing in Mychal's head while he drove out towards Orloff's commune to see the girls again. He would make up something to minimize his interest in it in his next letter to Teresa. He was always amazed that she never asked about Janey. Too painful, perhaps. Still he loved her, and with Bibi having cooled on him, and The Crossing imploding, he had crazy thoughts about reuniting with Teresa. It was a brief fantasy of taking the Eye of Shiva back to India and reuniting it with its guardians. Teresa would be impressed, and they could perform together once again and be a family. But this Third Cleansing, devastation thing, absurd as it sounded, torpedoed that peaceful, idyllic imagining. They had a hot potato on their hands, and there seemed to be danger at every turn. It had been months since Marie and Suzie went into hiding at Noman's. The two were still wanted for questioning by the FBI and Mychal felt he was being followed far too often. Like now. Mychal was certain the dark sedan a distance behind had been making the same turns as him. Concerned, he pulled to the side of the road. The car drove by him and he saw a dark-skinned man at the wheel. When that car was out of sight, Mychal doubled back the other way. It wasn't just the FBI on to them.

The girls were hoping to let things cool off and then be safely heading elsewhere. Without the Eye. Which begged a major question. What could they responsibly do with it without getting caught up in something that complicated and threatened their lives and maybe the world's? In goofy, Magic 8 Ball speak, it was, "Answer hazy, ask again." In their I Ching readings, it was, "Patience is needed." So the calendar pages turned, and the girls found some level of existence in the bad news commune. They worked in the kitchen and tried to stay out of Orloff's horny clutches. It was early December 1969 and the weather was determined to suck for the next five months. Suzie had started getting strong migraines and she was glad that Mychal had brought some painkillers along with new paintbrushes on his visit. Marie was happy to have tampons. Mychal helped out and scrubbed pots while he told the girls about the Aghori's prophecy.

They want to find the Eye so that it can be used.

-They want to set it off?

Yes, a total cleansing of a civilization is how it was translated for Teresa.

--For real?!

Marie had seen pictures of the Shiva faithful in India. It was hard to believe Patel could be an Aghori. They were dirty, ragged, disgusting-looking creatures. It seemed impossible that one could be living among them, let alone teaching at an Ivy League university. Mychal wasn't sure, but damn well believed Patel was after it.

If I hadn't have lost him this morning, he'd have followed me out here.

Next visit Mychal promised he'd have papers for both of them. New identities that could get them into Canada where there was a good draft resister infrastructure to welcome them. Suzie gave him a big kiss and Marie joined in with a hug. He was their hero. Both the girls wondered how he and Bibi were doing, and Mychal told them the truth.

We split. She thinks I've been lying. Going off to gigs she never heard of.

-You blew it with the belle of Belchertown for us?

No one can know where we are. Better she thinks I was cheating on her.

The crate with the Eye of Shiva was buried in a shallow hole secretly dug by Marie and Suzie inside their shelter, now winterized by large swatches of flapping, plastic sheeting. They didn't dare leave it there once they left for Canada. It was Marie who voiced what Suzie was also thinking.

We should put it back where we found it.

* * *

Patel had been tailing Mychal. It was easy monitoring his movements. He had rented a place up the street, and with a less than full workload at the university, Patel had time to obsess in Shiva's name. He believed the girls had the Eye and were hiding out from the FBI. He needed to get to them before the U.S. authorities did. Patel had lost Mychal this time, but he was getting closer he could tell. Late that night he checked the odometer on Mychal's car parked on the street as he had done after each of Mychal's road trips. In his studio apartment, Patel worked out vectors of possible hiding areas in the radius and felt quite productive. His notated, daily journal was meticulous and would be a valuable resource to his masters and those that followed him. Successful or not, he was doing the work that was asked of him since taking on the mission the year before. Better men before Patel had been in the Finger Lakes and not found it. Of this, he convinced himself. The journey was everything and had been since it was stolen in the eighteenth century. Outside, on University Avenue on a stroll, Patel wondered if his faith was still strong. He took out a handkerchief and bent down to clean up some fresh, dog poop a careless owner had neglected.

He would eat it later.

CHAPTER EIGHT

The Aghori who murdered the traitor Jovan was hiding out in the bush since the attack. Fitan was a stranger in a strange land, far from his home in Rajasthan. Growing up, he was always the strongest and meanest boy in the village. He was terrible to everyone, even his family. To make matters worse, he was intelligent and evil. At fifteen, he was sentenced to death by hanging for murdering his mother and grandmother with a kitchen knife. Saved from execution by Aghori monks, they made him one of their own and he found strength inside the faith. When a monk was needed in the Finger Lakes to find out what had happened to the rogue Jovan, twenty-one-year-old Fitan was entrusted with this most important task.

Crouched by a creek, he watched his reflection in the water, braiding his long hair slowly and carefully, tying it with rawhide, American Indian style. A headband was fitted next. He'd been in the area long enough and was ready to pick up the search for the Eye. The holy search that Jovan had forsaken. In buckskin leggings he had stolen from a local outpost along with a mussel shell necklace, he looked like the real thing. *Indians can be Indians*. He laughed so loud it spooked a busy beaver, upstream. Fitan knew the white man would not be able to discern the difference between brown-skinned people if he kept his mouth shut. He would walk into town and find the Englishman who stole the Eye. The authorities were looking for a crazy, half-naked Hindu, not a native tribesman speaking in hand signs.

***

After a few weeks, the manhunt for the Aghori who had murdered Jovan turned up nothing. The sheriff believed he was long gone. Aruna, Emily, and Philip did not. They were not going to wait to be attacked by the madman. Philip had spent seven years in India and had seen how the locals hunted lions. He floated a plan with options should things go awry. Being a surveyor, he knew where Wading Bird's village of longhouses had once been situated and it made sense that the chief had buried the map to the cursed *gift* near. It was private land presently with an absentee owner who had not developed his grant of land from the government. They would take a wagon with supplies out after dark and work all night in shifts.

Searching for the Eye?

–Digging. It will take only two or three nights if we're lucky.

Besides Aruna, Emily, and himself, both their grown children Caleb and Liza, would be needed. The kids were an engaged couple and Aruna begged Philip not to involve them. Caleb and Liza, however, would not be denied the opportunity to help.

While Caleb stood guard with a long rifle, Philip and others packed the wagon with shovels, lanterns, and three gunnysacks. Philip had them loading in the daylight in the hope the monk was spying on them. The women stowed a basket of vittles and drink, and they were off with the setting sun. Fitan was spying. Curious, he made an impulsive decision. He stole a horse from a neighboring barn, picked up the trail and followed the wagon for over an hour in the moonless night from a good ways away. Aruna was the first to hear a horse behind them. Caleb tightened his grip on the rifle. While Liza and Emily huddled, Philip led the hitched horse at the same pace, nice and easy. Aruna whispered that the someone following was keeping a safe distance. Philip sensed it too, upper lip stiffening.

Tally-ho.

CHAPTER NINE

It was happening. Janey had asked Max to lower the lights. Like her, he was happy to enhance the mystery. So many places to touch first time, new bodies, skin, flesh, sweetly caressed, rubbed, sucked. He felt no shame or guilt. Her lips were cushiony petals. He couldn't stop kissing her and her tender nipples. She knew her way around him like she had the secret menu of his pleasure centers. Their bodies lined up perfectly at one point, unwrapping the same present and then spun around again, an encore symphony of primal sounds. Exhausted, rejuvenated, staring up at the ceiling, Max laughed first, deeply. Janey joined in. Neither asked what was funny.

They went with two adjoining rooms at the Taughannock Inn. In her bathroom after, Janey luxuriated in the antique tub. Like her mother, she had a vocal gift and was singing one of her dad's songs without even realizing it. In his room, through the opening connecting door, Max could hear her. Entranced, he didn't recognize Mychal's original but liked the chorus.

Baby girl, there you lay
Glad your momma went away
Staring right back at the moon
Knowing she left you a little too soon

A cell call interrupted, and Janey called out, asking Max to screen it. Max in his boxer shorts and Security Event T-shirt, checked the chiming phone on her bed's nightstand.

It's an Agnes Brito?

-Great. Give it here. That was one of Marie's caregivers.

Max brought it into the bathroom. Janey had stepped out of the tub and was draped in a fluffy, white towel. The light was not low, and Max took it all in. She was Rubenesque in the best sense, a visual delight of curves, color, and texture. She felt him gawking and playfully flashed the goods, before turning away and answering the phone.

Hello, this is Professor Flatman.

Max was transfixed on her beautiful back. Her towel, hanging low, just above the crack in her marvelous rear, revealed a stylized tattoo. The tramp stamp of the '80s. It was etched in colored ink. DUERMO POCO, SUENO MUCHO.

Sleep a little, dream a lot.

A motto to live by. A paean to passion and possibilities. Damn, he was falling hard. It seemed impossible to be feeling that feeling after he loved his guts out with Mei, marrying her twice and leaving it all out on the floor, so to speak. But that was then, this was now. Mei U, who grew up in pain and so valued pleasure, would understand.

She'd have to.

* * *

Things were not so orgasmic in Ella von Tragg's room. She'd asked Franz for an oil massage while on her tummy, and he totally read her wrong and tried to passionately engage her without permission. He should have known better. *Dunderhead!* To further the chill, Franz was asking inappropriate questions.

Did the detective tell you where Tom Tom buried the Eye of Shiva?

When are they going to look for it?

Ella was irked and had one answer that fit.

Are you paying Detective Dean? If not, pay it no mind.

Franz didn't like being dressed down and feeling frisky, he decided to let her know.

My time with you may be running out, my lady.

Ella tried to read him and didn't need to peruse too deeply. He had something better on the back burner, thus this new independent attitude. That kind of grating companionship would not work for Ella von Tragg. She dismissed Franz on the spot.

Next!

* * *

Janey had to sit down. Still wrapped in her towel, she landed with a bounce on the four-poster bed and tried to emotionally steady herself. Max, concerned, landed next to her. He wondered if Janey was suddenly weird about their epic, mattress mambo, or was it the phone call? He went with the later.

What did Agnes Brito say? Was she with Marie at the end?

-Yes. She knew her as Carla Evans.

Agnes had a history with Carla. They were friends since Carla first arrived in Johnson City and helped out at the high school drama department. Agnes was a student. What had set Janey's world spinning was something else entirely. She said Carla had a friend, a folk singer, who came to visit her in the early days. Carla thought of him as her hero. Janey could barely share more without choking up.

His name was Mychal. Carla told Agnes he was murdered.

CHAPTER TEN

Suzie was too sick to help. Her headaches had continued, and Marie knew that there was a brown spot on Suzie's temple that did not look right. Suzie had been sluggish and unable to do anything strenuous, including her art, which further depressed her. Marie and Mychal tucked her into a comfy quilt that Mychal had borrowed from The Crossing. Stoking up the fire in the shelter, Mychal promised Suzie they'd be back before dark. Marie still had Wading Bird's map. They would put the Eye back under the falls where they had found it. It had been safe there for centuries, and Marie, Suzie, and Mychal all believed they could sleep nights knowing it would bring no harm once stashed there again. Mychal loaded the damned Eye draped with an old, beach towel into the backseat of his Nova. He tried not to draw too much attention from a few of Orloff's sketchy communards who came and went, up early themselves on this unseasonably warm, early December, Sunday morning, 1969. Mychal had checked. The pool under the falls was not frozen and he was sure they could get through. The water would be 'cold as a witch's tit,' he warned an amused Marie.

Thanks for the visual. Where did that come from? I shouldn't take it person-ally, right?

Mychal apologized. He confessed it was a favorite saying of his father, John, a WW II Army Air Corps vet stationed in Alaska. It was stunning to Mychal that he could not remember the last time they had talked. They certainly had not been close since Mychal left California and flunked out of NYU. Right after that, his father had offered Mychal a job in their printing business to bail him out. Until he got drafted, of course. Mychal was amazed his old man would think he would consider it. He was not going to work the straight world and live in the suburbs like his brother with three kids, a demanding wife, and a mortgage to choke on. And all the color TVs, buying more and more useless shit. And he was not going to get drafted either. Mychal took care of that. He got a 4-F in the mail from his draft board disqualifying him without even going to a physical. He was out, clean. Don't ask how.

"May human voices never wake you, Dad."

It was coming back to Mychal. Those were the last words he said to John who was born way too early to understand the changing times. It was taken from the last line of T.S. Eliot's "Love Song of J. Alfred Prufrock," and it ridiculed the mindless conformity his father embraced. They were on a long-distance call and his father was relating how proud the family was of Mychal's young cousin Max Dean who completed his basic training and was getting sent to Southeast Asia. His little cousin Max, whom Mychal had thought had writing talent, was Viet Nam bound. What a waste of a child, Mychal mused. He hadn't spoken to his father since. His real family became his Crossing family.

He'd borrowed two pairs of wading boots from a trout fishing friend, and Marie was up for the difficult task at hand. With a bikini under her faded, oversized Cornell Hockey sweatsuit, Marie had dressed as best she could for the mission. She knew she could find the spot again. Mychal handed her a ski parka.

May be better. Not cute but water-resistant.

Driving out through the commune gates and onto a rural, easement road, Mychal expressed his concern about Suzie. Soon, they needed to get her to Canada. She could get some medical attention there and would be safe with the ex-pat community. Marie patted his knee in agreement. He was such a good man. She wondered if he could be her man. Or if anyone could be with her living on the run. The whole Canada thing brought up her fantasy of living in the North Country with Suzie and Tim and Che. Before she found the old Indian map. Before Tim and Che were blown to bits. Before

Suzie got so sick. Marie told her not to sleep with it! Something was so wrong with her. Marie pretended to push some hair off her face and wiped a few tears away. Mychal didn't notice. It had been a terrible few months. She thanked him again for their new identity papers.

Carla? I think it flows nicely on the tongue. Carla feels Sicilian, you know. I like that.

Trying to keep it light, gesturing like an Italian, Marie glanced over at Mychal. He was focused dead-ahead on something up the road when she gave him a sweet *thank you* kiss on the cheek. Seemingly in response, Mychal gunned his Nova's eight-cylinder engine, and the Chevy lurched forward with testosterone, charging down the dirt road, rocks spewing, dust swirling. Up ahead a distressed vehicle with its hood up blocked their path, the driver stepped out, and waved for help. Mychal swerved off the road, right around the car and driver and rocketed away. Marie was horrified.

Mychal, your karma! You're a good soul. Go back!

-It's that freakin' shit, Patel! He knows where you are.

What!? Fuck! Him!

Patel could only watch them disappear off into the distance. He slammed his car hood shut and got in his car. The sedan started right up.

CHAPTER ELEVEN

Around the lakefront, it was dark and still like death, like nothingness, like Philip had hoped. They would need every advantage to bait the trap. On the wagon ride out in the blackness of the new moon, Philip told the others the stories he had heard growing up in Cornwall-by-the-Shore. The local legends of the Mooncussers. They were plundering land pirates who cursed the moon and waited for the moonless nights to do their damage. On those dark eves, the Mooncussers would stick a lantern on a donkey placed on a high hill above some notorious, rocky sea shoals and wait. An unwitting ship passing would mistake the light for the Cornwall Lighthouse and lose her bearings. Caught on the unforgiving rocks and in distress, it would be easy prey, ambushed by raiding buccaneers who never had to risk going to sea.

The wagon was parked on a small rise above Cayuga Lake that had once been the home of Wading Bird's tribe. The first hour illuminated by lanterns set on two tree stumps, Philip, the surveyor, aided by Aruna, carefully measured out with a ball of twine a section of earth that was ten-foot-long by fifteen-foot-wide. Emily and Liza drove the stakes into the ground marking the rectangular section. Caleb stood guard with the long rifle. It was a windless April night and they worked in silence. They knew somewhere beyond, in the velvet void, among the bushes, or up in a tree, he was watching.

Philip broke ground first, easily excavating the loamy soil. Aruna took her turn on guard, and Caleb, Emily, and Liza with shovels joined Philip in the dig, each working a corner. The dirt piles outside the marked area grew higher and higher till dawn crept near and Philip called it quits. That first night their hole reached a depth of four feet. The second night, following the same script, the same path out, the same timeline, working through the night, stopping at dawn, the big hole was almost nine feet deep. Their excavation yielded arrowheads, pottery shards and animal bones. If they had dug fifteen paces further away from the lake, they might have actually uncovered Wading Bird's map in its pottery jar and saved Walter Newton, and a century later, Marie Sayles, the trouble. Luckily for Philip, they didn't find it, nor did he want to. He only wanted to appear to be looking for it.

On the third night, Fitan was certain the infidels were close to discovery, and he would make his move when they did. After he had drawn some suspicion a few days before from a local Indian who could tell he was a pretender, Fitan knew he had to be more careful out in the open. He waited till after dusk to come out of his hiding place in the cave behind the big falls. It kept him safely out of sight during the day when farmers and traders frequented the area, moving along the lakefront. He was blessedly ignorant to the fact the Eye of Shiva, the missing cornerstone upon which his faith had been built, was stowed away in a dry chamber of his lair, a spitting distance away. As he had the two nights prior, Fitan got himself into a strategic position in a treetop under a canopy of blinding darkness and waited. This time, the hours crept by, but their wagon did not come. Curious, Fitan stepped out of the anonymity of the woods and crept nearer to better see the big dig, up close. He lowered himself into the hole and was pleased to spot a shovel stuck in the dirt that had been left behind. He grabbed it. It looked small in his enormous hands. He started digging himself, powered by the fury of righteousness. He was into it. So much so, he did not realize until they lit their lanterns that the deep pit he was in was surrounded. Like the trapped animal he was, he lashed back, gnashing his teeth, swinging his shovel. He would have thrown it right at Aruna's head had Caleb and Philp's tossed netting not first landed on top of Fitan, tangling him up and restricting his movement. Fitan howled with wounded pride loud enough to be heard all the way back to the Punjab.

CHAPTER TWELVE

Artie, short of sixty, short of the correctional facility, had a job. He was on Max Dean's payroll for the day, sipping the dregs of a Starbucks mochaccino to go, and enjoying the fuck out of employment. Pulling up to the Taughannock Inn at eight a.m., as requested, he was feeling so damn responsible. Reconnecting with Janey again was serendipitous. He still had fantasies about one of her stepmoms. Artie always felt he may have had something to do with Bibi breaking up with Mychal. Things got weird fast when The Crossing commune imploded so many years ago. Who would have bet on Artie being one of the lucky survivors forty years later? He certainly went to a lot of memorials and tried to remember them all—Tim, Elaine, Robert, Morris, Happy Jack, Danny V, Bibi. His ex-wives both refused to die, further proving they were not human, Artie joked to himself and then wished he hadn't. With a spring in his step, he opened the trunk of Janey's Prius and started unloading scuba gear into a neat pile at the front curb. Seeing a bellman come out, Artie gave him the high sign.

The bellman was rolling Franz's luggage. Franz, head down, followed, on a walk of shame. Unlike Artie, Franz was now unemployed. Artie intercepted the bellman.

Dude, I gotta park this, baby. Can you get that gear up to Max Dean's room?

He slapped a twenty-dollar bill into the bellman's palm. Max would be good for it. The delighted bellman folded the upgrade into his pocket and hailed Franz's cab. Franz brightened like he was the one who was tipped. When the cabbie asked where to, Franz gave Sabu's address.

Upstairs in their separate bathrooms, Max and Janey tried on the scuba suits. Max was groaning louder than Janey trying to squeeze in. Eventually, they met at the adjoining doors and laughed.

Perfect. Fits you to a T.

−More like an O.

You look amazing.

Max assured her with a kiss, and to his shock, he was getting an erection again, pushing hard against all that latex. Janey pushed him away with a probing look.

You never did tell me about your marriage between the two times with Mei.

−With Jonelle? It was draining. After our "I do's," every day was like Game 7.

Sports metaphors are wasted on me.

−I'll remember that.

Max melted into Janey, and their rubber suits harmonically squeaked when a kiss got more intense. The ringing phone separated them. It was Wilbur in his truck outside. It was time.

Downstairs, Ella had already met Artie in the lobby. Max had arranged for him to be with her for the day until she could sort out some help or head home to monitor events remotely, an idea Max had been championing. Frau von Tragg would have none of that talk. Tom Tom deserved her all. A soldier all his life, he always believed nothing got done without boots on the ground.

Or in Ella's case, her stylish, Vionic, orthopedic pumps.

CHAPTER THIRTEEN

The sun was setting, but you wouldn't know it from the cloud cover. It wasn't only a low-hanging blanket but an active fog creeping over the now choppy lake water casting ominous shadows after a good boating day. The "sheep were on the meadow," as the Cayugans would describe it. Cresting, foamy, white caps slapped against *Blue Lightning*, Tom Tom's fiberglass, twenty-six-foot Crownline powerboat with fewer than five hours on its 5.7-liter, 300-horsepower, twin merc-cruiser engines. It was a rocket, a sexy accessory Tom Tom had bought at a boat show the year before on a drunken whim and immediately regretted it. He guided it with care on to a short-term tie-up at the bustling Aurora Marina on the east side of the lake and grabbed an empty scuba tank to get it refilled. It was a habit with him. Use a tank, fill it right back up and you never have to worry.

Tom Tom hadn't been underwater since the ill-fated St. Malo salvage trip with his wife three years before. He dared that memory all day long and did what he had to do. The Eye of Shiva was stowed beneath the lake in a submerged, old canal lock's maintenance chamber. It would be safe there temporarily and buy him some needed time to talk to a trusted D.C. colleague and sort things out. Especially sort out who the good guys were. He knew the bad ones. Tom Tom was also in Aurora to meet that persistent East Indian.

In the far reaches of the parking lot, graduate assistant Sabu Shera had been waiting with Rama Patel in the professor's car for the last hour hoping Gill would show up. His mentor did not approve of Sabu's plan but had none of his own. Patel had spent nearly thirty years failing to find the Eye of Shiva. His best chance had been long ago when it had been found by two silly girls only to be lost again. He knew Sabu treated him with derision and he felt it was undeserved. He had been a beast in the early days when he stalked the girls' folk singer friend.

Getting a chill, Rama was ready to go home. Gill would not show. Sabu believed he would. Sabu had used his leverage with the FBI. After the surprise raid at Tom Tom's house did not turn up the holy artifact, to avoid further federal harassment, an agreement was reached. Tom Tom promised to surrender the map to its Hindu guardians. The FBI accepted Gill's story that he had not searched for it, let alone, found it. He was a respected man in the community. A man of his word. They were right. Gill had come as planned, and Sabu was ready. He left Patel in the car to intercept Tom Tom on his way back from the dive shack.

A few dock slips away, Wilbur Red Hawk, late for a great aunt's birthday party, was getting into his truck with a decent day's catch of smallmouth bass. Across the parking lot, through the thickening fog, he noticed the turbaned student heading for *Blue Lightning*.

On that very same dock, hoisting a full, scuba tank, Tom Tom looked off and saw Wilbur's truck pulling out. He shot him a big wave, hoping to catch up soon. Wilbur honked twice, hit the gravel access road, and sped off. It was the last time he saw his friend alive.

CHAPTER FOURTEEN

Fire!

-No!

--He said...fire!

-No!

First, Aruna refused Philip's order, then Emily's. She was against it. She knew it was hardly the time to argue amongst them with Jovan's killer in the pit below them, but she couldn't help herself. Philip and Caleb had secured a second netting at four corners on four tree bases and stretched it tight. Fitan, the Aghori, was trapped below in the hole they had dug. Caleb had his rifle sight set on him, and Emily had a flintlock pistol cocked. Philip was not a bloodthirsty man but believed the fiend deserved execution and wanted it quick and done. He thought he had worked this out with Aruna only now she was making others have second thoughts. Liza, Caleb's wife, a devout Christian, started questioning whether there should be a trial, and guns were lowered. They would not shoot him in cold blood. Not without being tried. Emily hocked up a ball of spit and aimed it at the murderer. She knew he was guilty. She saw him slit her husband's throat.

Below Fitan recoiled into a ball and sprang up. He grabbed hold of the rungs of netting, his feet dangling off the ground. He pulled himself up till his enormous, dark-haired head pushed into the hemp line, crosshatching his face. He spat right back at Emily. Philip smashed the stock of his gun down on Fitan's hand, but the swarthy giant never lost his grip. Invoking all his strength with a bestial roar, he drove his arms out, straining into an iron cross and then with a mighty growl, he pulled them back in faster, back and forth, netting in hand, over his head, bellowing, till the sinew in his neck and biceps popped. The very ground around the pit shook testing the rope binds. The trees themselves seem to buckle under his effort, the earth under their feet seem to shift. Liza's boot was caught in a tangle of stretched cord. Losing balance, she stumbled forward, rolling out on to the taut, netting cover. Before she could crawl off, Fitan's dirty, massive hand was upon her from underneath clamped across her narrow waist. Then another hand squeezed down on her. She cried out till her cry was cut short.

Caleb jumped in, throwing himself on the netting to free his fiancée with a knife. He hacked at Fitan's arms while Philip tried to get a good shot in the low light and Aruna screamed, helpless. Emily, beside herself, dropped her pistol. She lurched closer to see and accidentally kicked over a lantern. Whoosh! The netting caught fire. The burning hemp netting gave way in a breeze-driven flare up and Caleb and Liza tumbled down into the bottom of the pit along with the beast, Fitan. Caleb was on his feet first and bull-rushed the big East Indian, who still had hold of Liza, slamming him against the dirt siding of the hole. Fitan was shaken and Liza seized the moment to bite down hard on his arm and break free.

Fitan unleashed his anger on Caleb, pounding him back with a teeth-jarring, forearm smash. First right forearm, then left. Liza crawled off to a corner of the pit. Emily, on her belly, helped pull her up to safety. Philip had his musket aimed hoping for the clearest shot which was not clear at all with the furious mano a mano below. No time to lose, he had to take it. The shot rang out like an explosion splitting the night in two. When the smoke settled, Philip could see it was a wasted round, only grazing Fitan's shoulder. While the ex-soldier reloaded with his son's life on the line, the monster had Caleb's head in his hands and looked like he was going to rip it right off its torso. Hands quaking, Philip couldn't get the damn wad rammed into the barrel when a shot rang out. It was Aruna firing Emily's flintlock. She hit the giant with a bullet right between the eyes. Shocked, mortally struck, the goliath crumbled all at once in a heap. Caleb, out of the Aghori's vise-like grip, fought for breath, bent in half, panting for a good, long while before his father helped pull him out. Aruna was frozen, pistol still in hand, aware of what she'd done. Aware when she was firing with rage, it was another monster's face she saw. Singh, the bastard who raped her, Caleb's real father. Compelled to finally share the truth the words came much easier than she'd ever imagined. Philip held her. He was the one sobbing. Emily took back her pistol and reloaded. Training on Fitan, she fired into his lifeless body. And so it went. She passed a loaded pistol to each of them and they fired at the boogeyman. All in it together, all guilt shared and amortized. Fitan's blood covered what was once his face until only two empty eyeholes stared up at them.

Together they gathered brush in the early morning hours and covered the body. Setting it ablaze, they let the corpse burn in a building bonfire while they attended to Caleb and Emily's wounds. The smell of his meat cooking seared their nostrils for decades, but Aruna and Liza knew until their dying days that justice had been done.

* * *

If the history of the Aghori in North America is ever written, it will tell a tale of righteous believers who were martyred attempting to find their holy grail. Young Rama Patel was determined not to become one of them. But he got the shit beat out of him just the same.

After Mychal's Chevy had blown by him near Noman's, Patel decided to drive up the rocky road and enter Orloff's rustic, outlaw enclave. He had spied only two people in Mychal's truck, so that meant one of the girls could be around. He was not going to waste this trip. He parked just outside the open gates and walked in. It reminded him of seeing villages of nomadic mountain people north of his home in Rajasthan. Except this was 1969, the modern world, yet these young people were living off the land. By the evidence, bicycle generators were generating what little electricity they used. Though he was not a big man like the legendary Fitan, Patel was well-versed in martial arts and did not feel threatened as two curious citizens approached. Orloff was not a racist, unlike the criminal collective's carpenter who accompanied Orloff in checking out the visitor. To Vincent, an ex-con from Suffolk County, anything that was darker than a summer tan made the hair on the back of his neck bristle.

Maybe you could help me, please? A young girl. Red-headed...

BRAHMA, GOD OF CREATION

—What the fuck are you, a sand nigger?

——What he is, man, is trespassing.

It didn't get better after that. Vincent picked up a 2x4 piece of scrap lumber lying roadside and kept jabbing at the East Indian professor's chest, pushing him back toward the gate. Patel would get knocked down and get up each time, trying to explain he meant them no harm. More curious commune members stopped what they were doing to come see. Patel could take it no more and grabbed hold of the lumber with a two-handed twisting move that put Vincent flat on his ass. After a shock and awe moment, Patel was jumped by six others who whaled on him with their fists and feet for a good three minutes before tossing him, minus all the money in his wallet, out the gates into a pile of cow dung .

Eat shit, yak humper!

Broken, Rama Patel still had to laugh at that. He'd done both. A shotgun blast from Orloff's Ithaca Gun, Buck Buster, exploded over Patel's head. He crawled to his car and got in. Half-blinded, bleeding and battered, he managed to drive off.

The sun was melting into the horizon with brilliant December hues by the time Mychal and Marie returned to Noman's. They'd done what they had to—hid the Eye of Shiva right back where Wading Bird had stashed it. It was freezing for them forging through the falls' creek and they'd stopped to warm up in a gas station's men's room. The forced air heat from the hand dryer was heavenly for Marie. Like a smart-ass, twelve-year-old, she swiveled its chrome head around teasing Mychal all over with blasts of air. Then he teased and tempted her. She couldn't stop smiling. She sat on the sink and she and Mychal made love for the first time. They'd been through a lot in the last six months and it seemed like the perfect reward. Marie felt this joy was earned and was so sated on the drive back that it felt illegal. She'd brought a big piece of pumpkin pie for Suzie and it was still warm in her lap when she stared ahead at the gates. Suzie Sunshine was outside in a blanket on the ground, propped up against the outside of the fence with a pile of their belongings.

187

Mychal rushed out of the truck so quickly he almost forgot to put the vehicle in park. Suzie was coughing up blood but managed to say.

We were evicted.

Marie took Suzie in her arms.

Bastards!

-Patel was here looking for me! Orloff freaked.

A shotgun blast shattered a tree limb to their left. Orloff stood behind the gates.

Move it, losers! You're done here.

Mychal knew they could head for Canada in the morning. If Suzie would last that long.

CHAPTER FIFTEEN

Driving out to Interlaken with Wilbur was always a trip. Max and Janey shared the back seat of the old Bronco. In the front, riding shotgun was Wilbur's step-uncle, Em Homer. Sitting behind Max and Janey, cramped into the cargo hold, was Wilbur's grandniece, Tiffany, with a load of scuba gear, air tanks, and her BB gun. Max wasn't sure why the Cayugan had brought them along but went with it. Janey couldn't stop chattering about her scuba experiences and Max was enthralled. She seemed to be playing to an audience of one which was okay with Max. Janey asked Wilbur how deep they'd be going down and he didn't answer right away. First, sharing a glance with Em.

Oh, you both won't have to go in.

Uncertain, Janey looked to Max for an answer. All he could do was shrug. No idea. Part of him had a helpless, sinking feeling in his stomach, and the other part was buoyed by the fact that he wouldn't be getting wet. Not that he couldn't dive. Mei U had loved to on their vacations to Belize and Hawaii and he had to keep up. She challenged him to face his post-St. Malo fears and he appreciated that part of their relationship. He wished he hadn't started feeling guilty again for his unfaithfulness. He wished that would wash away. Janey tugged at his jacket sleeve and whispered.

What's going on?

Max assured her he didn't know. He suddenly felt as in the dark about the direction of his life as he once had felt in Birmingham, England. It was during his short but memorable stint as a writer with the WWE, the premier, TV wrestling promotion. He'd been given a plum assignment to write the verbiage for the great wrestling legend Eddie Guerrero who had turned heel and gone against his old friend and tag team partner, the baby face *luchador*, Rey Mysterio. In their ferocious battle in Chicago, the week before, the newly despicable Eddie had supremely humiliated Rey by pulling off his mask and stealing it away. The Birmingham audience would be super hyped for this kind of melodrama, and its blue-collar, mullet-headed, heavy metal-loving crowd was filling the arena. Max wrote the hell out of a three-page promo speech for Guerrero's entrance. He punched it up twice and believed it let the wrestler say a lot of harsh, personal things to burn his old bud. Right before showtime, Max got the script to Eddie. The great warrior read it and handed it back to Max.

I think I'm going to just say nothing.

–What?!

Guerrero walked away to get ready, and Max panicked. His employment with the company was already on shaky ground and now this? How could he ever explain to his boss, she-who-can-not-be-named, that Eddie was going to say NOTHING on live television? Max was sure to get canned before the flight home. The spot came up, and Eddie Guerrero entered the ring. The crowd was hushed. With a flamboyant gesture, he held up Rey's purloined mask for all to see. The crowd went crazy, incensed, booing him. He held it higher, shaking it, the boos doubled in intensity. It was music to a heel's ears. Eddie waved that mask and worked that crowd into a fireworks-finale-like explosion of hate directed at him for over five minutes without speaking a single word. Max got the credit for it but was relieved to be fired three months later. He never understood that business. Never. Always felt like a confused child, not unlike how he was feeling at the moment. This was not the retrieval plan they had laid out the day before. Max didn't have a clue what Tom Tom's old friend was up to. He put an arm around Janey and hugged her close. At least on this front, the clues were adding up. Max was falling in love with her.

CHAPTER SIXTEEN

Tom Tom expected Sabu to be waiting for him and hoped to be done with it all. He knew the whole *cleansing* thing he had heard from Marie, who had heard from someone else, who had heard from who knows whom, might only be a scary tale with little to fret. Or else it was as advertised, and it was what he'd researched, a weapon capable of massive destruction. Tom Tom always had lived by the Boy Scout code, *Be Prepared*. He'd lived a life trying to stay ahead of the game and true to it. He'd put the Eye of Shiva in a safe place, and in case anything happened to him, he'd hid a map in the old Freeville farmhouse. He'd tell Wilbur about it later. With his scuba tank topped at the serve-yourself shack, he let the graduate student think he was surprising him.

Oh, hey, hi Sabu. You came?

-Of course. It's extremely important to the faithful.

Come. I have what you want. I don't want any more trouble.

In the plush, little cabin of *Blue Lightning*, Tom Tom laid out Wading Bird's deerskin map on the polished mahogany table for Sabu to see for himself. The East Indian's fingers traced over it, examining the document with extreme reverence.

Exquisite, huh?

-Yes. Where did you get it?

From a woman a few weeks ago, before she passed.

-This would be Marie Sayles?

Tom Tom explained Marie was a friend of his late wife's. He repeated his untrue story that he'd never searched for it himself and was glad he hadn't.

It's all yours. Cayuga friends think it may be somewhere under the falls. Good luck.

Tom Tom cut it short and rose from his cabin chair. Sabu followed. He had come prepped for success and carefully put the old map into a Tupperware container and put that into his backpack. From a zipped compartment, he slipped out a pen-sized object that he palmed in his hand. With backpack on, Sabu climbed up the few rungs back to the deck and Tom Tom followed thinking this was the last of it. He snaked ahead of Sabu to help him off the boat when Sabu stuck Tom Tom's shoulder blade with a needle tipped in a poison used by indigenous people, it was derived from the strychnine plant. With the nerve endings of the voluntary muscles attacked, it paralyzed the victim while leaving the mind alert. Tom Tom's legs went wobbly first and Sabu came to his rescue, sitting him up at the helm in his captain's chair. With his mouth turning to cotton, unable to protest, and his limbs dissolving into jam, Tom Tom knew he had been bested. Though he was feeling mighty full of himself, Sabu did not rub it in out loud. All the decades that Patel had failed, he had not. Let Patel write that in his journal. In one year, Sabu had the map! He worked in silence, starting up the boat and casting off the lines. Reaching over the seated Tom Tom, Sabu grabbed the ship's wheel. The speedboat pulled away from the dock leaving more wake than allowed. He pointed the craft right into the mountain of fog and increased the speed. Before jumping off the side to swim back to shore, Sabu pushed the throttle up to full.

Tom Tom could feel the speed of the boat powering through the milky white abyss. Thoughts shifted in his head slowly like anchors in a rushing tide. Wanting to die, he'd written a suicide note ten days before, and now he had his wish, which was no longer a wish. He got comfort knowing that Sabu would find nothing under the falls. A nanosecond passed and he remembered how much he disliked *Blue Lightning*. He had gone to the boat show in New York City with an old pal from Freeville Elementary who said Tom Tom was too old for it and dared him to buy the speedy craft. Since he was a young boy, he could never back down from a dare. Tom Tom had an apple shot off his head, jumped out of crop dusters without a chute, climbed sheer cliffsides, and here was the one schoolyard dare he would not survive. He wished he had told Ella how joyful it was to have her in his life. It was not a romantic pang but that for a wounded bird, he had healed and given life. And Jeanie! With no seconds to spare, he framed his final, living thought on his beloved, stamping her into his soul for all time.

I love you!

The boat smashed head on into a fixed, wooden dock at ramming speed. The sickening explosion that followed could be heard on both sides of the lake. A dripping wet Sabu was climbing up a ladder at the marina when he saw the bright red fireball diffusing into the eerie fog and smiled with extra relish. He knew there would be little left of the boat and body. The locals who came running through the mist to see the eerie, rainbow-colored conflagration knew that unfortunate dock well and couldn't stop commenting. It had been owned by the iconic '50s sci-fi writer, TV host, and Ithaca resident, Rod Serling.

One last trip into... *The Twilight Zone.*

NANDI—
THE BULL
OF SHIVA

CHAPTER ONE

The first thing DeShaun DeMott did on getting out on early release from the Tompkins County Correctional Facility was to call his ex-bunkmate Artie. He was hoping to find some sweet paying, easy work, and Artie did not disappoint. Artie met him in the lobby of the Taughannock Inn and both were happy to see one another again on the outside. It's funny how life goes. They'd bonded over saving Max and now they were working on his case. DeShaun gave him a side-eye.

What case? Don't fuck with me, dog. I need to know.

-No, you don't.

Artie assured him that all was kosher and handed him a burner phone. With Max and Janey off with Wilbur Red Hawk, Artie needed DeShaun to go shopping in the town. He handed him a list. It was mostly pharmaceuticals and skincare products for Mrs. von Tragg. DeShaun had a rented car pre-paid by Artie, petty cash, and the promise of one hundred bucks for the day. He felt like an OG in paradise. He watched Artie move off with a classy-looking grandma in a wheelchair and caught sight of himself in the ornate, full-length mirror. He'd been off crack and cocaine for months and was Denzel Washington handsome in his Fubu jacket, T-shirt, and jeans. And he was Dwayne Johnson built. Pumping iron at the correctional facility weight pile had paid off. He'd gotten his shit together and was the best DeShaun he could be. The one thing he was missing was a honey. He longed for something more than a one-shot thing. After thinking about it for his nine months in stir, he was ready for a commitment. He'd put himself out there for real. No matter how many times he would be rejected, he was going to find Miss Right. And if it meant going right through a parade of Miss Right Nows, he'd love them one at a time, no more than two. *As if…*

Driving away from the inn toward the highway's access road, DeShaun passed the same blue Prius that was parked there an hour before with the same tawny-skinned beauty at the wheel. DeShaun couldn't help himself. No time like the present. He slowed down parallel to the parked car and stopped, window lowering to show his most rakish, yet vulnerable, smile.

Hey, are you lost, hon? Need any help?

Waving her cell phone, Pradeep assured him she was fine. She'd been on a business call and would be getting back on the road. *Thank you.* DeShaun knew that was bullshit and turned on some pent-up charm.

I always say, we're not here for a long time. So, make it a good time.

Pradeep decided to engage. She'd never experienced an African American.

Are you staying at this beautiful old inn?

-Nah, working for one of the guests. Dope old lady.

German?

-Yeah, maybe.

Well, maybe you could be of help.

DeShaun flirted with that idea until he remembered Artie's shopping list. He winked.

Back in a flash.

-Oh, stay. Please.

DeShaun was a lifelong thief and lived a life rarely on the up and up. He knew something was extremely funky with the Indian chick. As much as he'd craved funky and was curious about this exotic baby's skills, he slipped the car into D and threw a K.

Don't go anywhere.

DeShaun drove around the bend and called Artie right away to let him know the inn was being watched.

What kind of shady shit you got me into?

-Just know, you are with the good guys.

Damn. Is that good?

***

At the same time, Pradeep was calling Sabu to tell him about the black man. He was in his campus office, tight-lipped, and not alone. Franz, Ella von Tragg's former consort, was seated before him looking frustrated. Sabu kept the conversation with Pradeep short. Call over, he calmly explained to Franz that he appreciated his help but had paid enough for very little of use. The fact that scuba gear had been delivered to the inn was not worthy news. Sabu thanked Franz for his time and wished him well. He took a twenty-dollar bill from his billfold and offered it to Franz for goodwill severance. With Franz's own admission that he was no longer in the old woman's employ, it was hard to imagine how he could continue to be valuable. Franz matched the East Indian's calmness with a steely, determined demeanor of his own.

I can be valuable by what I don't do.

Franz reminded Sabu that he had some incriminating things to tell the police concerning the death of the limo driver.

Do you really want to open that can of worms?

Sabu appreciated the metaphor because it reminded him of how Westerners view the body's decaying process. He had plans for Franz and answered the unemployed Hungarian ballroom dancer's question with a question of his own.

Do you believe when you are born, you are crying from your death in a past life?

That stumped Franz and nervous, he decided to leave well enough alone and make for the exit. Sabu closed the door.

Have some tea. Let me explain.

* * *

Naba could tell it was going down. From her vantage point on a nearby rise, she had good sight of Wilbur' truck below. It was parked sideways at the bottom of a dirt lane, which led to a weed-strewn, forgotten, boat launch into the lake. Seated by the truck's front bumper with his back to Naba was Em Homer in a beach chair. The old musician was fast picking a bluegrass rag on his well-worn acoustic. By the rear end of the truck on the opened tailgate sat Wilbur's grandniece Tiffany. She stood guard with her rifle in hand scanning around for any trouble. Naba wished the vintage green and cream-colored Bronco didn't block her view of the others. She imagined they were already in the lake and called in to Sabu to report the latest.

Out of Naba's view, on the far side of the truck, Wilbur distributed sandwiches from a mini-cooler. Max and Janey, in their wet suits, sat with their feet in the water. Wilbur told Max and Janey he had endured enough. Someone was watching his reservation home last night. Before that burned down too, he wanted to give the watchers something to see and a little something to take home. Taking a page out of his friend Tom Tom's playbook, Wilbur lowered the backseat and grabbed a heavy, Syracuse U. lacrosse bag from the payload. With care, he maneuvered it out the passenger door. A quick zip open and Wilbur gave them a peek of an ornate chest within.

I got it at Pier One on sale with a coupon.

He zipped it back up, and Max could swear the crate was humming.

That would make sense.

Max and Janey hoped he would elaborate, but nothing more was forthcoming. Wilbur wanted to kill a half an hour before exposing and flushing out the watchers. So, they relaxed at the water's edge enjoying the bologna and cheese sandwiches, the music, and the wondrous spring day. Max liked the sleight-of-hand plan. It reminded him of P.T. Barnum, the greatest showman, whom Max obsessed over when he was living in Barnum's hometown of Stamford, Connecticut, working for the WWE. Barnum hated lingering audience members at his sideshows. To move them along and out of the exhibit, he had a sign created, *THIS WAY TO THE EGRESS.* Most of the suckers, rubes, and marks assumed it was another attraction and followed the sign. They had no idea it meant *EXIT* in Latin and before they figured that out, they themselves were out. Max figured Wilbur Red Hawk deserved a play and out of his element, out of ideas, Max let it ride.

At the thirty-minute mark, Wilbur let out a big whoop, and Em and Tiffany gave focus. Wilbur made a show of revealing himself and joined Tiffany at the tailgate, before moving out of Naba's sight again. From the hill above, Naba watched and dialed her cell phone. The call to Sabu connected and she described to her master that Wilbur had a large carrying bag that was dripping wet. She watched Wilbur load the bag into the rear of the Bronco and close the tailgate. There were high fives all around when Max and Janey in wet wetsuits joined the merry celebration.

They have it!

Before Max and Janey could properly dry off and change in the bushes, a black sedan charged down the lane blocking them in. Out of it stepped two federal agents right out of *Men in Black* with dark shades and bulges under their jackets. Flashing FBI IDs, they laser-stared at voluptuous Janey, who was half zipped out of her suit. Max stepped in front of her, his wet suit top hanging down, chest bare, ready to rumble.

Boys! What's the problem?

–Stolen artifact. Ask Professor Flatman. We'll take that bag.

Wilbur surrendered the wet, equipment bag. The Feds stowed it carefully in the trunk of their Dodge Challenger. The old Indian threw out a sincere suggestion.

I wouldn't open that, friend.

-Thanks. We won't.

The dark muscle car vanished up the hill. Max and the others shared a sigh of relief. Except for Wilbur who was mad at himself.

Well, that didn't go like I imagined. I hope you don't get into trouble, Professor.

-Not for a fake, she won't. What about the real thing? We going in or not?

Tiffany got it yesterday. Found the chest right where Tom Tom's map said it would be.

Tiffany let out the first smile Max had seen from her. Wilbur had Barnum-ed him. They had the Eye of Shiva. The big Cayugan held open the truck doors and motioned them in. That was not quite enough for Max.

Tell me it's somewhere safe.

-It's somewhere safe. Right, Em?

Em strummed the opening chords of "Deliverance." That was enough. Max got in.

Which way to the Egress?

CHAPTER TWO

Little Janey could feel him kiss her on the forehead as she slept. She was sure it was Mychal. He always had that smell of distant pine. When she raised a sleepy eyelid, she caught him slipping out of the room. Under the night-light's soft glow, he looked like a spirit in the dark. A ghost that was dead already but didn't know it. It was almost Christmas, 1969. Mychal, Suzie, and Marie had snuck back into the rainbow-painted house on University Avenue the night of their eviction from Noman's. They waited till all were asleep and entered through the back door, crashing in the living room like fugitives in the dark. To shield their sleeping housemates from any danger, they planned to be headed for the Canadian border before the sun came up. Before early riser Robert. Before the FBI or Patel found them. The less their friends and enemies knew, the better. Then, Elaine, who prided her-self on soundness of sleep, came stumbling out of a nightmare and tip-toed downstairs in the dark to make some calming tea. She was in the perfect position to catch sight of Mychal tip-toeing himself from Janey's room off the kitchen. Suzie and Marie didn't try to hide from her. They rushed to embrace their earth mother. Unstoppable tears interrupted sighs of joy in a muted celebration. They'd been in hiding for over three months and as bad as Suzie looked, Marie and Mychal looked no better. The toll on each of them these last months was significant. They knew too much about the threat of the Eye of Shiva and trusted no one. Mychal was the first to speak before Elaine could. He laid out a tale that the girls were in an FBI Witness Protection Program, and their location had been breached. Elaine pondered this in her inscrutable way.

The FBI is hiding them? Then why have their agents been here looking for the girls?

-No. No. That's their misinformation campaign. That's helping protect the girls from the Weathermen. I can't say more. I can't.

Mychal was sweating it. Elaine was their conscience. For a moment, he almost told her the truth. Instead, he bit down hard and spun the narrative that they would be meeting a safe house contact in the morning. Elaine should forget she ever saw them. Mychal hoped she'd keep an eye on Janey while he was gone.

Of course. And what does it all have to do with this Professor Patel?

This caught them off guard. Elaine explained, Patel had come around a few times to see if Marie and Suzie were back. Marie joined the fib fest.

Don't talk to him. I think he has a thing for me.

-Dude is super bogus.

Suzie coughed, chiming in. Elaine could tell she was ill. She'd lost a lot of weight and needed to be looked at by a doctor. Mychal assured Elaine that Suzie would be checked out once they got settled. They all said their goodbyes and Marie couldn't break her hug with Elaine. It all felt disloyal to abandon her, Elaine was their leader. Elaine let them off the hook with an Elaine story.

Summer of 1789 and the incited rabble were running through the streets of Paris. Robespierre, the architect of the French Revolution, was right behind them, A shopkeeper saw him and asked, 'Robespierre, why are you following that mob?' Robespierre replied, 'I have to, I'm their leader.'

It felt good to laugh without any guilt. At least for a moment. For what it was worth, Elaine knew they were lying and let it go at that. She watched them walk out toward Mychal's parked Chevy in the predawn darkness. Their images sparkled in the heady mixture of moonlight and dew until they seem to atomize into nothing. Elaine surprised herself with a primal sob that came from so far down in her soul that her universe quaked. She'd tell Robert today.

The Crossing was over.

CHAPTER THREE

The FBI had transferred the confiscated lacrosse bag with the artifact inside to the waiting Naba for Sabu to authenticate. She carefully drove it back from Interlaken to Ithaca and pulled up in front of the professor's house on University Avenue feeling very excited. It had all gone according to plan, and she expected to be given some special dispensation for what she had helped deliver. Sabu could hardly contain himself. He met Naba halfway down the front path and took hold of the bag.

It's lighter than I thought.

-Wilbur Red Hawk told the FBI not to open it.

Sabu got a good chuckle out of that. Into the house, they passed Pradeep in the kitchen cooking up their golden mustard curry. She joined their march toward the basement door until Sabu aborted it.

No, no. This is for me alone to experience.

He entered the basement, closing the door, shutting out the girls. Down the rough, cedar steps, Sabu's veins surged with an overwhelming satisfaction of what he had accomplished. He laid the bag out on the ritual altar that Rama Patel had carved from a Bengali banyan tree. He could feel the surge of energy when placed near the antipodal point of its original home. The Third Cleansing would be righteous. The preparation would begin at once. He let it breathe there while he took off all his clothes and took three deep breaths. Naked, he approached the lacrosse bag with two hands and slowly unzipped it, chanting to the rhythm of a sacred song. He pulled the sides of the bag back. Inside was a shiny chest of wood with brass fittings that looked practically new. From within, he could hear a low hum as if the Eye was alive. Humbled, he got down on his knees and gave a prayer to the almighty Shiva. With both hands, Sabu raised the chest lid and was stunned to see a gray hive, alive, and hundreds of angry, flying insects coming right at him. They attacked all over his body until his flesh was covered in black, stinging Vespula.

Naba and Pradeep listened by the basement door, startled by Sabu's screams from within.

Should we help him?

-Not when he's getting closer to God.

They closed the basement door and went back to cooking dinner to the tune of Sabu's pitiful wails.

* * *

Wilbur confessed his prank box contained a large, wasp nest he needed to remove from his sister's house.

Two birds, one stone. The kids call it multi-tasking.

Hilarity abounded in the Taughannock Inn's private dining room. Frau von Tragg had invited all to join her for dinner, and like a big, diverse family, they supped well, enjoying each other's company and a fine, free meal. Max, Janey, Wilbur, Em, Tiffany, Artie, and DeShaun all sat around a big, perfectly set, oak table digging into a traditional, hand-carved turkey dinner. DeShaun was on a straight and narrow path with all these good influences and was trying to keep up. Artie and Tiffany were swapping proto-punk bands-they-liked stories, while Em and Wilbur played the spoons in between courses to Ella and Janey's delight. Only Max was not enjoying himself. They were no closer to getting justice for Tom Tom or Eddie. They knew it was Sabu behind the deaths yet had no evidence or witnesses. Plus, he worked with the FBI and that complicated things more. Max was certain that Sabu would go ballistic at being fooled again. He'd come back at them hard to get what he wanted. Wilbur seemed oblivious to the danger he had put himself and his family in and that bothered Max. Next to him, Ella was having an iPhone discussion with Artie. Her ex-friend Franz had left with one of Ella's cell phones and didn't have the decency to answer or return it. She'd left messages and even offered a small reward.

He's probably in Manhattan by now.

–What's the number? I can track it with Find My Phone

Janey, too, offered to help. Everyone was bent on singing for their supper. Max caught up with Wilbur on his way to the men's room. The Cayugan understood the situation and the risk. To him and his tribe, the Eye goes back to the ancestors who had believed it would protect them.

Someday, I will tell you about General Sullivan and his excuse for soldiers.

Like Max, Wilbur expected Sabu to come after it and planned to be ready. He had the Onondaga irregulars watching the reservation. They would not be packing BB guns, he assured Max.

What do you plan to do with the Eye?

–Good question. You know it's warm to the touch. That can't be healthy.

Max was relieved Wilbur knew the score. Back to the dinner in time for the dessert tray roll out, Janey jumped up to let Max and Wilbur in on the latest.

Ella's phone that Franz took? We traced it to a faculty building on the Cornell campus. Sabu's building!

Max should have been puzzled by that. Instead, he embraced the coincidence.

Let's go get it.

-Tonight, how? Break in?

--Someone call my name?

All turned to DeShaun, who finally had a way to contribute.

CHAPTER FOUR

Marie made fun of Canada the minute they crossed the border and stopped at a gas station with a candy counter by the register.

What is this? Smarties? Looks like M & M's someone sat on.

She was trying to be funny to keep Suzie's spirits up, and it was working. The drive north from Ithaca to the border had been hairy as hell in a driving snowstorm. Mychal's ragged Chevy Nova truck spun out twice. Miraculously, he pulled out cleanly each time and they continued on. Suzie slept through that part which was a blessing. Marie was in awe of Mychal. She regretted she didn't have these warm and fuzzy feelings for him earlier. She always had felt sorry for the drop-out musician, saddled with a small child. A fierce believer in zero population growth, Marie knew she was not mother material, she was an artist. She wondered about the theatre scene in Hamilton, Ontario, where they were headed. If there was a stage, she would find it. Mychal had contacted a draft dodger friend and they expected to be well received by the ex-pat community. The Canadian customs guard eyed Mychal with some suspicion in a car that reeked of incense masking pot. Mychal had a valid driver's license and at twenty-nine, was too old for the draft to question. When prompted, he told Customs they were visiting some friends for the holidays. The guard was getting pelted by icy pellets of snow by this time and hardly looked at the girls' fake passports in the rough weather. He waved them all through. On the highway along Lake Ontario, the storm subsided, and the sun exposed itself like a homing beacon. It was only Suzie's uncontrollable coughing and vomiting outside St. Catherine's that burst their bubble of hope.

**

On the second of January 1970, there was a good, strong west wind on a frozen, full moon evening. Rama Patel set the fire, and nature did the rest. It burned wild and unchecked through Orloff's sleeping commune and its makeshift, dome homes. The Noman's inhabitants fled for their freaky lives with whatever they could carry, whomever they could carry. There was no combating it with the hoses on a below-zero night. Patel could not stand for their disrespect. Downwind, the Aghori in a foreign land longed for a nostalgic whiff of burning, human meat like the acrid smells he grew up with on the Ganges. Weary of it all, he needed a fire to give him a spark. It had been weeks since the musician, his only link to the Eye of Shiva, had returned to the rainbow-painted house. Patel was wondering if he ever would. Without any connection to the whereabouts of the Eye, Patel was stuck. The prophecy would go unfulfilled and his karma would reflect the shame. His journal had documented the journey in the two years he'd been in Ithaca. It read like a tragedy of near misses and blunders. With too much time on his hands, on winter break from his classes, Rama Patel's thoughts were bleak. He wondered if he could die eating his own flesh as penance. He had dreamed of ending his life as part of the Third Cleansing, the glory, the uplift. That dream was being crushed by fate itself. Restless, walking through the neighborhood the following day, he saw a realtor planting a For Sale sign on the lawn of the garishly painted University Avenue house where Mychal lived. He spotted the owner on the porch and moved up the path to Elaine's chagrin.

Normally, Elaine believed in a *chains off* approach to life. She did not suffer fools or have a filter. This turbaned Cornell professor, however, did not deserve the truth. The second Patel got close Elaine held up a hand to halt him.

The girls are not here or coming back. They've gone to Canada. Leave us alone.

The *Canada* part Elaine threw in as a misdirection, not realizing it was actually the truth. Contrite, Patel shrugged and shuffled, making it up as he went along.

I'm not here about any girls. The house, what is the cost?

Elaine, who understood her way around a dollar, adjusted and called over the realtor. By spring, with financial backing from India, Patel would take over the ownership of the property and it would be rainbow-colored no more. Patel would settle down in Ithaca for the next thirty years, never finding the holy Eye. In his weekly journal entry of February 10, 1970, besides noting the start of escrow, it also detailed the torture and killing of Mychal, a wasted effort, garnering no useful information. Patel would never get closer again.

CHAPTER FIVE

Max found the cell phone that Franz had taken from Ella inside Sabu's desk. He also found Franz's feet in the office mini-fridge wrapped in a freezer bag like next night's dinner. At this point, they didn't know for sure to whom those extremities belonged. Max only checked the fridge because he thought there might be a water bottle and he was parched from the whole, crazy day. When he let out a gasp of surprise, Janey, keeping watch in the corridor, came in and calmly confirmed Max's discovery of *humanis pedes*. They both agreed they were at least size elevens. DeShaun, on the other hand, was afraid to look at the dead peds and busied himself inspecting the closet. He had shimmed through Professor Shera's office door lock and got them in. It was well past midnight on the quiet Cornell campus and Max was glad he had insisted they all wear disposable gloves. He had left Artie at the inn to watch out for Ella while they searched for some evidence tying Sabu to the Aghori death cult. The disembodied feet seemed to qualify. As they discussed the pros and cons of bringing in the police, Max put the bag back in the fridge where he had found it. Sabu was living a double life with a mission to unleash ritual destruction. This stopped being a murder investigation long ago. It was an End of Days ticking clock. That thought was courtesy of Janey. DeShaun tried his best to block out their scenarios. He was a simple thief working a job for some crazy white and half-white people. Before they closed up, DeShaun spied an old, oblong, lockbox at the back of the closet, under a storage blanket. He sprung its lock with a safety pin. Inside were some musty ledgers or journals which Max thought could be incriminating. They took the books and left the feet.

Sabu was being treated in Emergency, lying down in a curtained-off cubicle with an IV inserted in each arm. A Filipino male nurse with a winning disposition, dabbed at his bites with antibiotic antiseptic on cotton balls.

Tell me if this stings. Oops, bad choice of words, sorry.

Sabu said nothing. He shook his head at the idiot and scowled. Closing his eyes, the East Indian fanatic felt as useless as the monk he replaced, the pathetic Patel. He had been tricked by the infidels and kept from his prize. The pain of the wasp attack was nothing; the shame was everything. Sabu had endured an eventful day. After the chauffeur had threatened to expose him, Sabu had to spend the next three hours killing and dismembering Franz, all by himself. Sabu was no rookie. He had experience as a hunter of homeless men needed for sacred ceremonies and that helped guide his efficiency. He also had access to the hotel school's test kitchen, and it provided the perfect, private space with all the amenities to do the trick. He had used the same poison on Franz that he had on Tom Tom, years before, and it allowed Franz to a least enjoy Sabu's artistry until his heart stopped. The industrial, meat grinder made short work of chopped Franz. Sabu tossed it all out, doubled bagged in the trash bin behind the building, except for the feet. Those were special.

Naba and Pradeep were killing time in the hospital waiting room criticizing the models in a discarded fashion magazine when a candy striper came out to say their presence was requested. Sabu was done playing games. He had a good idea of how to force the issue and let the prophecy's fate write the rest.

CHAPTER SIX

Good night, angel child,
Sweet dreams and all
I'm about to fall asleep
I'm about to fall

See you in the morning
Until then good night
There's a night bird taking flight
Putting out the light

Mychal had written the lullaby for little Janey. Suzie asked him to sing it, and he did, playing an awesome Gibson he borrowed from a long-haired oncology intern at Hamilton Memorial Hospital. He got all the way through the song and Suzie was with him. The final strum and Suzie Sunshine was gone. He brushed from her eyes the few strands left of her once fabulous, red hair and kissed her forehead, a tear dropping on to her moribund, gray skin. This end of Suzie seemed so unjust, against all karma. Fuck the Eye, fuck the big C, fuck God. Mychal returned the guitar and felt so empty he couldn't sit down and wandered the depressing corridors, passing room after room of ill and dying. He was sick too, at heart, all alone.

After the Hamilton apartment they had shared with other Americans was raided by the RCMP, Mychal had relocated Marie to a small town outside Binghamton. The Mounties were acting for the FBI looking for two girls, Marie Sayles and Susan Shapiro, wanted for questioning about the Weathermen. Fortunately, Marie and Mychal were off visiting Suzie when it went down. No one at the house gave them up even after marijuana roaches were found. Marie and Mychal made a swift escape and were in the wind. With Suzie hospitalized, Mychal got Marie—called Carla Evans— back across the border. In Johnson City, New York, selected randomly with the help of the I Ching, Marie rented a small trailer that needed fixing, and within a week had a job at the high school helping out with their drama students. It was paradise for Marie especially with the plans that she and Mychal were making for the summer. They would be a family with Janey. If Patel or the FBI really wanted her, they would have to look harder. Mychal called her from a payphone in the hospital to tell her that Suzie had passed. Marie had been preparing herself for this for a few weeks. She knew it was a relief for all, especially Suzie who had suffered so. Mychal planned to drive down in the morning to visit Marie and toast their late, beloved friend. Goodbye kisses thrown back and forth on the phone were a sweet affirmation of life going on minus one beautiful, talented soul.

Soon, minus two.

CHAPTER SEVEN

Max set himself in the corner booth, so he had a solid view of the street. They had not been followed and the late-night snacks were on him. The Shortstop Deli on Seneca Street was an open-all-night joint specializing in something called pizza subs. DeShaun took full advantage. He silently sipped a chocolate milkshake and devoured his second house special, called the Big Willie, while observing Max and Janey across the table. Neither had touched their orders, Janey's vegan burger or Max's Reuben wrap. Both were nose deep into the journals of Rama Patel. DeShaun stifled a burp, excused himself, and took off for the men's room. Alone with Janey, Max slipped an arm around her.

You okay?

-Oh, my God. September 1969, Patel was at the Stop the War rally I was at! He confronted Marie and Suzie. He knows they have it. In October, he used Mychal to find them. I'm afraid to read more.

I got nothing but descriptions of shit-eating and dog-fucking. Then in 1996, he is replaced by Sabu and sent back to India. Sabu, unfortunately, was not one for journal writing.

Max pulled her close and kissed her cheek. It felt awkward and forced, and Janey knew it.

I want you to know, you don't have to love me to make love with me. We're adults.

Janey planted lips on his with a kiss that was anything but awkward. Max didn't get a chance to answer it. DeShaun plopped himself back in the booth with a chuckle.

Get a room, kids. Oh, I promised Artie we'd bring him back cherry pie. Whipped cream on the side, cool?

-No worries. We could be awhile. Why don't you grab a cab?

DeShaun was all for that and personally delivered the takeout order to the well-worn waitress semi-slumped at the end of the counter. Max took the first bite out of his not-so-warm-anymore sandwich. Damn, it was still good, and more bites followed. Janey skimmed the pages ahead in Patel's earliest journal. She paused, taking quick breaths, concentrating on one entry near the middle. Reading it, she rocked in place with a moan that couldn't be contained.

Feb 4th, 1970, he kidnapped Mychal!

* * *

With Suzie's death in his rearview mirror, Mychal crossed the border from Canada into New York State after being held at U.S. Customs for a good three hours. It all made no sense to Mychal other than he wore his hair long and in a braid these days. His passport was actually his passport and he was not draft-eligible to give them concern. He had no warrants out for arrest and carried no drugs today, so he let them have their annoying, bureaucratic way with him. He only wished that his main inquisitor hadn't looked so East Indian. Waiting to be cleared gave Mychal a sterile space to let his consciousness stream. Suzie was gone, and the last letter he sent to his ex-wife Teresa in India was returned with no forwarding address. He winced with grim thoughts and shook them off. Teresa was the freest of spirits, she could have split India and been in the Sahara if that's where her heart took her.

Back on the highway south, reality nagged at him. The whole border experience left him brimming with a lack of confidence. That last letter, Teresa seemed to be in some danger from the cultists. *They knew that she knew that…he may know.* God, Mychal hated to let his thoughts travel down this dark, paranoid road. The cultists were bent on massive destruction if the story held true. And who could Mychal and Marie turn to for help? Who could they trust without putting themselves in risky positions? Damn, he was bumming. Mychal calculated the trip to Johnson City would take him about four hours. He was grateful to have wondrous and loving thoughts of Marie to propel him through the monotony of the road. That and FM radio. He found a strong signal on his self-installed Blaupunkt. It was a station out of Rochester playing a sweet, sad song by some lonesome picker named Bat McGrath. He turned it up louder. The guy was freakin' authentic. Mychal wanted to cover this song himself. It was so good it made him well up with emotion. So captivating that Mychal failed to recognize the same dark Dodge that had been trailing him for the last five miles had also followed him off the exit ramp to the gas station.

Rama Patel was at his wit's end. He knew he had to do something out of the box, and it occurred to him that the house owner Elaine could have been telling him the truth. If the girls and Mychal were in Canada, maybe he could pick up their trail with the help of a college friend from Lucknow, India. That friend had a job at the U.S. border as a Customs Officer. Patel told his friend that Mychal Dean was a former student and tenant who had stiffed him on months of rent. His friend promised to let Patel know if Mychal's name came up as a border crosser. Patel prepared the supplies necessary for the day that call may come in and, to his surprise, it did. He canceled his classes and drove hard for two hours to catch up with Mychal outside of Batavia. In Shiva's name, he pledged to succeed.

Mychal gassed up and parked next to the side of the Sunoco station's men's room and walked in to relieve himself. He did not walk out. The next conscious moment for Mychal, he was jolted awake with a pail of water thrown over him. It sparked a cable clamped on his arm that sent an electrical charge throughout his body all the way down to his testicles. His agonizing screams of unimaginable pain and sheer terror were muted by the white handkerchief stuffed in his mouth. He was tied up, hands over his head, and bound at the ankles, as well, naked in a tub of water in Room 104 at the Sunset Motel on Highway 5. Patel wanted answers and methodically read through a list of prepared questions. Every answer Mychal gave was met with another electrical charge from the cable attached to a car battery that Patel had bought on sale. If the question was repeated, it demanded a new answer, a true answer. How much could Mychal take? Mychal told some, he did not tell all and lied big where he could. He never gave up anything of value and on some answers, never wavered, no matter how many times asked and shocked. In his journal Patel noted the following things:

The girls died of cancer caused by exposure to the Eye.
They all knew about the Third Cleansing.
They got rid of the Eye where no one could find it.
They never told Mychal or anyone else where.
Shock.

Never told Mychal where.

Shock.

Never told him where.

Shock. Shock. Shock.

After Mychal went into cardiac arrest and breathed no more, Patel had no choice other than to believe him.

Janey's heart was in her hands. She closed the journal. She was still sitting in the booth at an all-night deli. She couldn't speak and was beyond tears, Max had been reading along with her and nodded, mute. He wished his own father was still alive to hear the truth about his black sheep brother. Mychal was no ordinary uncle.

As brave as any soldier I knew. He protected Marie with his life.

–He may have saved thousands, tens of thousands. He stopped Patel.

Janey had always wondered about the car crash that claimed his life. Mychal's body was burned beyond recognition in a one-car accident outside of Batavia. The fire department was too late to extinguish the fiery wreck of his Chevy which had smashed into a hundred-year-old maple tree at the bottom of a rural hill. The police surmised the brakes had given out on the older vehicle and it rolled free. Patel was clever but Mychal was cleverer. He had beat *the man*. Janey had never loved him more. A mention in the journal about Teresa, her mother, lingered inside Janey.

Could she still be alive?

Max took it as a rhetorical and didn't respond, lost in his own cobweb. He and Janey shared Mychal. They were family, and thankfully, they were not. Mychal was not the lost soul Max had grown up believing. Janey had it right. Mychal beat *the man*. Patel had thought little of Mychal's power in their final test of wills and that had cost him. Janey's head tilted on to Max's shoulder and her eyes drifted low with the sweetest sigh. It was time to go. Before Max could get the check, DeShaun called.

All cool, brother? Artie's pie survive the ride?

Janey could tell something was wrong. The answer should have been simple and cute. Max was listening way too long. Way! He mouthed it slowly and silently for Janey.

They. Have. Ella.

CHAPTER EIGHT

The Aghori high priest, Sabu Shaan had been alerted that the British were ransacking the city. He enlisted a trusted acolyte to help him carry the sacred Eye of Shiva down into a catacomb sanctuary where it could be safeguarded with their other valuables. They removed it from its shrine in a water-fed sarcophagus, despite the passionate protest of the ancient, dying Baba Ram, once Sabu Shaan's mentor. The wise man's words made no sense. He was telling Sabu to leave it be. Let fate take it. Before expiring from the effort, Baba Ram screamed to Sabu that he would receive it back, forever. It was 1772, Varanasi, India, and though unnerved, Sabu Shaan found little guidance in his ravings. He believed he must protect the Eye with his life like he had been trained. The Eye was rushed into the dark tunnel below. Before Sabu Shaan and his helper could stow it within its hiding place, they were confronted by torch-carrying, thieving soldiers led by Lieutenant Philip Pearce. Backed into the wall, Sabu sprang forth with his dagger to surprise the Englishman. Pearce dodged it and skewered the high priest with a thrust of his blade. Sabu Shaan's death would be honored for centuries.

***

Sabu Shera believed he was the embodiment of that high priest. The ignominy of not being able to live holy like his namesake was frustrating and fed into Sabu's hatred of the unholy world. He was over fifty years old and believed it was all coming to an end. He welcomed it. His previous deaths had led his soul to this karmic peak. He knew in his bones his death would

NANDI—THE BULL OF SHIVA

have no meaning without the Third Cleansing. He knew in his blood it was within his reach. Before Sabu was released from the hospital, bandaged on face and extremities from the painful wasp attack, he had spoken to his FBI ally and confirmed the artifact was a fake. No charges would be issued for Professor Flatman. Sabu apologized and confessed he had naïvely believed some hearsay and felt used himself. In fact, he may have been the victim of a hate crime, he floated, always an easy third rail. He asked the agent to please pass that complaint along to the local police. That was that. It had to be done and, in the aftermath, will matter less than the dust that will remain from the obliteration of the entire region. It was almost sunrise on Sunday morning and he had driven himself to the campus. He'd been distracted the day before and had left some items that would be needed. Walking to his office building in the crisp, creeping shadows before dawn, the campus seemed lifeless, which soothed him. Sabu's phone kept vibrating. He had turned off his ringer to ignore the repeated phone calls from Max and Janey Flatman. Let them sweat it out. His interns had taken Ella von Tragg and if Max wanted her back in decent condition, he would have to cooperate. He was banking on Max and Janey not going to the police. If they did, his girls had their orders. The detective had no reason to doubt Sabu would take a life. Naba and Pradeep had used their skills and devotion to great advantage, and he was sure they would be rewarded in another life. Sabu had been wise to recruit help from home unlike Patel who was overmatched alone. Sabu was feeling particularly sensitive after a Fed Ex-ed letter announcing an Aghori elder would be visiting him in the fall. Was he being replaced? This hurt more than the wasps. Sabu dismissed his own insecurity. He believed he could be a day away from completing the prophecy. Monday was Shiva's special day and what would be sweeter? Once Sabu got word from Naba that the situation was stable, he would make his deal with Max. More vibrating from his phone caused a glance. It was a text from Naba. No message, only a photo attached of eighty-eight-year-old Ella von Tragg, gagged and sitting naked on the floor of the cage in Sabu's basement.

* * *

Sabu's plan had worked better than they had thought. They caught Artie outside the Taughannock Inn smoking a late-night joint by a dumpster. They came at him from behind, and when he turned, Naba flashed him, showing her tits. While he stared, Naba rushed him with a topless, bear hug. Pradeep hopped atop the dumpster and fitted a mask on Artie gassing him with nitrous oxide from a small canister that Sabu had secured weeks before from the dental school. Artie went limp. His pockets were searched, and he was tossed in with the garbage. They locked the metal bin with a thick stick for a lock hasp. Ella was easier. With Artie's room keycards, they found Frau von Tragg asleep in her pajamas. They gassed her with a mask as well, carrying the old lady wrapped in a blanket, out the back door. Ella came to in the backseat of their car as it pulled up to the house on University Avenue. Around the time when Max and Janey were picking at their diner food and eye deep in the journals, a conscious Ella was outraged and let the girls feel the heat.

You fucking cunts! Take me right—

Before she could finish, Pradeep punched her in the face. They waited for a car full of frat boys partying on a Saturday night to pass by and then dragged a dazed Ella out of the car when the street was clear. Ella fought through the pain. She could feel something in her pajama pocket. It was her room keycard. She dropped it at the foot of the entry path to Sabu's house. Inside they carried Ella down to the basement and into the sanctuary room. Naba locked the door, and together, she and Naba stripped off Ella's clothes while she struggled. Without any concern for her condition, they tossed her into the cage. Pradeep aimed her cell phone camera at the defiant Ella.

Smile.

Ella gave her the finger. Naba took a broom and swatted at Ella with the handle to get her to behave. Naba liked being in control and let the broomstick smack back and forth against the old woman's once-siliconed breasts. Ella grabbed the broom end and with a burst of strength honed from years of personal trainers, jerked the pole back all the way, surprising Naba and driving her face-first into the cage's bars. Close, Ella spat at the co-ed. Naba glared back and ran a tongue around her mouth to take in the full expectorate and swallow it. Ella backed away, arms crossed for warmth, suddenly shivering in the cold, damp room.

Sabu was not expecting to find a Post-it note on the desk in his office. He read it out loud to hear it himself.

Is that breakfast or dinner in the fridge?

In the fridge wrapped with the human feet was Franz's cell phone. The arrogant, East Indian fanatic did not like being violated and would take measures when appropriate. His office phone rang, and he answered it. It was Max. There was no reason to waste words.

If you want her alive, deliver our stolen treasure. The real one.

-Oh, glad I caught you. You mean your bomb?

Sabu answered with silence. At the Taughannock Inn, Max and Janey were in the library, huddled with Artie and DeShaun. The clock was striking seven a.m., and Max had Sabu on speaker mode. Finally, he spoke.

Do you have it or not?

-Don't have it.

That's unfortunate for your client.

Janey's phone chimed. It was Sabu. He forwarded the photo of Ella in captivity.

Let me reframe this so you absolutely understand. Bring it to my office within the next hour.

-Where is she? How do we know she's still alive?

A place you can't reach her. You'll have to trust me.

-We'll need more time. Soon as I get it, I'll text you a picture. Give me two hours.

The extra hour is on you. I'll send pictures too. Oh, And the answer to your clever Post-it question is...lunch.

Sabu hung up, grabbed the package in the fridge, and hurried home. He didn't bother to lock the office. He wouldn't be coming back.

* * *

Max had once briefly inherited the command of a squad of military police investigators in Viet Nam. He had never been in a leadership position, so a veteran detective sergeant took him aside and gave him some sage advice. He explained that Max would be asked to make a lot of decisions very soon. The important thing was he make them quickly. It didn't matter what they were. That could be changed later. Max thrived on that nugget for the whole three weeks until he was relieved of command. The advice still held. He proclaimed:

We have to call Wilbur and get it back. We're not getting Ella killed.

-We give it to Sabu, he'll try to destroy everything in the Finger Lakes. They're a suicide cult!

Janey startled Artie, who didn't know that little wrinkle and started to rise to excuse himself. Max motioned him down.

Prehistoric legend. Can't be true.

-Except these maniacs will kill for it.

--And they sexually abused me.

Artie added, feeling vulnerable at letting Max and Janey down. Candace, the inn manager, interrupted with a bit of luck. A newspaper delivery kid had just called. He found a Taughannock Inn room card on a sidewalk down the hill from the campus. It was Frau von Tragg's key. The boy said he picked it up on University Avenue across from the cemetery. Max choked on that thought, a good choke, almost a chuckle. Coincidence finally was working in their favor. It had to be Sabu's house. Ella was a survivor and had left a clue. It would make sense to get a peek inside to know more. Max, Janey, and Artie knew what that meant. DeShaun could feel their imploring looks. He was forty-eight hours out of Correctional. He should be getting his diddy thing off. Instead, he was side-eyed, listening to honky talk, seeing wrong shit like frozen feet with no body.

Really, dog!? Can we talk about hazard pay?

-I should mention, Frau von Tragg is very rich and very generous.

DeShaun warmed to the sound of that. Artie relished the thought. They would be Mr. Inside and Mr. Outside. A rescue mission was not out of the realm of possibilities. They headed out to assess the situation and report back. Alone with Max, Janey voiced what he was thinking. Money was a motivator for them, but it would be no help in buying Ella's freedom from Sabu. The only chance they had was somewhere hidden on the Onondaga Reservation, sixty miles north. Max thought it best they split up, with Max headed for the reservation where cell coverage was spotty. Janey was to stay behind at the inn and coordinate it all. She was the lifeline to Sabu. After a short protest about gender bias, Janey bought in and agreed. Max dialed up Wilbur's cell number and let it ring and ring.

He's not answering.

-Who's not?

It was Wilbur joining them, carrying a crate covered by a bearskin throw. This time Max did chuckle as Wilbur explained.

We don't want it anymore.

CHAPTER NINE

Ella had been anally penetrated by bigger dicks than Sabu's. And certainly bigger than Hitler's tiny weenie. This was not her first *arschficken* rodeo. Ella had not helped her situation as a hostage. After she refused to cooperate with Sabu, who wanted to take a time-coded photo of her, ungagged, outside the cage, she let loose an uncontrollable tirade of swearing at him and his disgusting assistants and kicked away his phone, cracking the display screen. Sabu decided he'd teach her a lesson in another Aghori ritual. He had his assistants smear her naked body in ash and set up for a carnal sacrifice. The girls held the octogenarian Ella down, spread her legs and ass cheeks and Sabu had his way with her derriere. With him thrusting inside her, Ella realized her life had come full circle. This was her hell and she knew she had earned it. She only hoped Max and the others found a way to never surrender the damn artifact to these animals. Her life passed before her eyes while getting pounded from behind. The good, the bad, the best. That would be her Tom Tom. If he was alive, he would gut this creepy psycho like a lake bass. Ella thought about her wedding night in Munich, 1941, with the dashing officer Ernst von Tragg when she had pretended to be a virgin. If he knew, he was chivalrous enough to never let on. Then the horrible war took him and left her to her own worst instincts. She understood life and its temptations because she had tasted so much loss. She'd survived rough sex before this and howled and whimpered every so often so Sabu would believe he was hurting her. Quite the opposite, damn. She had to give him credit for one thing, he had stamina. Naba was getting off on watching and decided to participate. Sabu knowing her future was perishable, did not stop her. She lay down in front of Ella and scissored her legs around the old lady's head so that her muff was in Ella's mouth. Naba humped from the front, while Sabu humped from the back. Ella could tell by Sabu's breathing that he was finally going to come. She was feeling a strange rush too. It seemed to be broadcasting over every cell in her body. She hoped it might be an orgasm coming like she had never experienced before, but she was wrong. It was death, and death only. It was her time. With a violent, full-bodied contraction, she was gone. The grand lady of Augsburg, Germany, darling of the finest spas in Europe and the Caribbean, decorated breeder of Black Forest stallions, hedonist extraordinaire, and philanthropist, thanks to her friend Tom Tom, had expired in a dark, basement sanctuary in Ithaca, New York. Cumming mightily, Sabu power-wailed and called out to Shiva, to Kali, to Agni, to Nandi. Naba screamed louder. Sabu assumed they had worn Ella's spirit down, not out. He was wrong, as well. The muscles in Ella's glutes toned from decades of horseback riding, clamped shut and would not release. Sabu could not get his penis out of her dead ass. It was stuck. He shook at her and pushed… nothing. Naba tried to get to her feet and was in a pool of blood, the lips of her labia bitten clean off and still clenched in Ella's spectacular, implant incisors. Naba hopped around in agony. Sabu struggled to pull out of Ella. He beseeched Pradeep to help him, but she was helping Naba to the bathroom. With a mighty groan, almost hyperventilating, Sabu yanked out his sad member and cried. His dick looked like a twisted, bloody, and broken taro root. A text beeped on his phone. It was from Janey and showed a photo of the Eye of Shiva, chest opened, revealed in all its glory, with a TV in the background and chyron time code. The text message read.

I showed you mine, now show me yours. Proof of life, please.

Sabu gasped. His phone screen, damaged by Ella, fritzed out in a flash, going blank in his hand, as lifeless as Frau von Tragg. Pradeep appeared with the wounded, crying Naba and started for the stairs. She was taking her friend to the hospital. Sabu screamed back at her to stop. Pradeep kept going.

You can punish me when I return.

Everything seemed to be unraveling. For a moment, Sabu felt like Rama Patel must have. But he was not Patel! His greatest moment was right before him and he should not waver. He took off the tarp from his stationary bike in the corner and covered Ella's body. There could be no proof of life now. Charging back in his phone, he prayed.

* * *

At the inn library, Candace laid out some bakery buffet on the breakfront. She knew this all had something to do with her boyfriend's suspicious death, and she wanted to be part of it. Max understood and rolled with it. At this point, everyone was needed. If things went horribly wrong, they were all doomed anyway. Max sat with Janey, Artie and DeShaun, Wilbur, Uncle Em and Tiffany around the conference table with the Eye of Shiva in the middle and waited for a response from Sabu. None was forthcoming which had everyone on edge. Max assumed it would be instant and then it would be nut-cutting time. He couldn't pull a switch on Sabu but maybe he could make the madman come to them. Janey marveled at the sight of the relic. It seemed unfair and unimaginable to think something ancient, so simple and eloquent in design, could hold the power described in the Hindu writings.

One way to find out.

Uncle Em reached for the disc. They looked on in horror until the old jokester raised a finger and cackled. He got them. And he did, tension cratered. The searing "Free Bird" guitar riff from Max's phone cut through the short-lived levity.

* * *

It was broad daylight, almost ten a.m. Artie and DeShaun stationed themselves behind the cover of the stone wall of the cemetery off from the main gate where they had the best view of the house. It was a house Artie knew well from The Crossing days though it looked a lot duller without the rainbow paint job. Behind them, if they bothered to notice, were two old, white, and worn headstones in a shared plot, which time and gravity had drawn together and left leaning one against the other, like lovers. The couple's name engraved on the marble stones was Pearce, Aruna and Philip, still together through the ages. Unknown defenders of the Finger Lakes, like the unlikely Artie and DeShaun. The Pearces' son Caleb and wife Emily were buried near as well. Further up the hill, poor Walter Newton lay in an unnamed grave. (Never trust an older brother).

Artie saw the girls first. The two female students exited the front door in a rush. One was in terrible distress, walking oddly, holding her crotch and moaning. Something was up. The other was supporting her. They got into their car. Artie called into Max.

I think our lady may have inflicted some damage.

* * *

With Artie's news about the girls' exit, Max agreed with Janey. If the two were gone from the house, Ella could be there with only Sabu. Janey had tried calling the professor's office landline. No one had answered there, so it was possible he was across from the cemetery. Unless he was elsewhere and no one was guarding Ella whom by the evidence, they were keeping in a cage. Artie's rough map to the house's backdoor and basement bulkhead gave DeShaun the intel he needed. The smooth criminal thought he could work his way to the rear without drawing any attention and learn more. There was a low, perimeter fence and the window casements looked to be sweet targets of opportunity. DeShaun was primed on rescuing the rich white lady and living like a happy camper ever after. Max asked him to slow his roll. Sabu was calling Janey.

* * *

Sabu's disdain for Westerners started early in his life. Englishmen still held positions of power in his Punjabi city and they knew nothing of the history of the continent. The West always claimed to have invented civilization. First, the late-to-the-party Europeans, then worse, the Americans. They controlled the history books, and what was taught had little regard for the great worlds whose shoulders they stood upon. The East was ignored. Revisionist history prevailed. The A.D. designation, denoting the birth of

Jesus Christ, reset humanity's calendar, ignoring the great civilizations in India, China, and Mesopotamia, where modern knowledge of math, science, ethics, and trade began. His own hotel school students knew nothing of the architectural acumen of the Harappa Empire or the early Persians' breakthroughs in medicine. They were blind to the holy path to the Supreme Being that man was meant to follow. The arrogance of the West was overwhelming for Sabu. A strike at its heartland, near the antipodal point from where Shiva and Buddha thrived, was ordained and righteous.

This disdain may have caused Sabu to underestimate Max and Janey. On the phone call, he did apologize for not responding right away and explained his cell phone battery needed charging. He ordered Max to bring the artifact to the office.

You know…where you broke in earlier.

With Janey's phone on speaker, Max asked to speak to Ella, and threatened Sabu should she be hurt in the slightest way. Sabu could have answered that threat a number of ways and covered his phone mic to let out an ironic sigh if an ironic sigh was possible. The troublesome, old lady friend of Gill's, of course, was no longer alive. From blunt truth to ridiculous whopper, the options were open to Sabu and the stakes were high. He played it right down the middle. He said Mrs. von Tragg was being kept in a secret location, no longer a cage anymore. He also reiterated how unwise it would be to alert any authorities. Sabu would have her released when they complied. He added if Max and Professor Flatman didn't, his devout assistants would have no compunction at all in taking a life.

They will gut her. And eat the tastier parts when hungry.

While Sabu waxed on, Janey used Max's cell phone to call the professor's office landline again. No one answered. Max stayed on point.

Have your devout colleagues please call in so I can speak to my client.

-No cell reception there. Sorry.

This was never a good answer in the few times Max had dealt with kidnappers. Proof of life is a common currency and absent, it usually means proof of death. Max did not share this with Janey. Instead, he proposed that Sabu meet them noontime in a more neutral place, the lakefront marina, end of the dock, and to bring his client, unharmed. Wilbur had recommended the marina. It fit the bill for Max's plan for the exchange. With their backs to the water, they would be able to see Sabu and friends coming and if Ella was not there, the old Indian had a small boat and could evacuate Max and Janey. It was 11:02. With no immediate response from Sabu, Max added:

You know. . . The marina where you killed Mr. Gill.

***

Outside the University Avenue house, DeShaun could see Sabu through the rear window talking on the phone in the living room, angry, upset, hands waving for emphasis. DeShaun slipped toward the basement bulkhead and played with the padlock for a few seconds using a straight pin tool he kept in his belt buckle. The lock popped, and he was in, down the stairs without a sound, soft stepping his Air Jordans toward the basement landing. It smelled very strange, a pungent mixture of incense, shit, urine, bleach, and sweat. Worse than any prison block he'd experienced. He got the sense there was no one in the basement so he went into the adjoining, sanctuary room through an open, inner door. Lights were on low. The cage was empty. There was blood on the floor and a tarp covering something. His heart sank along with his dreams. There was a body beneath, he could tell. A peek underneath confirmed it was her. Before he could text Max, DeShaun heard footsteps on the stairs. Sabu was coming down. DeShaun knew how to be cool and quiet on a hot prowl. He faded into a corner, his blackness into the blackness of a kitchenette. He could hear Sabu in the main area moving the body. DeShaun's hand momentarily reached back and he felt something defrosting on the counter. More feels and he knew what it was. It was the freakin' feet again! He gasped out loud and gave himself away. Desperate, DeShaun threw the damn package of human feet right at Sabu and beat him to the stairs. His non-knock-off, official Jordan's were a blur, flying up the steps. Sabu was right behind him. DeShaun slammed the door in the puss of the pursuing professor and inside the living room, he sprinted for the front door.

Watching the house he once knew so well from behind the cemetery wall, Artie had been overloaded with memories of his younger self and all the promise of The Crossing. He'd spent the last forty years trying to rediscover that feeling of love and family he had so briefly experienced. He'd wasted his life as a fringe player, a street hustler of ducats doing whatever he had to, to not have a straight job. He was getting good and down on himself. It was easy. He'd been so bent on never being part of the establishment that now it was burying him. If he could afford to be buried. The Social Security he was due as a senior citizen was literally hotdog money because he never paid in and never really paid taxes. His retirement funds were in his wallet. Being with Max and Janey, despite the dangers, had been a pleasant distraction—make that a blessing. He felt he was doing something important. As if giving a pep talk, Artie reminded himself they could be saving the city where he was a laughingstock. They could be heroes. That delicious positivity triggered a flashback to one of Mychal's antiwar songs with the lyrics about *heroes* and *herpes* being just one letter apart. Before he could savor that, he saw DeShaun burst out of the house and down the path, coming across the street, Artie's way, with a dark-skinned, turbaned man trying to catch him. *Herpes or Hero*, Artie grabbed a bouquet of memorial flowers off a nearby gravesite. As DeShaun bolted through the cemetery gates, Artie waddled like an innocent, old mourner right into Sabu's path and took one for the team. The colliding mass went pinwheeling, ass-over-teakettle. Sabu landed hard, head bouncing off the footstone of one Aruna Pearce, who got a lick in from the great beyond. On the ground, Artie played it up.

Oh, my God! Watch where you are going! My neck! My shoulder!

Sabu could no longer see DeShaun. Struggling to get to his feet, Artie put out a hand, looking for help. Sabu glared back.

You will die soon.

With eyes on Artie, Sabu's right hand reached around for something behind his back. A buzzkill jolted Artie, who feared the reaper. A veteran of county lock-up, he contracted into a tight ball to protect himself and his most important parts. To Artie's relief, Sabu ran back off to his house, a cell phone clutched in hand.

In an old mausoleum at the far end of the cemetery, DeShaun hid. He knew he should text Max immediately, but his hands were shaking too hard. He tried deeper breaths to steady and calm himself. It didn't work.

Fucking cannibals!

* * *

LADY DEAD

The text from DeShaun was all caps and deserved to be. There was no more to the message. Max, Janey, and Wilbur were in Max's room upstairs at the inn. They were cooling the Eye's chest in about an inch of water in a beautiful, period bathtub. Wilbur had insisted. Janey had been taking photos of it and the news of Ella's demise had her quaking every few minutes. The message from DeShaun hit Max worse than he expected, since he expected it. She was some incredible female and if half of what he had heard was true, she had gotten her money's worth out of this go around. He hated the fact that he and Sabu shared a belief in reincarnation, which made it all instantly repulsive and wrong. Truth was, Mei U was not coming back. The end of the trail is the end of the trail. Max was now ready to die on this grim hill.

With no Ella, the fanatic Sabu had still agreed to meet them at the marina dock at noon and Max, Janey, and Wilbur were of one mind. Besides getting Sabu Shera's confession to the murders, they also needed to put the Eye of Shiva where no one could get hands on it. Wilbur knew just the place.

With ole Greeny.

The Cayugan believed the sea serpent lived somewhere near the lake's middle, which was bottomless. With a storm brewing, his little boat could reach mid-lake going flat out with two of them and the Eye. They could drop it down where it would be watched by the creature of the lake. Max liked his story for the *bottomless* aspect. *Perfect.* That thought was immediately re-thought. His insurance agent old man, older brother of Mychal, lived life like an actuarial table. He would always say, *"perfect is the enemy of good."* *"Good gets it done."* Max hated reincarnation and particularly hated that his father ruined *perfect* for him. Dreams had to be achievable. A man's reach should *not* exceed his grasp. Don't gild the lily. One comforting thought got Max back on track. Wilbur had to be exaggerating. The lake couldn't really be bottomless. But real, fucking deep would absolutely work.

Let's rock. Beat Sabu there.

Janey felt left at the altar. Wilbur shrugged.

Sorry, only two. Sheep are on the meadow.

Max translated—White caps on the water. Rough going out there.

So, it's about my weight?

-I love your weight. Please stay with Em and Tiffany. Have some lunch.

I don't need to eat.

-They do.

Max kissed Janey to seal the deal. It was a mansplaining thing to do, and he immediately aborted. Janey let him off the chauvinist hook and pulled him into a real kiss. She had someone to wait for. He had someone to come back to. Not perfect, but good.

CHAPTER TEN

Naba's vagina hurt like hell. It had been stitched up but had lost its pleasure ridge and sensitivity. Her arm in the cast was itching, and she was angry enough to scratch out the eyeballs of every infidel within spitting distance. Pradeep kept her focused.

Sip your soup and keep your head down.

Sabu had called them at the hospital and ordered them to get up to the Taughannock Inn and grab Dr. Flatman by whatever means they could. Their immortal souls depended on it. He threw in the embarrassing fact that the old woman had shamed them. Sabu needed a live hostage and hoped Janey would be more durable. They were seated out of Janey's view in a high-backed booth in an alcove corner of the inn's crowded dining room, which was serving a buffet lunch. Every so often, Pradeep peeked off to the other side of the room, watching the table with Professor Flatman and the two Native Americans. They were to deliver her to Sabu at the marina dock ASAP and would need some luck to get her separated from the others. Blessed Kali gave them their opportunity. Janey rose from her table, excusing herself and headed for the restrooms in the hallway. Pradeep slipped a hypodermic needle out of her fanny pack and hid it up her sleeve. A look to Naba and they were off. Pradeep stepped out of the dining room. Naba kept a few steps behind.

Janey strode into the unoccupied ladies' room and sought out a stall. Before she could close the door, Pradeep was on her like white on rice. She hit her with another goody from the dentistry school, a hot shot of

Novocain. Janey went numb. Pradeep caught her before she crumbled and waited for Naba to help.

Naba didn't get far. Coming out of the dining room, she crossed paths with Candace. Suspicious, the inn manager asked Naba for a room number. Naba ignored her. Candace persisted and with an arm out, tapped her shoulder to hold up. Naba let loose like a tightly coiled spring and attacked Candace, plaster cast and all. Candace, armed since her boyfriend's death, had a mace can on her belt under her blazer and blasted Naba with spray. To the East Indian grad student's extreme discomfort, Candace followed with her version of a karate kick that she'd learned at her sorority's one-day self-defense seminar. Her Tory Burch, metal suede loafer connected right in Naba's tender groin. The damaged cultist howled so loud, and so long, everyone in the building came running, including a security guard with a gun raised.

Pradeep used the fortuitous commotion in the dining room lobby. She grabbed a rolling, luggage cart from the empty hallway and loaded a comatose Janey on to it and ran out the inn's rear door.

* * *

Wilbur apologized for the size of his boat. Since Tom Tom's passing, and the lake house's sale, he'd been living inland in Freeville and only kept an underpowered, twelve-foot Boston Whaler for some summer fishing or good weather cruising. He tossed Max a life vest and put on one of his own. With the wind whipping up, and the water a nasty shade of gray, the marina dock was deserted except for the *Footloose*, a bigger, sleeker, powerboat with a Sunday fisherman tying back up. Max cast off the lines and they were away by 11:45 and heading into the rolling and rocking lake surf that was splashing over the gunnels. They must have looked insane to the *Footloose*'s owner, a podiatrist with a small pan's worth of lake trout to show for his early morning effort. He waved to Max despite it and Max waved back. Knot by knot, the determined outboard motor cut through the wind with a teeth-jarring sound. Max tightened the bearskin around the troublesome artifact. Was it right what they were doing with a storied piece of antiquity? From reading Patel's journal, Max knew generations of cultists had been trying to fulfill the prophecy for one reason. To set off an explosion powerful enough to level the city and the nearby towns. It could kill tens of thousands if the legend held. Certainly, the Aghori believed it and had stopped at little in its pursuit. How many people had their agents killed over the centuries? Max thought again about going to the police or the FBI, CIA, or even the President of the United States. Would Barack understand? Max was feeling uncertain. Wilbur tried to read him. The Cayugan spoke so he could be heard.

This is right. Some power cannot be trusted to anyone.

And who would listen to them? They were already on the FBI's radar, perceived as relic hunting thieves. Perception was a tough mistress. Only a bit worse than expectations in the psychic damage it can do. Whether you are trying to live up to your perception like a doomed John Belushi or trying to change perception, you will do things you shouldn't. Max remembered his friend Jeffrey, a music industry lifer. It was 2001, and he drove a 1963 Ford Falcon V-8 convertible that he had restored. It was the much-adored vehicle of his high school days, a precursor to the Mustang and a sweet, vintage ride. Jeffrey got his dream job at Capitol Records and pulled into the parking garage on the first day. The garage attendants stuck him in below, down in parking Siberia. To them, it was an old car which meant the driver was a nobody. In Hollywood, you are what you drive. Next day, Jeffrey traded in the beloved '60s Ford for a late-model Mercedes SL with an expensive lease. When he next drove into the garage, the attendants parked him on the first level. He had it made. Right around Thanksgiving, Jeffrey got fired. Before Christmas, he defaulted on the Mercedes' lease and by New Year's, he'd lost his mind. Moral being—don't chase, don't change. Be true to yourself, authenticity is everything. Max, of course, didn't say any of this to Wilbur Red Hawk. He nodded instead and Wilbur knew like Max knew, they were where they needed to be.

We're close. In Wading Bird's day, you could see the top of Taughannock.

You couldn't see the falls anymore from the lake with the growth of the trees, but you could feel its thunder, amplified by the natural, bowl acoustics. The mist the falls generated was drifting over them with the smell of the forest and more—the earth, the sky, the water, it soaked them with the rich sweat of history. Wilbur cut the engine. It felt divine, the sun pouring out from behind a dark cloud. A flash of bright goodness fell upon them before it surrendered back into another sinister, cloud layer. It was amazing to Max with all the roar he could hear his cell phone. It was Janey.

Max, dump it!

–Do that, and she will die before your eyes. Drop anchor. We are coming.

It was Sabu.

He had Janey and Pradeep aboard the *Footloose* with a .44 automatic trained on a frightened podiatrist piloting the craft under extreme duress. Janey was still woozy from the anesthetic. They had her tied with bowline to the captain's chair. Pradeep stuffed a rag in her mouth. She'd said enough to get Max's attention. Pradeep tried to keep her balance on the rolling sea. Janey stretched a leg out and tripped the tall grad student who slid forward bracing herself for a collision with fishing gear. Twack! Aagh! Pradeep removed a hook from her cheek and would have chewed Janey's nose off her face, had Sabu not stopped her.

Need her bright and shiny. Pray!

The podiatrist, whose name was Dr. Al Prit, one t, assumed Sabu was talking to him and started reciting the Lord's Prayer. Sabu clocked him upside the head with the steel in his hand.

I'm sorry. I didn't go to church today. I'm sorry!

Janey had forgotten it was Sunday. She was due at a summer session faculty meeting first thing in the morning. It would be nice if Professor Shera would honor that. It would be nicer if there was a Monday morning. Janey always loved the start of classes, the excitement. The chance to create that same excitement in her students. Fuck. Fuck. Fuck. She bit down hard on that fantasy and thought about Max instead. He was older, kinder, more capable than any man she'd met. What a shame it would be if their one-night stand was a one-night stand. But what a night. There was much more for them possible. The water splashed harder, stinging her face. The boat was speeding up because Sabu had taken to smacking Dr. Al on the head to ensure it. Janey could only wipe away the building foam with her tongue. She couldn't believe she was following her dear guardian Mychal's righteous path into the great beyond. What was the song he used to sing her to sleep?

Goodnight Angel Child
Sweet dreams and all…

Strange, how proud she felt, like a partisan spy going to her own execution. But her death would mean nothing if Max turned over the Eye of Shiva.

***

The Tompkins County Police Report filed Sunday, May 11, 12:06 p.m., noted the following:

The Suspect, Naba Gupta, age 23 of Lucknow, India, was charged with disorderly conduct, battery, and resisting arrest. She was read her rights at the scene. After being forcibly removed from the Taughannock Inn by Officers Cellario and Ganbaum, she was secured in a squad car. During the time that Cellario and Ganbaum were away interviewing a witness, Ms. Gupta beat her head repeatedly into the vehicle's grill partition and had to be rushed to the Cayuga Medical Center. Her condition at this time is unknown.

***

Max and Wilbur could see a boat approaching them from the south. With their anchor down, their little tub was rocking hard, back and forth in place. If it was a rhythm, it would be a wild, salsa beat. They both held on to whatever they could to stay upright. It was Max's idea to secure the anchor's line to the Eye of Shiva's chest instead of a boat cleat. Wilbur had threaded the rope head through the handles of the heavy, iron crate, tied it up with a hitch knot and with care, dropped the anchor over into the water. It disappeared beneath till the rope went taut. The weight of the iron chest on the deck held the boat in place. The sun, a gray disk as ominous as the Eye itself, ghosted behind the clouds, haunting the tableau below. Coming towards them from the south, the *Footloose*'s Sealine 330 dual engines slowed to an idle. Dr. Al let the boat drift closer, side to side, while Pradeep dropped the boat fenders. Sabu tossed Max a line.

Tie us up.

Max could see Janey was alive. He wrapped the line around the cleat on their rail, and the two boats were hitched. What happened afterward could only be verified by the survivors. And even their stories all differed, depending on what direction they faced when the sun came out again.

CHAPTER ELEVEN

Sabu had the Third Cleansing dream more than once since he arrived in the Finger Lakes in 1996. He had already seen himself in fantasy opening the holy chest and removing the sacred Eye. It was amazing to feel the power, strong as Nandi's heart, and to place it within a ritual altar dug into the earth. In his dream, he drenches himself in the golden bull's fluid and sets himself ablaze, falling atop. He becomes the very fuel that ignites the Eye to everlasting glory halfway around the globe like the prophecy proclaimed. He would not have that luxury now. Sabu had not been able to take care of the old woman's body, and police could already be at his house. There was no turning back for Sabu. His double life was over. This was the End of Days for him and Pradeep. With Naba's situation unknown, the two of them would ride Shiva's fiery Eye into the next life. They would shake off the karmic shackles and become demigods themselves. Sabu had Pradeep untie Janey and move her up toward the boat's rail.

Here's your professor, unharmed.

He pointed with his gun at the bearskin covered crate on the floor of their boat.

Is that it?

–Where's my client Mrs. von Tragg?

She expired from natural causes. Show me the chest. Bring it closer.

–When Janey's in our boat.

Open it first. I need to see the Eye with my own.

It had to be swift and certain, Sabu knew. Once the infidels opened the chest and showed him the Eye was real, he would shoot right at it and let loose Kali's blessed hellfire. Sabu could think of no better spot than this lake. No better day. It was fate, he believed.

He wasn't the only one believing that afternoon. Wilbur believed the lake had a protector. Max believed he loved Janey no matter how many breaths he had left. Janey believed Max would save her. Pradeep believed she'd made a mistake. Dr. Al Prit believed he saw an enormous sea serpent. That belief proved to be the most impactful, seconds later.

Wilbur adjusted his stance to balance the boat as Max removed the bearskin and lifted up the crate. Pradeep helped Janey up to the port side gunwale of the rocking boat. Sabu had his gun pointed at Max. Janey violently shook her head in protest, resisting. Max tried to calm her.

It's going to be all right. The chest is attached to the anchor. Sir, lower your gun. Do as I say, or I'll toss it over.

It was a desperate negotiation on open water. Sabu lowered his .44. Wilbur, with feet wide for stability, reached for Janey. She took a step across steadied by Pradeep. The *Footloose*, still idling, was rolling on the white caps making for a treacherous transfer. Sabu, clinging to a support wire with his free hand, stepped a foot down onto Wilbur boat's gunnel rail to keep the crafts close and to closer view what was in the chest.

Let me see it!

Max unclasped the iron box that originated from the seventh century before Christ. At that same moment, the sun freed itself from its cloud fortress, beaming down glorious, golden rays. The chest lit up with glow in Max's hands. When he lifted the lid for Sabu to see inside, a shadow fell on the boats and beyond across the water. The air chilled. The moment froze. It was the dark specter of a long-necked, enormous creature. Its shadow head lifted, rearing back, jaws opening, and Dr. Prit, directly facing the source of the shadow, screamed in terror, pointing.

All turned except for Sabu, who was focused on the sacred disc in the chest. It was real. He could reach out and touch it. Instead, he raised his pistol to take aim.

Namah Shivaya!

Janey reacted first. Quick as a cat, she jumped down hard onto Wilbur's boat, heavy as her weight would allow. Sabu caught in the sudden, rocking movement, saw his shot go heavenward. Max slammed shut the chest and copied Janey. He jumped up and down, Wilbur too. Sabu, trying to keep his balance, straddling both boats, lost his toehold on Wilbur's craft and was dangling off the side of the bigger *Footloose*, fighting to keep his grip of the support wire. Needing two hands, he tossed his gun on to its deck. Fingers stretched, he reached for a helping hand from Pradeep. Instead, she jumped up and down, rocking the *Footloose*. Sabu looked back at her with helpless eyes and lost hold of the wire, his only hope. Gravity did the rest. He slipped between the boats. Professor Shera, accomplished as he thought he was as a swimmer, did not handle panic well. Thrashing to stay afloat, his right leg got tangled in the anchor line. Max seeing his chance, summoned a mighty burst and threw the Eye of Shiva, clear over the stern. It plummeted under the black water, dragging the fanatic Sabu with it, to a bottomless forever.

Max had not written a song since Mei U had died. He'd struggled after with his creative direction and his purpose. At once, it became clear. His purpose was simply to love and be loved. Holding Janey in his arms, he had a damn, good opening for a love song. He whispered it into her ear in his best Leonard Cohen drawl.

> *You can have your skinny Minnies*
> *You can have your perfect tens*
> *My Janey love weighs heavy*
> *She's the stuff of true le-gends*

Janey kissed him right through the whole bullhorn announcement that crackled over the lake.

This is the New York State Marine Patrol. Identify yourself.

A grateful Dr. Al Prit yelled back his boat's name rank and serial number in a blaze of letters and numbers. Max, Janey, and Wilbur waved off to a policing craft rapidly approaching, cutting through the rough water with Uncle Em and Tiffany aboard.

Everybody okay?

The uniformed officer's voice boomed over the engine's whine. Everybody was not okay. Max realized they'd lost track of Pradeep, the young Aghori cultist on the *Footloose*. She'd picked up her master's gun and froze the moment, all eyes on her. Pradeep's hate for Sabu Shera had overtaken her beliefs. She had doomed herself in two different worlds and sought another. She swallowed a bullet, and no one shed a tear.

EPILOGUE

Ella von Tragg's last will and testament requested there be no funeral or memorial. Her ashes would not be collected. Her estate, which was valued at two hundred-thirty-five million dollars, had stipulated, among other directives, that should she die prior, one hundred million would be given as a reward to whoever delivered justice for the murder of Mr. Thomas Gill of Freeville, NY. The nine who qualified and shared in the bounty were all at the wedding a year later.

In the natural bowl of Taughannock Falls, creekside, Uncle Em, in an outfit Hank Williams would have been proud of, played the wedding march on a new Stratocaster and portable amp. Max and Janey exchanged *I do's* with Wilbur Red Hawk presiding. The bride and groom wore rain ponchos to avoid being drenched by the mist. All the attending did as well. *The Ithaca Journal* reported notables in attendance included Artie Hicks, the rock concert promoter, DeShaun DeMott, security alarm company owner recognized by his cable TV commercials, the retired podiatrist Dr. Al Prit of Key West, Florida, and the new Onondaga Reservation Industries Board of Directors. Janey had old friends and colleagues there and Max had friends come from as far away as St. Malo, France.

At the party that followed in the Taughannock Inn's ballroom, personally decorated and catered by Candace, now its co-owner, Max and Janey danced their first to the song that Mychal wrote for her. She had taught it to Eddie's Eagles cover band, who were providing the entertainment. The happy newlyweds, Janey and Max, took the floor alone and swayed to it with grace and dignity.

Goodnight Angel Child
Sweet dreams and all
I'm about to fall asleep
I'm about to fall

See you in the morning
Until then good night
There's a night bird taking flight
Putting out the light

The assembled gushed. A striking, older African American woman in colorful African garb joined the throng. She was seventy-something, blessed with the style and smooth skin of a much younger woman. Besides Janey, she was the only one in the room familiar with Mychal's lullaby.

Orion, arise
Mighty hunter of the skies
Can I use your eyes
To see where
my Angel flies

Others joined in on the dance floor when it was appropriate, and the song ended to applause. The mystery woman approached the bride and groom dispensing with any formalities.

Janeykins! I heard you're marrying a detective. I need one.

And that's when Max met his mother-in-law, Teresa.

THE END